COUNT HUGO,

OF CRAENHOVE.

By Hendrik Conscience,

AUTHOR OF "THE CURSE OF THE VILLAGE," "THE HAPPINESS OF BEING RICH," "VEVA,"
'THE LION OF FLANDERS," "WOODEN CLARA," "THE CONSCRIPT," "BLIND ROSA,"
"RICKETICKETACK," "THE POOR GENTLEMAN," "THE DEMON OF GOLD,"
"THE VILLAGE INN-KEEPER," "THE MISER," "THE AMULET,"
"THE FISHERMAN'S DAUGHTER," ETC.

Translated Expressly for this Edition.

BALTIMORE:
PUBLISHED BY JOHN MURPHY & CO.,
44 W. BALTIMORE STREET.

Preface to the American Edition.

In "Count Hugo of Craenhove" — independently of the charming romance that invests the story — there are dramatic descriptions of scenes during the plague that desolated Europe in the fourteenth century, which fully equal — if they do not surpass — in vividness, the tragic details of Boccacio and De Foe, and, in fact, realize its dreadful incidents with that palpable distinctness which we have only found in the celebrated "Representation of the Plague" preserved in the *Museo d' Istoria Naturale* at Florence.

CONTENTS.

COUNT HUGO OF CRAENHOVE.

CHAPTER I.

THE TWO SHEPHERDS.

ABOUT the year 1360, there lay between the villages of Wyneghem and Santhoven, some three leagues from Antwerp, a wild and gloomy forest. The oak — the wood-king of the North — lifted there his towering crest toward heaven, while the faithful ivy clung around and covered with love-wreaths his rugged trunk, and the odorous sprays of the honeysuckle adorned his broad foot as with golden sandals. Near to each other, like children of one mother, rose the beech, with its shining leaves, the silver-stemmed birch, and the poplar, with its ever-rustling leaves; while the slender willow, like some lovelorn maiden, bent its drooping branches over the numerous water-pools.

The borders of the forest had about them an aspect of enchantment. The bramble threw its purple twigs from stem to stem, and wove around an impenetrable curtain, while at its foot cowslips and daisies glistened like scattered pearls. Deeper in, however, everything bore a different character. The ground showed evident tokens of some mighty revolution; here and there stretched barren tracts of sand; treacherous fens and stagnant marshes consumed the half-decayed branches of uprooted willows; in place of the bright green honeysuckle, the dull and yellow moss enveloped the trees, which, spotted over with fungi and excrescences, as with so many leprous tumors, seemed like an aged and toil-worn company, who stood awaiting their final hour.

Never did a beam of the noontide sun pierce through the tangled branches and penetrate to the damp earth; a continual dusk, a gloomy stillness, ever brooded over the spot, save when from time to time a solitary owl uttered its funeral screech, or a swift fox sped with rustling steps through the fallen leaves, breaking for a moment the deathlike silence only to render it still more awful.

Beyond the forest stretched a wide and immeasurable waste, and on the verge of the horizon hung an impenetrable curtain of black pines.

On a spring morning in the year 1366, ere the sunbeams had pierced through the dense night-mist, there sat two shepherds on the wild heath. One was an old man of more than sixty years, with snow-white hair, and shoulders bent with age: the other was still a youth; but seventeen years shone as yet on his ruddy and engaging countenance; his blue eyes glanced softly beneath his broad forehead, and his hair, blended as it were of silver and gold, floated in graceful negligence down his neck. Both were clad in coarse garments, and were employed in stitching their thick woollen stockings, while at some distance on either side their flocks browsed on the scant grass and the few flowers which the wild heath afforded.

After a few moments, the elder shepherd, laying aside his work, drew from his scrip a book, which he opened. No sooner did the younger man perceive this than the iron needles fell from his hand, his eyes glistened with curiosity, and, drawing near his companion, he bent himself over the open pages, and looked with eager attention at the characters. Then, with a deep sigh, he said:

"Thou canst read, Albrecht? Hast thou learned from this book how to govern the winds? to make good and bad weather? to bewitch the cattle? or to remove a charm? Oh, I would give twenty of the best years of my life, could I but understand those characters as well as thou!"

The old shepherd smiled at this outburst, and replied:

"Is it thus, Bernhart? Dost thou already believe what the old wives of Santhoven say? Because I know how to read, folks proclaim me a magician; I have, however, in my whole life had no other book in my hand than this one, and what dost thou think it contains?"

"How should I guess? Tell me, I pray."

"Well, then, it is the narrative of the passion of our dear Lord and Saviour. In my youth I dwelt with an old priest; he it was who wrote the book for me, and with much labor taught me to understand the characters. May God be merciful to the soul of the good man! At the end of the book he likewise wrote for me certain powerful remedies most useful in diseases of sheep. In the knowledge of these remedies, Bernhart, lies all my magic skill."

Bernhart, however, was not content with this.

"Oh, let me but hold the book in my hand for once!" he begged, impatiently.

The old shepherd gave it up willingly. Bernhart threw himself upon the ground, laid the book open before him on his knees, and with almost feverish attention turned over one page after another. There was something wonderful in the demeanor of the young shepherd, and, above all, in that motionless head, from which drooped on either side his fair flowing locks. With a benignant smile old Albrecht gazed down upon him, and at last said:

"Wouldst thou likewise willingly learn to practise magic, Bernhart?"

The other lifted up his glowing forehead, and answered:

"Practise magic! No, no! but I would willingly give two fingers of my right hand to him who would teach me how to read."

"Readily would I teach thee, could we more

frequently let our flocks graze together; but that, as thou art well aware, happens scarce ten times in the year; thou wouldst in this way learn to read with some difficulty."

The words affected the young shepherd deeply. With a heavy sigh he gave back the book, resumed his needles, and, bending down his head, a heavy tear rolled from his eyes. For a long while there was a painful silence between the two shepherds; at length Albrecht turned compassionately toward his sorrowing companion, and said:

"Bernhart, this desire of knowing how to read is a singular malady. I cannot conceive why thou shouldst grieve thus; it is only by a fortunate chance that I myself understand it. Why shouldst thou not be able to console and calm thyself in this, seeing that, for the most part, knights and noble dames, yeomen and burgesses, know as little about the matter as thou? And even if thou couldst read, where dost thou hope to obtain a book, since thou wilt never be rich enough to purchase one?"

Bernhart shuddered despairingly at these words; his tender limbs seemed almost convulsed, and deep grief showed itself on every feature.

"Assuredly, Bernhart," continued old Albrecht, "thy eagerness for knowledge is not natural; it must have a hidden cause. Truly thou art a marvellous youth; no one knows whence thou art; thou knowest neither father nor mother, and dost speak and act altogether differently from us. Still so young, and thy life already shrouded in dark mysteries! I have pity for thee, for I see but too well that thou dost suffer, and art unhappy."

These loving words sank deeply into the heart of the young shepherd, and he now ventured to disclose to his friend his inmost feelings. Drawing nearer, therefore, to the old man, he took him by the hand, and said:

"Albrecht! no one knows me here. Promise me to observe silence, then thou shalt learn at least who I am; then will I reveal to thee why this eagerness for knowledge so possesses me, and why deep grief harrows my bosom. I am of noble lineage, Albrecht; thou wilt not credit it, but it is nevertheless true, thy companion, the shepherd Bernhart, may style himself Burgrave of Reedale."

"Thou of noble blood!" cried the old shepherd, amazed; "thou Burgrave of Reedale! Speak on, I can keep your secret."

Bernhart wiped the tears from his eyes and sat himself down upon the heath, and Albrecht following his example, he began thus:

"Ay, sit thee down likewise, Albrecht! for my history is long and mournful. I still am young, yet have I suffered much. Listen. Scarce ten years have gone by since I was living with my father and my mother in a noble castle in the environs of Grimberg, in Brabant. My days were spent in the exercises which became a boy of noble descent; my father, who was a famous warrior, taught me to wield the sword, and to tame the fiery steed; and although still very young, I soon

gained much adroitness. Our fortune was not
large, and our table would often, to say the truth,
have been ill calculated to bear testimony to our
station, had not our constant practice in the chase
compelled the woods to yield us abundant game.
In order to be able to accompany his prince, John,
the conqueror of Brabant, with becoming honor
in the war against the Flemings, my father had
mortgaged his only country-house to certain usurers of Brussels. On this account the duke had
made him large promises, none of which, however,
he kept. Thou hast perchance heard, Albrecht,
how, in 1356, the Flemings, under Count Louis
Van Male, captured Brussels, and got possession
of the whole of Brabant. My father was one of
those who, with Everard Serclaes, made an attack
upon Brussels. One night they penetrated into
the town, and, seconded by the townspeople, drove
the Flemings forth. Flushed with triumph, my
father hastened to the walls in order to plant
thereon the standard of his prince, when an arrow
pierced his side, and on the day following he was
no more.

"I was meanwhile with my good mother in the
castle at Grimberg. We had heard of the capture
of Brussels, and already rejoiced in the expectation
of soon having my father with us again. Comforted and tranquillized, and reckoning securely
on happier days, my kind mother said: 'Duke
Wenzel will certainly now, at least, richly remune-
rate the few knights to whom he owes his throne.'

Hereupon she kissed me tenderly, gave me more than one shining kreutzer, while tears of hope and love glistened in her eyes. Tranquil and happy, we sank to slumber.

"In the middle of the night a loud cry suddenly struck upon my ear, and, O God! I beheld naught but flames around me; the dense smoke nearly suffocated me; I heard my mother cry for 'help!' and outside the castle were wild shouting and the clash of arms. Every object danced before my eyes, and all consciousness, nay, life itself, seemed ebbing fast away from me. Then suddenly a swarthy human form dashed through the flames, approached my bed, and encircling me with both arms, fled with me through the glowing pile. Quite bereft of my senses, I let myself be borne along. What further happened to me I know not."

Overpowered by bitter remembrances, Bernhart remained silent awhile; tears streamed down his cheeks, but no sigh accompanied them. The old shepherd at first did not venture to speak; at last he began:

"And thy mother, then, Bernhart?"

"My mother, sayest thou? my poor mother? Oh! burnt, burnt to ashes; only her calcined bones were found."

A cry of horror escaped from Albrecht's breast, and his eyes, long dried up, were bedewed with tears. Bernhart mutely pressed his hand; and thus they sat for a long time in silence. Bernhart first spoke, and thus continued his narration:

" The officers of the Flemish, who had been
driven out from Brussels, had recognized my
father during the affray, and after their expulsion
from the town they had hurried forthwith to our
castle, and heaped up piles of wood which they
set on fire. Now was I a poor orphan, bereft of
all; I was still too young to serve as a soldier; my
ancestral castle was a heap of ruins; and even had
it not been so, what advantage could it have procured me, seeing that it belonged entirely to the
usurers? What remained to me, without possessions, without parents, without a relation? I saw
but one opening before me. I might procure
employment somewhere as a page, and so at least
attain a position suitable to my age and my noble
birth. At first I resided in the dwelling of a
neighboring peasant, with the brave-hearted fellow,
in fact, who, at the peril of his life, had saved me
from the flames. Some days afterward, a knight,
who had been on a pilgrimage to our dear Lady
of Halle, passed by the ruins of our castle; he
entertained a heartfelt pity for our ill-fortune,
which grieved him so much the more because he
had been a cordial friend of my father's. The
peasant conducted me to him; my bloodshot eyes
and sorrow-stricken features affected him deeply;
he accepted me as a page, and promised to the
good peasant that he would treat me his whole
life long as his own son. I followed him. The
deportment of this knight was somewhat inexplicable. On the first day he spoke not a word

2

during ten whole hours, let the bridle of his horse hang unconcernedly over its neck, and bent his head forward like one wrapped in slumber. His eyes, which were scarce ever bent upon me, lay half hid under his bushy eyebrows, and seemed to me like the surface of some dimmed mirror. No wonder, then, that anxiety and dread sunk into my heart, and that more than once I was haunted by terrible forebodings; but then the words of the knight, which I but seldom heard, were so soft and sad, that at last compassion took the place of disquietude. After a journey of two days we perceived the tower of Antwerp in the distance, and stood, an hour later, before the bridge of a large, stately castle, which was flanked by four towers and surrounded by strong fortifications; and scarcely had the warder perceived us when he blew his horn, the portcullis was raised, the bridge fell, and the heavy door creaked on its hinges. A large band of retainers and men-at-arms, all as mute and still more mysterious-looking than my benefactor, received us with great show of honor, and I soon became aware that we were standing under the knight's own roof. After I was somewhat rested and refreshed, Count Arnold Van Craenhove (so was my generous benefactor called) ordered an old domestic to saddle two horses, take me with him to Antwerp, and there get me clothed in his livery. Five days we remained in the town, and then I received my new dress. Oh, how handsome I felt, Albrecht! The right side

of my attire was of sky-blue silk, the left a rose-
red; on my head waved a rose-colored plume, in
a brownish cap, and around my neck wound a
silver chain, from which there hung on my breast
a silver hunting-horn. So handsome was I and so
gay, that they scarcely could tear me away from
the mirror, and were fain to threaten to take away
my silver hunting-horn if I did not cease blowing.
On the sixth day we returned once more to the
'Lanteernenhof.' Immediately upon my arrival I
was led before Count Arnold. He seemed well
content with my array, and not less with my proud
bearing; yet (and this I had already noticed on
the road) his voice soon again became hollow and
dull, his smile forced and painful, and when I
covered his meagre hands with kisses, he let me
do as I would, but remained cold to all my demonstrations of affection. After some moments of the
deepest silence, he rose from his seat, took me by
the hand without speaking a word, and conducted
me across several apartments to a beautiful chamber, where a maiden of my own age was seated
by the window, and gazing with wearied air upon
the prospect without. As soon as our eyes met, a
mutual smile hovered on our lips, mutual joy
beamed in our countenances.

"'Aleidis, my sister,' said Count Arnold, in his
hollow voice, 'I bring thee a playmate and a brother. Thou wilt now no more yield to sadness,
wilt thou? Be you happy in each other's company.'

"And with these words he left me there, and withdrew. Abashed, and without venturing one step forward, I fixed my eyes upon the ground, the young maiden, however, hurried up to me impatiently, seized my hand, drew me with her to the window, and asked, in a friendly tone:

"'How art thou called? and whence dost thou come? Wilt thou remain here always? And canst thou already sound thy horn bravely?'

"I answered all these questions as well as I could, although she scarce left me time to speak; she then rapidly drew a stool before her own, and said, half entreatingly:

"'Sit thee down here in front of me.'

"And when I had sat down, she looked with still greater curiosity at each of my features, and at every part of my dress. After this scrutiny had lasted some time, she began twisting one of my locks round her fingers, saying:

"'What smooth, pretty hair you have, Bernhart! It is like silver threads.'

"I, who had bashfully fixed my eyes upon the maiden, replied:

"'Not so beautiful as your fair locks, Aleidis! for they are like the gold that is woven in your bodice.'

"With a friendly smile, she continued:

"'And what lovely blue eyes are yours, Bernhart! they look as gracious as the heavens.'

"'Not so lovely, Aleidis, as yours, which are more beautiful than the glistening silk of my garment!'

" ' And what blooming cheeks and lips you have, Bernhart! they are more rosy than the feathers that wave upon your head.'

" ' Oh, not so beautiful as thine, Aleidis! which show like the coral around your neck.'

" This dialogue seemed to gratify Aleidis; on a sudden she sprang from her seat, pulled me away from mine, and said:

" ' Bernhart! you will always remain with me, will you not? You must not go away, do you hear? for then I shall be so lonesome, so disconsolate, so forsaken! You will be my brother, and we will always, always play together, shall we not?'

" We immediately set to work at our play, ran hither and thither, skipped and leaped about, until fatigue compelled us to rest; and then I blew upon my silver horn, or recounted to Aleidis how dreadful a calamity had fallen on our house. I made her weep, and at intervals again forced her to laugh. So intimate, in short, did we become, that she could not be persuaded to partake of the midday repast until they allowed me to sit down beside her. In the evening she wept bitterly because the day had flown by too rapidly, and she must needs separate from her playmate, in order to betake herself to rest. What more need I add, Albrecht? Each day rendered Aleidis more dear to me, and me more dear to her: never were we found apart. Two young vine-tendrils do not entwine more lovingly, two lambkins of one mother do not keep company with each other

2 *   B

more faithfully than we did.   Abandoning myself
unsuspiciously to my feelings, I did not perceive
that my good-fortune had already thus early found
many to envy me.

" It behooves thee to know, Albrecht, that Count
Arnold was scarcely ever to be seen; the apartments which he inhabited in the castle always remained closed, both against us and the whole
household, one man excepted, who, altogether as
pensive and taciturn as the Count, seemed to possess his entire confidence.   A strange being was
this man, and I still tremble while thinking of him.
Nature had bestowed features which were anything
but agreeable; and my dread of him, inspired by
the awful and harsh expression of his face, painted
him in the most forbidding forms.   Thou knowest
how dull and yellow are the eyes of an owl; even
such, Albrecht, were his.   Thou seest my dog there,
the hairs on whose back stand straight up, like the
leaves of the pines; such was his hair.   Thy book
is cased in two tablets of oak; even thus dull and
unseemly was his face at all times.   ·Hast thou
ever seen a fox which, taken in a snare, snarls at
the hunter and threatens to bite? such was his
sweetest smile.   So fleshless and curved were his
fingers, that I can only liken his hand to a falcon's
claw.   His name, too, resounded in my ear like a
blasphemy: he was called ' Abulfaragus !'   This
man, who throughout the castle and its vicinity
was reputed an astrologer, and one versed in the
abstruse sciences, never met me without fastening

upon me his distrustful and searching glance.
Oftentimes, when with Aleidis I was playing about
under the trees in the court-yard, I all at once perceived his yellow prying eyes looking out from behind some spreading trunk; and more than once
he crawled through the bramble-branches, like any
hound, in order to listen to our conversation. All
this kindled in my bosom the deepest hate toward
this man. I was not the only being who trembled
before him: every inhabitant of the castle quaked at
his voice, partly because the ever-invisible Count
Arnold spoke by his mouth, partly also because
each one feared that he would, by some super-
natural means, take vengeance for the least dis-
obedience shown toward his authority.

"Near the 'Lanteernenhof' grew a little copse
of elms, and beneath their impenetrable foliage lay
a tombstone, with an inscription graven upon it.
In this spot, when he was not required to be with
Arnold of Craenhove, Abulfaragus was wont to
linger. No one knew what the soothsayer did
there, nor why he stayed so long. Everybody
shrunk from this sepulchral monument through
sheer terror, and hardly did we dare to play in its
neighborhood. Aleidis well knew that this stone
covered the grave of her parents, who had been
removed from her by an untimely death, yet never
had she ventured to enter the elm-copse.

" The servants of the castle had received orders
from the astrologer to gratify Aleidis in almost
everything she wished; and thus was she the real

mistress of the castle, or at least seemed to be so.
When she wanted anything, or wished at any
time to give some capricious order, I was always
the messenger to convey it to the servants. Thus
I acted as master in her name, and on such occasions I often remarked no slight vexation in the
looks of the old servants of the house. I, however, in my light-heartedness, took no heed. I
answered them with sportive laughter, while I
blew a merry peal upon my horn, by way of
scornful greeting to these envious people. What
mattered to me the disfavor of a world where one
joyous bound brought me back to my paradise,
where a loving angel awaited my coming?

"Thou knowest, Albrecht, that to the unfortunate, time drags onward with slow and weary steps,
whereas, to him who quaffs joy from a brimming
cup, it speeds more swiftly than the eagle's flight.
Thus had I reached my thirteenth year without
having reckoned up a single day. During this
period, by means of what Aleidis told me, and
from words casually thrown out by the servants, I
had been able to get some insight into the reason
of the strange behavior and gloomy disposition of
my protector. Listen then to what I learned.

"Two years before my arrival at the 'Lanteer-
uenhof,' Count Arnold resided there with his elder
brother Hugo. Although the latter only bore the
title of count, and was, by right of primogeniture,
sole owner of the castle and its dependencies, he
lived on the most equal terms with his brother.

Their attachment to each other went so far, that
in order never to separate, and further, to insure
the education of their young sister Aleidis, they
promised each other they would never marry or
even form acquaintanceship with any woman.

"During the first four years after the death of
their parents, they remained faithful to their vow;
but then they broke it with mutual consent, and
betook themselves almost daily to a neighboring
castle belonging to a foreign lady, styling herself
Countess de Merampré. No one knew what
means she employed to deprive everybody who
came to her of their wits; many persons believed
that she had recourse to magical arts and powerful love-potions. However this might be, people
whispered under their breath that already more
than twelve knights had perished through her
means; and that it was almost an impossible thing
for two individuals to come near her, without one
thirsting after the life of the other. It seemed,
however, that the two brothers Van Craenhove
had not allowed themselves to be ensnared by her
artifices, for they remained as heartily united as
before. Another misfortune, however, befell them.

"One day, toward evening, Arnold rode out
from the castle, and took the road which led to
the abode of the countess. Some time after, his
brother Hugo followed him, accompanied by Abulfaragus. They both remained absent a very long
time, and already sleep began to weigh upon the
eyes of the sentinels, when suddenly a shrill cry,

not unlike the screech of a bird of prey, was heard
before the drawbridge. The guard distinguished
the voice of Abulfaragus, upon which they let
down the bridge and threw open the gate. Without deigning any one a look, or uttering a single
word, the old man hurried to that part of the castle
which was inhabited by the two brothers, and as
speedily returned, laden with a heavy travelling-
bag; again the bridge was lowered, and he disappeared in the darkness. Thou mayest easily conceive with what curious and anxious minds the
night-watchers longed for some solution to this
strange enigma. They were still lost in conjecture, when the piercing cry of Abulfaragus was
heard anew. Again they opened to him, and this
time he spake to them: he related, with brief
words, that the Lords Van Craenhove had been
attacked by a band of robbers, and had both been
killed; that their bodies were still lying bleeding
in the road, and that he had come for assistance to
convey them to the castle. The astounded retainers obeyed with tearful eyes, and followed the
impassible Abulfaragus with broken sobs. At a
quarter of a league from the castle, they arrived at
a cross-road, where they found Sir Arnold weltering in his blood; earnestly, however, as they
sought for the body of Lord Hugo, they found no
trace whatever of it, not even the mark of the spot
where it had lain bleeding. Arnold's steed was
grazing peaceably near him, but Hugo's was nowhere to be found. What the astrologer had done

with the travelling-bag no one ventured to inquire.

"Arnold's body was borne to the castle and laid on his bed, and thereupon Abulfaragus ordered the household to repair to rest, and shut himself in with the body. On the following morning he announced that Arnold was not dead, and might perchance recover; he then caused his mid-day repast to be brought to him, and closed the door anew. For fourteen days he acted thus, and one morning appeared with Lord Arnold in the entrance-court. The latter was pale and worn, like one just risen from a lingering illness; on his forehead there was a deep scar, which I have remarked there to this day. This is all I am able to recount to you of the history of the house of Craenhove.

"Aleidis and I had reached our fourteenth year; although no longer so wild or frolicsome as before, we were still quite as inseparable as ever. At this period, Abulfaragus appeared one morning in our chamber, bearing under his arm a book; he sat down upon a stool, and with a gentler accent than was his wont, he spoke thus to Aleidis:

"'Damsel, thou hast now attained thy fourteenth year: it is high time, therefore, that thou shouldst begin to learn whatsoever it becometh a noble maiden to know. Bernhart can teach thee nothing, for he is altogether ignorant.'

"For the first time in my life, some unknown feeling sent the warm blood to my forehead, and I

glared with angry looks at the old man. He only
laughed, however, and continued, unconcernedly:

" 'Thy brother wishes thee, Aleidis, to adorn
thy mind with graceful and elegant sayings, and
with tales of the heroic deeds of knightly prowess.
The time for play is over; at some future day thou
must appear at the court of the duchess, and what
would the world say if Aleidis Van Craenhove
comported herself like some ignorant peasant
girl?'

"The maiden read in my countenance what
deep trouble was oppressing my heart; she stood
forward, seized my hand with tender pity, and
thus replied to Abulfaragus:

" 'I will not learn. How! wouldst thou then
separate me from my brother here? Nay, in this
thou shalt not succeed.'

" 'Thy brother, sayest thou? thy brother! Dost
thou not then know,' growled Abulfaragus, 'that
he is thy servant?'

"This insult forced from me a cry of indignation and sorrow.

" 'Vile caitiff!' I shouted to the soothsayer, 'art
thou then so devoid of shame as to call the Burgrave of Reedale a servant? Why does not noble
blood flow through that despicable body of thine?
then would I teach thee how one chastises such
blasphemy. But, no! I will treat thee as one
should treat a serf.'

"Blind with rage, and excited by the jeering
smile which played on the features of Abulfaragus,

I caught up a willow rod and lifted my arm to strike him; but on the instant his yellow eyes shot through me a piercing glance, while an icy shudder crept through my limbs, without my being able to account for the secret power which had thus suddenly made me a coward. I sank back upon a couch as if crushed to pieces. Abulfaragus laughed aloud, while. Aleidis wept with deep sighs.

"Abulfaragus, little heeding our state of mind, began to read from his book. At first we were steadfastly resolved not to listen; Aleidis went away and stood by the window, and I turned my back upon the astrologer. He had read but for a short while, when some mysterious influence attracted us to him; slowly and unwillingly we turned toward him, and soon were our ears eagerly open to his words. Oh, what glorious things did that book contain! and how captivating, how thrilling, became the voice of the hateful Abulfaragus! I was forced against my will to take pleasure in his reading; and as for Aleidis, she hung upon his lips.

"After reading to us aloud for two full hours, he closed the book, and quitted the apartment with these words:

" 'To-morrow we will continue.'

"Entirely given over to the impression of the beautiful things we had heard, we remained sitting there in silence for a length of time. At last we began to converse about what we had heard. Aleidis could not cease speaking of the Knight

8

Walwin and King Arthur, whose adventures Abulfaragus had read to us. During that entire day
nothing was heard resembling our former conver-
sations; and with all my efforts I could not succeed in turning Aleidis's attention to anything
else. She said to me repeatedly:

"'Oh, why canst thou not read, Bernhart?
How delightful that would be! Thy voice is so
clear and sweet, and then we should no longer
need that abominable Abulfaragus.'

"With a powerful effort I suppressed my chagrin, great though it was. Aleidis, however,
longed thus earnestly after a pleasure which it
was not in my power to promise her.

"The next day, and the day following, Abulfaragus came at the hour appointed for the reading.
Never did he appear too soon for Aleidis, and
always went too soon away. Although she still
preserved the same love for me, I felt, nevertheless, that I was no longer all in all to her, and that
Abulfaragus's readings absorbed in no small degree
the thoughts and feelings of the young maiden.

"The thirst for knowledge, at which thou dost
marvel, preyed upon me like a subtle fire; night
and day I meditated by what means I might learn
to read. Often did I endeavor to peer into the
book over the old man's shoulder, but he shut it
until I had resumed my seat. More than once I
wished to break into some room by force, in order
to seek for a book, but each time Abulfaragus was
to be found leering behind me.

" One morning it occurred to me that there were characters written on the gravestone in the elm-copse; my curiosity quickly overruled my terror, and in deep agitation I penetrated into the thicket. Withered flowers bestrewed the earth round the tombstone, on whose characters I stared with flushing cheek and bewildered thoughts. Suddenly a distant rattling broke upon my ear; I turned round and beheld Abulfaragus, who was advancing toward the grave. Seized with alarm, and half dead with terror, I concealed myself under the thick foliage, held in my breath, and secretly observed the movements of my enemy.

" Abulfaragus slowly approached the stone, drew from under his cape a basket filled with flowers, and strewed them on the grave; so powerful was their balmy odor that it penetrated even to my hiding-place. Meanwhile I heard how Abulfaragus prayed, sobbing, ' O Lord Jesus! through thy dear blood grant to the souls of my benefactor and my dear sister eternal rest! Amen.' And then he bowed down his head upon the stone, and wept so bitterly, that I also could not refrain from weeping. The movement of my hand in wiping away my tears excited Abulfaragus's attention. I saw his flaming orbs so keenly riveted upon me, that a cry of dread escaped me. The soothsayer seized me by the hand, drew me forth from the overshadowing leaves, and said, in a voice which deeply agitated me:

" ' Thou hast seen and heard, audacious wretch!

If thou darest to utter one word of this, death shall close thy mouth forever!'

"While I was entreating for pardon on my knees, Abulfaragus withdrew, casting on me, even from afar, a threatening look. I did not remain long in this spot, for the elm-copse had now become more awe-inspiring than ever. I wandered about for a long time before I could entirely recover myself, and at length returned to Aleidis. However earnestly I strove to fathom the meaning of Abulfaragus's words, and however willing I might be to clear up the mystery as to whether the mother of Aleidis had been the sister of Abulfaragus, on no account did I dare to speak of my visit to the place of entombment. Abulfaragus came daily to read in our apartment, and seemed now to have quite forgotten that I had spied his movements. I, however, began to waste away and lose all my color, so keenly did this unquiet desire to learn, coupled with jealousy of Abulfaragus's knowledge, burn in my heart.

"One day—oh! never shall I forget it—the old man had brought with him a fresh book; for we had heard, the day before, the conclusion of the charming history of Floris and Blanchefleur. Aleidis fixed her earnest eyes upon him, and let not one syllable escape, so gratified was she with what Abulfaragus was reading. Suddenly the features of the old man assumed an expression inconceivably mild; his eyes beamed with more noble fire, and his voice assumed a softer tone.

Turning directly toward Aleidis, he read the following words; even now I well remember them,
so deeply did they impress me:

> 'Lovely maiden, formed so sightly,
> In all virtues shining brightly,
> Manners noble, modest, winning,
> Never against pity sinning,
> All to thee precedence granting,
> To depict thee words are wanting.
> Goodness, truth, and beauty claim thee,
> Mirror fair of grace we name thee:
> Pure thy lips, with music ringing;
> Peace is thine from conscience springing;
> Temple to all uses holy,
> God has surely blessed thee wholly.'

Inmost joy beamed from the features of Aleidis;
the more overjoyed she was, however, the more
did I feel my soul pierced through with chagrin
and envy. Tears streamed in abundance down
my cheeks, and I did not cease weeping until the
old man withdrew. I followed his footsteps up to
the door of his own chamber, there threw myself
on my knees before him, and besought him, with
agitated voice:

" ' Oh, Abulfaragus, for God's sake give me a
book! Teach me then to read. I will serve thee
as thy slave! At least have pity on me; thou
seest how the thirst for knowledge consumes me!'

"And with these words I embraced his knees
and watered them with my tears; but he let me
utter all my entreaties without returning one word;
with calm and chilling demeanor put the key into

3 *

the door, and, spurning me with his foot, entered his chamber, from which a jeering laugh resounded in my ears.

"With broken heart, and weighed down by shame, I returned with lingering steps to Aleidis. I cast myself, like one exhausted, upon a low seat, and began to sigh and weep, and conduct myself like one deranged. Aleidis would fain have consoled me, but I repelled her from me, and desired not to speak with her any more. Her tears at length broke down my resolution, and I exclaimed:

"'Aleidis, thou hast told me I was to be thy brother always: thou hast broken thy word; Abulfaragus is my mortal foe, he would fain destroy me. But this very moment he spurned me from him as one spurns a dog. A sister can scarce love him who treats her brother thus; she doth not yearn after his presence, nor find an odious voice like his agreeable. I am of noble blood, Aleidis; I cannot, and will not, any longer endure that a vile caitiff should jeer and insult me. Ah! thy friendliness toward me cannot any longer make me forgetful of the scoffing. To-morrow I abandon this place, and, relying on God's mercy, shall go into the wide world; never shalt thou see me more. I know that my going away will no longer grieve thee. Thou hast thy Abulfaragus; he can say to thee better than I:

'Lovely maiden, formed so sightly,
In all virtues shining brightly.'

Oh, I will learn to read, and will learn quickly, but then others shall listen to my speech!'

"At these stern words Aleidis drooped her head, as though oppressed by some grievous burden; suddenly, however, she sprang forward without hesitation to kiss me, but her strength failed her, and she fell senseless to the floor.

"I was on the point of calling for help, but Abulfaragus was standing there beside me, and the words died upon my lips: he looked upon me upbraidingly, yet scoffingly withal; took Aleidis by the arm, and with one glance of his eye called her back to life, and then rapidly quitted the room. Now did Aleidis reprove my severity with her bitter tears; she spoke to me with such tender words, she gave me so many assurances of attachment, that I soon was begging for pardon on my knees. We became good friends again, and promised each other to forget the past.

"On the following day Abulfaragus came as usual with his book and sat himself down to read. Hardly had he begun, when Aleidis's forehead flushed over, she sprang rapidly toward the old man, laid hands on the book, and tore a good ten pages out; these she rent in pieces and cast upon the floor, while she calmly said:

"'So will I always act, if thou still darest to come here with thy books—and now begone, unbeliever!'

"A stifled cry was the soothsayer's only answer; he threw himself upon the floor, and with both hands gathered together the torn leaves.

"I saw two heavy tears roll from his eyes, which were doubtless occasioned by the destruction of so costly a book; he then rose up quickly, and rushed out of the chamber, exclaiming with doleful voice:

"'Woe! woe!'

"From that time forth he left us at peace; we lived again gladsome and content. The thirst for knowledge once enkindled, however, did not quit me, and I resolved, whatever it might cost, to learn to read. The more the faculty of memory was developed, the more earnest became the desire for knowledge, and the deeper grew my curiosity to know what that might be which both my invisible patron and Abulfaragus sought to conceal so carefully from me.

"One morning, when I had risen somewhat earlier than usual, I crept silently past the entrance to those apartments which had always remained closed to me. One of the doors was ajar: standing on tiptoe, I peered into the chamber with throbbing heart. Count Arnold was there, reclining on a couch like one who is paralyzed; his eyes were fixed immovably on the wall, whereon was suspended a dark effigy, underneath which golden characters were written; near to him sat Abulfaragus, reading from a large book. At the same moment I heard Count Arnold speaking:

"'Thou sayest, Abulfaragus, that Bernhart must quit the castle. Thou reflectest but little on the sorrow which will seize Aleidis when we take from her the friend of her childhood.'

" 'It is a serpent thou art cherishing,' answered
the old man: 'if he remain here any longer, he
will discover the fearful secret, and upon thy
father's house a murderous blot will —'

"'No, no! say no more of that,' returned Count
Arnold; 'there are but two hearts in this castle
which are familiar with joy; thou wilt not compel
me to break these.'

"'It must be!' exclaimed Abulfaragus, with imploring voice. 'Listen! This night at twelve the
firmament was sparkling with stars: I found our
several planets without any difficulty. Thy star
was glimmering but feebly, like to a flickering
lamp, beneath Bernhart's. Suddenly the latter
moved off from thine, but approached it anew,
and beamed upon it with the light of joy and consolation. By the power of my art I at once compelled destiny to speak out clearly. If Bernhart
retire not from here, then will he inflict two terrible blows upon thy house, and the name of Craenhove will be branded with lasting dishonor. If
he go hence now, he will one day return and fill
thy after-life with joy and happiness. So spake
destiny to me.'

" 'Oh, Abulfaragus, how cruel art thou! how
pitiless toward my poor Aleidis! No; let my sufferings be redoubled rather than that she should
suffer!'

" 'Arnold, Arnold!' exclaimed the old man,
impatiently, and pointing with his finger to the
golden characters underneath the effigy, 'hadst

thou always believed this prophecy of mine, it would not now be torturing thee, and the sting of conscience and remorse would not be leading thee to the grave. Dost thou yet know what it containeth? "When a woman shall step between you, then shall your own blood stain the house of Craenhove." Was it not even so? Open shame alone is now wanting to thy name; well, then, be thou the first to cast mire in thy face! defile thy father's pure name; write upon his grave that his blood is a blood of dishonor! Summon courage for the foul deed!'

"During this discourse I was trembling with alarm and terror, like the leaves of the quivering aspen; my last remains of strength were ebbing fast away, and I was obliged to cling to the wall in order not to sink down. I saw the head of Count Arnold drooping low upon his breast, as if bent under the weight of the old man's cruel words. After a long pause he again inquired, with earnest voice:

"'Well now, Count Arnold, what seemeth good to thee?'

"'That he should depart,' was the reply.

"'Thanks for that resolve!' cried the old man; 'but fate requires that he depart hence as he came hither, poor and rejected, that he may be humbled.'

"A heart-rending sigh broke from Arnold's breast, accompanied by this terrible sentence:

"'Be it so! Do with him as it pleaseth thee.'

"Thereupon I sank fainting on the threshold,

and my sobbing penetrated into the chamber.
Abulfaragus drew near, opened the door wide,
and leered at me like a very demon triumphing
over the fate of a soul. With mocking laughter
he advanced into the corridor. At a call from
him, which resounded through the whole castle, I
heard many doors open and shut, and the servants
rapidly running and hurrying about; a secret voice
told me that perhaps even now they were sepa-
rating Aleidis from me forever. I sprang forward
and hastened to the chamber where she was to be
found erewhile; but the door was fastened. How
loudly did I cry and shout! how fiercely did I beat
the door till my hands ran blood! yet no answer
came. I hurried through the castle in desperation,
left no one tower, no one chamber, unvisited, and
no doors at which I did not call aloud my sister's
name; but one and all remained closed and silent
as death. Oh, what a depth of misery was mine,
Albrecht! Now I wept before Aleidis's chamber,
now under the spreading trees of the court-yard,
or wandered sorrowing along the broad corridors
of the castle, but no succor came: my sentence
had gone forth and was already half accomplished
— I had lost my Aleidis.

"Toward evening I was sitting in the court-
yard upon the green turf. The old enchanting
past, with all its radiant imagery, rose before my
soul; and how painful was the remembrance! It
was as though each one of these joys had bidden
me an eternal farewell — just such a heart-rending

farewell as one utters to a friend whom one scarce
hopes to see any more. At length I lost all consciousness; I neither saw nor thought any longer.
I had become oblivious to everything, and was
slumbering with my eyes open. In this trance I
must have remained for a long while, for when I
awoke all my limbs were stiff. My first glance
rested on one of the old retainers of the castle,
who was standing motionless before me; he was
a soldier of some sixty years of age, called Roger,
who had always been most attached to me, and
now gazed down upon me with pitying eyes.

" ' Get thee up, Bernhart,' he murmured; ' I
have something to tell thee.'

" I rose up slowly, drew nearer to him, and listened with painful anxiety to his words.

" ' Bernhart, there is some terrible matter in
train against thee. It seems thou hast committed
some great misdeed; folks even say that thou hast
spread a rumor among the country people, which
reflects seriously on our young lady; severe punishment awaits thy calumnious words! '

" I? my sister Aleidis? Albrecht, I was as
though struck down by a thunderbolt. With a
cry of desperation, I began tearing my hair; but
the old warrior restrained my hands, and continued:

" ' Bernhart, dost thou know Abulfaragus? Art
thou aware that he can extract poison from honey?
that a murderer's weapon is a plaything in his
hands, and that infernal spirits work his behests?
Wert thou ever in the subterranean dungeons?

Oh, every ill awaits thee! fly, therefore! I have
left the postern-gate open; thou canst easily wade
through the castle-moat. Hasten, then; thy misdeed is great, thy virtues, however —'

"At this instant the yellow eyes of Abulfaragus
glared from behind a distant tree. The words
died away upon the lips of the old retainer, and
he rapidly withdrew, all trembling. What happened to me afterward, I know not; my eyes began
to swim, the trees and battlements danced round
with a rapid whirl, and I was forced to lie down
upon the grass for fear of falling. Absorbed in
the thought of my distress, I remained there a long
while; the words of the faithful old man recurred
to my mind, and I beheld cups of poison brimming
over before me, and glittering steel pointed at my
heart. Oh, Albrecht! the fear of death ran curd-
ling through my veins. I shuddered with affright,
and in my despair seized, as an anchor of safety,
upon that expedient which the retainer had offered
me.

"Favored by the advancing darkness, I glided
from among the trees toward the outer part of the
castle walls, where the postern-gate was situated.
A few steps more and I should reach it; this sight
restored my strength and courage. Amid my sufferings it was a consolation to me that I should
never more behold the hateful Abulfaragus. But
heaven willed otherwise; the soothsayer was
planted before the postern-gate! I stood as though
riveted to the ground with astonishment, when he

4

advanced toward me, seized my hand in his bony grasp, and addressed me in a voice unusually gentle:

" 'Bernhart, my young friend, thou art truly unfortunate! On whose shoulders dost thou lay the blame? On those of Abulfaragus, dost thou not?'

" 'Ay, verily! and with good right!' I exclaimed. 'Thou hast always tracked my steps like an evil spirit, and now, mayhap, there simmers on some fire the poison which is to destroy me.'

" A bitter laugh was the old man's reply; he remained silent for a while, and then asked:

" 'Bernhart, hast thou heard what I said this morning to Count Arnold?'

" 'I heard but too well,' I sobbed through my tears, 'how thou didst calumniate me, and how cruelly thou didst demand my death-sentence.'

" 'Hast thou heard naught else?' still inquired the old man.

" In order to drive my enemy to desperation, I acted as though the fearful secret were no secret to me, and quickly replied:

" 'Ay, indeed, more have I heard, but never would I dare to utter what I know, and still less what I conjecture. Count Arnold is my benefactor.'

" The silence which followed upon these words caused me no little wonder. The old man seemed suddenly to become more sad than myself. He drooped his head, and sighed painfully. After a pause he lifted up his head again, and said, in accents of deep sorrow:

"'Bernhart, my child, thou lookest upon me as a very wicked man, dost thou not? Didst thou but know, however, what I am doing, and wherefore I act thus — didst thou but know why I make myself an object of hatred, while all the time I have never done harm to mortal man — thou wouldst have compassion on Abulfaragus, nay, wouldst even lovingly embrace him, for thy heart is noble and pure.'

"How shall I portray my wonderment at such language, Albrecht? The man whom I believed a very fiend stood before me beseechingly, and his voice moved and agitated my very soul; my dread of him vanished.

"'Abulfaragus,' I said, with a sigh, 'thou dost astound me; art thou indeed uttering truth?'

"'Follow me,' he replied, at the same instant drawing me onward by the hand.

"It would seem that nothing could withstand the voice of Abulfaragus, for these few words of his had dissipated not only my hatred and anguish of heart, but even all my mistrust. I followed him willingly to the door of his chamber; there, however, a slight shuddering seized me; I was about to enter for the first time that mysterious chamber which had awakened my curiosity for eight long years. I quivered all over when the door swung open, and I stepped into the room. What I there saw, however, affected me less than

I had expected. Everything was uncleanly and
lying about in disorder; an iron lamp, casting
around a dim light, permitted me to perceive a
few skeletons of animals, some dried plants, and a
few books, and — whereat I was not a little astonished — a large image of our Lady, around which
two beautiful bunches of flowers spread a delightful fragrance. And this was all.

"Abulfaragus bade me sit down, and, placing
himself on a stool near me, took my hand, saying:

"'Bernhart, thou art persuaded that I hate thee,
and seek thy destruction; but thou dost err grievously, my friend: excepting those of the blood
of Craenhove, I love but one being, and thou art
that one. I have indeed given thee reason to fear
and even to hate me; but that destiny, whose servant I am, has compelled me thereto. I saw thee
arrive at the "Lanteernenhof," and thy coming
gladdened me. I left thee at peace till an invin-
cible curiosity impelled thee to search into things
thou shouldst not know. I then took a balance,
cast thee into one scale, and the honor and welfare
of the house of Craenhove into the other, and thou
wert found wanting, and must needs become the
victim. It was needful that thou shouldst depart
hence. I tracked thy steps, therefore, and prepared for thee many sufferings, in order to render
thy sojourn here wearisome; but Aleidis soothed
all thy pains, and thou wert rendered unconquer-
able. Thou hast a right to hate me, Bernhart, for
often have I loaded thee with trouble and chagrin;

and in order to cause thee to dread me, I have even seemed to find enjoyment in thy suffering. Thou art as yet too young, my son, to penetrate the motives which forced me to treat thee as I have done. Abulfaragus, my son, is bound like a slave to the house of Craenhove, and must, perforce, sacrifice every feeling, every inclination of his own, for the furtherance of its well-being. While loving thee with fervent affection, these bonds forced me to apparent enmity toward thee. Later on, thou wilt know wherefore I tear thee from Aleidis. Sufferings there are, wherewith thou art happily still unacquainted, which inflame and penetrate the heart like an all-devouring fire. What the stars have uttered thou knowest, and to-morrow, ere sunrise, thou must quit the castle; and thou wilt do so readily, wilt thou not? Thou wilt not compel me to be stern toward thee, to call for the retainers, to strip thee of thy garments, and have thee cruelly driven from the door? Therefore thou wilt submit thyself, act as I bid thee, and obey thy destiny. Promise me this.'

"I stood there with drooping head; scalding tears streaming down my cheeks, and I could only answer with my sighs.

"'Thou weepest, my son,' continued the old man; 'thou art thinking of Aleidis, art thou not? It grieves thee to be forced to abandon thy good sister.'

"'Alas, forever!' I cried in anguish.

"'The stars announce that thou shalt return

4 *

hither, my friend,' returned the astrologer, 'and remain here ever after.'

"These words sank softly into my bosom, and consoled me. I turned my grateful eyes upon the old man, and he no longer seemed hateful to me; his features bore a gentle, loving expression; he appeared to me even like a father who discourses with his son.

"'Bernhart,' he continued, 'promise me to do my behests, and I, in a few words, will tell thee what endless bliss destiny hath reserved for thee.'

"I took his hand and promised him willing obedience.

"'Well, then,' he said, 'when thou shalt have quitted the castle, I will take measures that no other youth ever approach Aleidis: all that a father can do for his own child will I do in thy behalf; I will keep for thee a pure and faithful bride. Destiny tells me that thou wilt one day call Aleidis thy spouse, and become lord of the "Lanteernenhof" and of Abulfaragus. Does this content thy love and thy ambition?'

"Struck dumb at the happy future which the old man's words unveiled to me, and overpowered by my mixed feelings, I rose up precipitately from my seat, and, with tears of joy and happiness, sunk upon my knees before him; I could only cry out —

"'Thanks! oh, thanks, Abulfaragus! Heaven grant that thou mayest not be deceived!'

"'I deceived, child! I! Verily, I have oft been

deceived; my art is not altogether infallible. Yet
be consoled; I will abide here to insure a part of
what I have foretold thee. If Aleidis become not
thine, she shall never become another's. Never,
besides, have the stars spoken more clearly; but
hear, Bernhart, what thou must do in order to deserve thy good fortune. In thy bedchamber thou
wilt find the humble clothing of a peasant; put
this on, and take with thee from this place nothing
which belonged to thee. Sleep a while, if thou art
able; before the rising of the sun I will awaken
thee. It is forbidden me to offer thee counsel:
thou must go and abide wherever inclination
urges; but never take one step hitherward to behold Aleidis or the "Lanteernenhof." A powerful impulse will reveal to thee when thou art to
return; but this will never happen unless thou
dost possess the full assurance of being able to
return to Count Arnold his lost repose and his
heart's content. This much alone can I reveal to
thee; the rest thou wilt soon discover.'

"Hereupon he took his lamp, and, conducting
me to my bedchamber, took leave of me with
words of peace and consolation.

"Difficult were it to relate to thee, Albrecht,
the fantastic visions that hovered round me the
whole night long, — so many and so various were
the emotions which the past day had brought with
it. Unfortunate I could not call myself, seeing
that the future reserved for me so happy a lot.
To deserve Aleidis! the very thought thereof

made me ready to undergo every hardship. Not only did I blindly submit, therefore, to the will of Abulfaragus, but I rejoiced with myself in my inmost soul at being destined to soothe, nay, to dissipate altogether, the anguish which so heavily oppressed my benefactor; and some day, perchance, I should be able to penetrate that secret which hung over the fate of the house of Craenhove, like some veil woven by enchantment. All this flattered my hopes, and almost made my banishment appear like something great and noble.

"When Abulfaragus opened my door and entered with his lamp, I was quite ready, and dressed in my old garments. I cast one long, sad look at my silver hunting-horn, and followed my conductor. The door opened, and the bridge was let down. When we were in the open country, Abulfaragus gave me a piece of bread and a roast fowl. Once again I pressed his hand, saying mournfully:

"'Abulfaragus, thou knowest full well that Aleidis will not hear of my departure without pain, and that she will, mayhap, bewail the loss of her brother.'

"'Be at rest as to that, my son,' he replied, benignantly. 'I will console Aleidis, and will do my best to convince her that thou wilt return; and with that intent, Bernhart, I will speak of thee day by day, for I earnestly desire that she should never forget thee.'

"Tears of gratitude gushed from my eyes, I pressed my arms around the neck of Abulfaragus, and eagerly kissed the man whom I had till then reputed the most malignant of mankind. He then addressed me a few more friendly words, and at last said :

"' Farewell, till we meet again ! '

" I hastened onward with hurried steps, and continued my journey the greatest part of the day, without growing tired. When I had reached Santhoven, I approached a peasant's cottage, and asked for a little milk to quench my thirst. After I had exchanged a few words with the farmer, I learned from him that his shepherd had quitted him to take service as man-at-arms under some nobleman; I offered myself as substitute, and was accepted. I have now served these good people for two years, and am content with my lot: for I have the assurance that I shall one day behold Aleidis.

" But I would not willingly return to Lanteernenhof without being able to read. I am fully conscious of the enjoyment Aleidis finds in listening to the history of the warlike deeds of knights and heroes; and this pleasure she once sacrificed for my sake; during two years her words showed me plainly how grievous must have been the sacrifice. An indescribable eagerness for knowledge still burns in my bosom. I believe even that Aleidis is not wholly the cause of this : some secret feeling, the reason of which I know not, appears to govern me. This is my history, Albrecht: say, is it not a strange and sad one ? "

The old shepherd had listened with so lively an interest and such deep attention to the narrative, that he did not immediately return an answer. He looked wonderingly at his young companion, and after some moments replied:

"Sad? ay, verily; but what is still more marvellous, the name of Abulfaragus has often caused me to tremble. Art thou quite sure, Bernhart, that he is of mortal mould?"

"What other should he be, Albrecht?"

"Thou art young, Bernhart, and thou dost not know what I know. What if I tell thee that there are men who bind themselves to the devil, and receive for their slave and servant an evil spirit? What if I further reveal to thee that these men frequently repent too late of their execrable compact, and then, pursued by remorse of conscience and the fear of hell, immure themselves and shun the light of day?"

"Well, Albrecht, what is it thou wouldst say?"

"That it is not difficult to conceive that Count Arnold Van Craenhove may have sold his soul to the demon of darkness, and that Abulfaragus is the spirit whom the devil has granted him for his slave servant."

These words, uttered with a solemn voice, made a deep impression on Bernhart's mind; but he quickly recovered himself, and remarked, with an incredulous smile:

"Thou deceivest thyself, Albrecht; Count Arnold went constantly to church, like any good

Christian. And with regard to Abulfaragus, if what you say were true, he would scarcely have an image of our Lady in his apartment, and would assuredly not take so much care to deck it always with fresh flowers. Did he not besides call upon the Saviour when he knelt before the gravestone? No, that is not the undiscovered secret! That terrible night of the visit to the Countess of Merampré conceals something else. He who knows where the body of Count Hugo Van Craenhove is to be found, will be able to give information on every other matter."

"Have they never sought an explanation from this same Countess of Merampré, Bernhart?"

"How should one have been able to inquire of her? From that night forward she never was seen in Brabant!"

"I am lost in conjectures. That mysterious night witnessed perchance some direful deed of vengeance, some terrible murder; — but, however this may be, we ought not to cast suspicions on our neighbor by our own surmises. It grows late, Bernhart; the sun is sinking behind the trees: we must drive our flocks homeward."

With these words the two shepherds separated, each one going to collect his master's flocks. While Bernhart was thus busied, the old man came gliding toward him with stealthy steps, and whispered to him solemnly:

"Bernhart, hast thou ever seen the Were-wolf?"

The youth was terror-struck; and, turning his

head in every direction round the heath, replied:

"No! why address this question to me?"

"Look then at the border of the wood, and thou wilt see him."

Bernhart remarked, in fact, the dark shadowy form of a man, which appeared to advance slowly and cautiously along the thicket.

"Ha!" he exclaimed, "so that is the Were-wolf of which people talk so much! I had figured to myself a ravening beast of prey; and this appears afar off to wear the semblance of a man. What then is a Were-wolf?"

"Dost thou not know, Bernhart? A Were-wolf is a man who, on account of some sin which cries to heaven for vengeance, is doomed by God to wander, without rest or repose, all night long, under the form of a wolf. These Were-wolves avoid the villages and habitations of men, for fear that the doors and windows of the rooms should be fastened upon them; for so surely as this should happen, and the time of the Were-wolf's transformation come about, he would dash his head against the wall, and doubtless perish the very same night."

"Hast thou ever seen this man under the form of a wolf, Albrecht?"

"Ay, often. It is now more than ten years since he chose this wood as his resting-place; and from that time not a soul has dared to tread upon that ground, partly through terror, and partly from a sacred fear of this judgment-place of God. During the night he wanders about or sits among the tombs of the churchyard; there he sighs and utters fearful moans. No one has ever heard him utter words; for he is dumb and cannot hold discourse. As to all else, he is as gentle as a lamb; whenever he goes by us he droops his head, and glides away with downcast eyes. No one can remember his ever doing either man or beast any mischief. Once even he offered a poor woman, who sat weeping near the wood, two gold-pieces; the woman, however, durst not take the gold, but ran' away in utter terror. This, however, is a proof that he had not a bad heart."

During this explanation Bernhart had not once turned his eager gaze from the wolf; and as the latter at each step advanced nearer to the shepherds, they were able to discern his form more clearly. He seemed a man of unusually lofty stature, and was clad from head to foot in a hairy garment, which seemed not unlike the head of some animal. In his right hand he held a long staff, on which he leaned, with hide bent down; his left hand was clasped firmly to his body, as though he were carrying something underneath. This object doubtless attracted Bernhart's attention, for all at once he exclaimed:

"What is he holding under his arm? Is it not a book?"

"I cannot distinguish clearly," returned old Albrecht. Soon after, however, he added: "It

certainly is a book; ay, and four times as large as
my own!"

Bernhart fell into deep musing, and sighed, in
a strange tone:

"The Were-wolf can read!"

As he looked again he observed the Were-wolf
stooping at the edge of the wood, and disappearing among the bramble-bushes. His comrade had
already twice reminded him to quit the heath;
Albrecht was already at some distance with his
flocks, while Bernhart still stood motionless in the
very same spot. He was gazing fixedly on the
place where the Were-wolf had vanished from his
sight. At length, giving his dog the signal to
depart, he quitted the heath, and, with a mind
anxiously excited and full of visionary dreams, he
took his way home, while from time to time he
repeated his first exclamation:

"The Were-wolf can read!"

ALL sleeps upon the heath. The leaves of the tender plants are still folded together; the flowers have not yet opened their cups, and look like animated beings, which, with closed eyes, lie sunk in calm self-forgetfulness. The night has flown, but the day has not yet broken. The west is still covered with a dark impenetrable veil; the east is slowly brightening, like a transparent sea, on which shines a yet uncertain light. Of all the stars, one alone twinkles in the firmament; it is Lucifer, the harbinger of the rising sun.

On the border of the forest there hangs a heavy veil of mist; but it is now ascending, and has already reached the tops of the trees; soon will it have mounted aloft, and been scattered in the blue depth above. Like to a discreet maiden that quietly tarries for the awakening of her mistress, so lies the earth in deepest calm, awaiting the approach of its lord. A rosy glistering colors the east, and the morning star grows pale. Yonder a goldfinch is shaking the dew from off his downy plumage. He quits the bough on which he had been resting, wings his flight upward, and settles on the loftiest tree in the forest. Joyously he gazes toward the east, where the sun is slowly beginning his career; clear, silvery warblings come pouring from that little throat, and joyfully bid welcome to the light of day. Happy bird! that dost behold the torch of heaven before the children of men!

The signal is given, and a thousand feathered songsters awake, a thousand hymns of praise give glory, as with one voice, to the Creator. Higher and higher still mounts the lark; she would fain pour forth her homage before the very throne of God itself.

The smiling sun now rises above the pine-grove. His clustered beams dart their radiance over the heath like so many endless magic wands, and whatever they reach at once receives light and life.

Listen how the grasshopper and the cricket bring their morning prayer to the Creator! See how the flowers open their eyes, and unclose their coronals and chalices as if they would fain receive into their very hearts a glowing ray from the all-loving God. Hail! all hail! thou glorious master-piece of the great Artificer!

If such a hymn of praise echoed not aloud from the lips of Bernhart, in the depth of his soul, at least, the praise of his Creator was intoned in still richer melody; already for a full half-hour had he been kneeling on the heath, and witnessing with prayerful heart this awakening of nature, while his sheep were browsing on the dewy grass.

However devout was Bernhart's prayer, he

looked, nevertheless, at the spot where the Werewolf had vanished on the day before. Suddenly he trembled in all his limbs; he saw the Werewolf creeping forward on hands and feet under the bramble-brake, and then, getting up, retire along the edge of the wood. This time he held nothing under his arm.

The book must have remained after him in the wood; and many other books, perhaps, might be lying in the Were-wolf's den. But, could any one summon up courage enough to approach this abode, — to penetrate into his lair? Would not a frightful death be the forfeit? would not the Were-wolf tear him asunder, and scatter his quivering limbs to the beasts of the wild wood?

Poor Bernhart! there he stands on the open heath, leaning upon his staff, and he looks down upon the ground like one distracted; his forehead burns, his knees sink under him, an incomprehensible power draws him onward to the wood. Now he ventures one step — another still — and then more; but he quakes and is terror-stricken, for now he stands directly before the bramble-thicket, the boundary of the Were-wolf's territory. Will he be hardy enough to stoop himself down like the Were-wolf, and tread the footpath that leads on to the dreadful abode?

An hour before mid-day, Bernhart is still standing before the bramble-brake, with sunken head and fixed gaze and feverish agitation; eagerness for knowledge was struggling in his heart against

5 *

the fear of death. The contest must now have
ended, for Bernhart bent himself down slowly to
the ground, and crept suddenly on hands and feet
under the thicket.

He was soon able to stand upright and look
about him, so as to find out where he was. Nothing unusual presented itself to his bewildered
gaze, save a melancholy and desolate scene which
lay wrapped in a dim half-light, and in a death-
like repose. With throbbing heart and increasing
agitation, Bernhart advanced onward, with slow
and cautious steps, like some malefactor. From
time to time the hoarse cry of some bird of prey
broke upon his ear, and made him tremble in all
his limbs; and again he would pause terror-stricken
before some decayed tree, which, like a pitying
mortal, stretched forth its withered hands, and
seemed to wish to hold him back. But a feverish
curiosity drove him irresistibly on toward that lair
at the end of the path which the Were-wolf's steps
had worn. At length he reached a glen where
the trees happened in their growth to have left an
open space, decked with a carpet of turf and flowers. A small and almost imperceptible brook
wound its way along this natural prairie, just as a
serpent hurries rapidly under the thicket in order
to shelter himself from the scorching rays of the
sun. Here all breathed life and gladness; the sun
cast his perpendicular beams upon the luxuriant
meadow, and lovingly caressed its thousand glistening flowers; birds sang in full choir on the

neighboring trees: in a word, this little spot was like a garden of delights, which nature in some capricious moment had planted in the desert.

Any other wanderer but Bernhart would surely have paused in this enchanting place; would have quenched his thirst in the clear brook, and, while his ear listened to the many-voiced song of birds, would have allowed his eyes to linger with ecstasy on the divers-colored carpet of flowers which lay before him; but Bernhart's one thought was — " Where can the books lie hidden? "

After gazing round him for a while, he perceived in the distance, at the opposite end of the prairie, a lofty sand-hill, and, between the tangled copse-wood, an opening in the same, which probably formed the entrance to the Were-wolf's abode. He turned his steps in that direction, but the nearer he approached, the slower grew his pace. With each moment his dread increased, and he remained standing aghast before the Were-wolf's strange dwelling, where, however, nothing very terrible could be discerned, either from without or within. At the first glance, one could perceive that it was the unassisted handiwork of some human being. He who had constructed it had first of all dug deep in the hillside a broad, square cavity, like to a chamber, over which he had fastened a kind of roof composed of heavy branches, and covered it with a thick layer of leaves and twigs. One extremity of this covering afforded sufficient protection from the wind and rain; in

the other was to be found an aperture, which
served for a window and let in the light of day.
The dwelling of the Were-wolf was not small; for
a man of lofty stature could conveniently pass in
without stooping.

Although the whole appearance of this abode
was little calculated to inspire awe, Bernhart did
not dare to enter. Some undefined terror seemed
to seize him, for he drew back a few steps and
looked on every side with an air of alarm, to see
whether the Were-wolf had yet appeared. Perhaps he would have returned to the open heath,
but as he again passed by the entrance, he perceived the large book lying on a desk-like frame
within the cave. His resolution was quickly
taken; the book drew him onward like a magnet,
and, as a ravening beast rushing on its prey, he
sprung forward with one bound and fastened on
the outspread pages with both hands.

How happy was poor Bernhart now! A rap-
turous smile played upon his countenance, his
eyes sparkled with the fire of curiosity, his breast
heaved, his heart beat with impetuosity, and his
fingers moved with impatient haste. Now, indeed, he held in his own hands a large and beautiful book! Had Bernhart not fixed his gaze so
intently upon the letters, he would have remarked
more than one strange object in that hut. The
desk, on which the book lay, was made of twisted
boughs and fastened in the ground; in one corner
of the cave was to be found a couch constructed

after the same fashion, stuffed with moss and half
covered with a tattered woollen counterpane; in
the centre stood a wooden cross, on one arm of
which hung a knight's surcoat covered with dark-
brown stains, like those of dried blood. Underneath was suspended a sword all covered with
spots of rust, apparently caused by wet, which
had somehow been spurted over it. On the side
of the couch was an open travelling-bag, and
underneath there lay, as it seemed, some scattered
gold-pieces. Farther on, a quantity of dried roots
of all kinds were hung upon the wall; and lastly,
was to be seen a discipline, and a girdle with
numerous iron spikes running inward.

These objects, however, did not attract Bernhart's attention: he was absorbed in the contem-
plation of the book, and occasionally turned over
a leaf without even knowing what he was doing.
Had it not been for this slight movement and the
deep breathings of his chest, one might easily have
taken him for a lifeless effigy.

But see! what figure is that which appears yonder at the door? Is it a man? Yes; it is the Were-
wolf with his heavy staff and brown garments!
From his deep sunken eyes there gleams, as it
were, a fire; his hollow cheeks grow pale, and
wrath convulsively distorts his mouth. He stands
still and motionless, while he fixes his gaze upon
the shepherd, whose countenance he cannot altogether distinguish.

Poor Bernhart, thus joyfully and self-absorbed

feasting his eyes upon the book! Could he but
see the flashing eyes that are fixed upon him from
behind!

For a long while the Were-wolf gazed wrathfully into the hut; by degrees, however, his features assumed a softer look, and he appeared again
to grow quite calm. The old shepherd had apparently spoken true, when he asserted that the Were-
wolf could not speak; for instead of words there
escaped from his bosom a heavy groan, which
broke upon the ears of Bernhart like a thunder-
clap. The youth at once sprang up in alarm, and,
turning his head toward the door, saw the hollow
countenance of the Were-wolf turned toward him,
and his glaring eyes fastened upon him. With a
loud cry he fled to the other end of the hut, and
lifted up his hands toward the Were-wolf in an
attitude of speechless entreaty.

The Were-wolf advanced one step nearer to
him; but the affrighted shepherd, who saw only
death before his eyes, sunk down upon his knees,
and crept onward till he came directly before the
Were-wolf; then, seizing one of his hands and
bathing it with his tears, he cried out:

"Oh! if it be possible for thee, have compassion upon me! Mercy! mercy! harm me not, I
pray thee!"

A smile replete with kindness and benevolence
beamed from the countenance of the Were-wolf;
he took both Bernhart's hands, raised him up from
the ground, placed his thin fingers caressingly

upon his fair hair, and, to the great wonderment
of the youth, said, in a gentle voice :

"Poor child! what fearest thou from me? I am,
indeed, an unfortunate being, who am obliged thus
severely to expiate my crimes; but I do no one any
harm. Calm thy terror, my son, and be no longer
afraid of me."

Bernhart, all amazed, looked gratefully at the
Were-wolf, and kissed his hands with fervor; suddenly, there dawned in his breast a feeling of affection for the unhappy man who had treated him
thus benignly, while he himself had only expected
death at his hands.

With a smile still full of entreaty, he continued:

"Thanks, master! oh, thanks! I shall ever be
mindful of thy goodness, and remain as silent as
the grave respecting this presumptuous visit of
mine to thy abode. Forgive me! I will quickly
leave the wood."

With these words he cast yet one sad glance upon
the book, as if he wished to bid a last farewell to
that object of his longing desire. When he turned
round again, he beheld the Were-wolf sitting on
the edge of the bed, and looking fixedly on him,
while a flood of tears coursed down his cheeks.

This sight drew Bernhart back : he looked compassionately at the unhappy man, and tears of
sympathy began to fall from his own eyes.

"Master!" he said, with his soft voice, "master!
thy suffering pierces my heart. Thou hast been so
kind toward me, that I would give much to be able

to console thee : but what can a poor lad like myself do ? Should I ever have it in my power to
render thee any service, I am wholly at thy disposal."

The Were-wolf rose up slowly, took Bernhart by
the hand, and led him out of the hut, saying :

" Come, my son, that I may gaze upon thy features; it will be doing a kindness to me, and will
be a consolation in my suffering."

He conducted the shepherd to the little brook,
sat down upon the grass, and said, pointing to the
ground before him :

" Sit thee here before me, my son, and marvel
not at the tears of joy which thy countenance
causes to gush forth. Ten years have already gone
by, since any smile from the face of man hath
beamed upon the Were-wolf, since any friendly
word hath reached his ear. And then — shall I
confide it to thee ? — there is but one being in the
world, who is dearer to me than the apple of my
eye, and whose gracious countenance still makes
me cling to life. This being has blue eyes like
thine, fair locks like thine, fresh blooming cheeks,
and a voice as sweet as thine. Hence the secret
power of thy countenance over my soul. Forgive
an unhappy being this strange and perhaps foolish
emotion."

Bernhart seized one of the Were-wolf's meagre
hands and stroked it softly, by way of showing
his affection, and, if possible, comforting him
in some measure for his sorrowful lot. Thus

they remained sitting for some moments in silence side by side. At length the Were-wolf resumed:

"But tell me, my son, how thou couldst dare to enter this dreaded wood? Curiosity doubtless hath spurred thee on; and thou hast had sufficient courage to obey it!"

Bernhart's soul was now moved in its very tenderest part; he could not help revealing the all-consuming desire for knowledge which burned within his heart; and, though trembling in every nerve, he still pressed the Were-wolf's hand lovingly, and thus replied:

"Oh, master! scarce do I dare to tell thee my thoughts; yet, nevertheless, thy kindness encourages me. Reject my presumptuous prayer, if it please thee not to grant it; but be not displeased with me! There burns in my soul an incomprehensible desire to learn how to read; and were it permitted me to explain, I could tell you also how this desire sprung up within my breast. It has become so strong, that the very sight of a book exercises over me an irresistible power: I thus feel my forehead glow, my heart beats impetuously, and I tremble with eager desire, like a very child."

"I have observed it," murmured the Werewolf.

"Well, then," continued Bernhart, "I perceived thee yesterday, passing by the border of the wood with a book under thy arm. That was enough.

6

From that moment I have had no rest; I did not sleep this last night, and I felt myself impelled toward thee by some secret power. I struggled desperately against this unknown agency, for I dreaded thee much; but all in vain! My fate was fixed, and I would have hurried through fire and water to seek out that book. Shall I confess to thee what bold, audacious hope filled my bosom? I dared to hope that the Were-wolf might teach me to read!"

There was a short pause, during which the young shepherd peered anxiously and tremblingly into the hollow eyes of the Were-wolf.

"Well, then, my son," said the latter, "thy hopes shall not be disappointed; the Were-wolf will teach thee."

A shout of joy resounded over the meadow. Bernhart sprang forward, sat himself down near the Were-wolf, twined his arms round his neck, and wept with joy upon his shoulder, while words of gratitude poured from his lips. A moment after he started up again, leaped about like one distracted round the Were-wolf, and continued, without stopping, his cry of joy —

"Then at last I shall learn to read! Thanks, thanks, dear master! I will pray to God for thee, and kiss thy hands, as those of my best benefactor. To read, — to know! Heaven be praised for such goodness!"

The Were-wolf stood up, and approaching Bernhart, said, in an earnest tone, "I must forewarn you that the fulfilment of my promise depends on certain conditions, which must be inviolably kept. Mark well then what I say, and impress my words deeply in thy soul; for if thou shouldst forget any one of them, I can never see thee more."

"Oh, speak!" exclaimed Bernhart; "I am prepared for all; never will I do any thing that may be displeasing to thee!"

"Attend well, then! Thou must never put thy foot in the wood, save in the early morning, ere yet the sun stands in the south. Never must thou return to the hut of the Were-wolf, happen what may; never must thou ask the Were-wolf any question concerning his manner of life or his exercises of penitence; and still less must thou speak to him of thy parents, thy sister, or thy brother. Let this last name, above all others, never drop from thy lips. Beware of penetrating by night into the wood. Thou knowest the punishment, which, through God's will, I am obliged to undergo: it is dreadful, and even perilous to witness. Guard faithfully in thy breast the secrets of this wood: an incautious word might cause me my death. This is all that I have to say to thee. And now, my child, behold the sun hath reached the south; one of my hours approaches. Leave me therefore. When thou returnest in the morning, seat thyself beneath yon oak, and imitate the cry of the wood-owl. It will be heard in my hut, and then I will come to thee with the book."

At these words he pressed once again the hand

of the young shepherd, and turning round, he pro
ceeded with slow steps toward his hut.

Bernhart lifted up his staff from the ground,
and took the path by which he had come. How
beautiful, how resplendent, now appeared to him
this woody solitude! How glorious the sunlight,
which shone warmly on his glowing cheek as soon
as he had crept from the bramble-brake, and stood
upon the open heath! How ravishing, how sweet,
the song of the birds, and the solitary chirp of the
grasshopper!

With light and bounding steps he hastened
toward his flocks, called to him his faithful dog
and his favorite sheep, and began telling them that
he was to learn to read; he sang all his choicest
songs, and danced untired upon the heath, until
the sinking sun called him homeward.

CHAPTER III.

THE STORM.

ON the following day, as soon as Bernhart had led his sheep to the heath, he crept forward under the bramble-brake and hastened toward the abode of the Were-wolf. No sooner had he begun to utter the appointed cry, than the Were-wolf came out from his hut and approached the youth with a benevolent smile. He sat down near him under the tree, and after he had opened the large book, he began, without other explanation, to show him the letters and to name them. When he had devoted two hours to this instruction, he got up, drew forth from under his garment another book, and offered it to Bernhart with these words :

" My son, take this little book as a present from me ; it will serve thee to repeat to thyself what I have taught thee. Thou must summon all the faculties of thy soul in order to retain well what I convey to thee, and when thou art alone strive to recollect the characters again. I have sufficient confidence in thee to be convinced that thou wilt not show this book to any one, and that, in case it happen to be perceived, thou wilt be silent respecting its owner."

Bernhart carried the book with rapture to his lips, and answered:

"Oh, fear nothing, master! I will fasten the book in a sheepskin cover, and wear it, suspended to a cord, on my naked breast. In this way no one will be able to discover it. I will only draw it forth when far from the reach of all mankind, in order to learn it undisturbed."

"Until to-morrow, then, my son," said the Werewolf, and withdrew.

Bernhart quitted the wood and betook himself to his flock. Seating himself on the ground with blissful pleasure, he opened the book upon his knees, and, quite absorbed in himself, he repeated carefully what he had heard. Occasionally a joyful smile gleamed over his features, as he recognized a letter, and greeted it as an old friend; at other times grief and disappointment might be read upon his countenance, and he would rub his forehead with impatient gesture when his memory had proved unfaithful, and he could not recall the name of this or that character.

Thus did Bernhart spend the first day of his school-time, and so also were spent the days following. He was not always able to quit his flocks and repair to the wood, for he was frequently obliged to lead them for pasture to some distant spot. Thus five or six days would often pass, before he could visit the stranger; but then he studied all the more diligently the little book which he constantly wore next his heart.

Since his acquaintance with the Were-wolf, Bernhart was not regarded with so much favor by the farmer in whose service he was. This change was occasioned by Bernhart's negligence: for instead of leading the sheep to the richest pastures, he was nearly always to be found in the neighborhood of the wood, where little herbage for cattle was to be found; and often had the passers-by looked about for the shepherd in vain.

It will not appear wonderful that Bernhart in a short time made great progress, and that before a year had passed he was able to read through his own book, and even to repeat by heart the beautiful prayers which it contained. From time to time the Were-wolf allowed him to read in the larger book; and this greatly rejoiced the heart of the young shepherd; for the volume, which contained the " Wonders of Nature," by Pliny, gave him a description of many strange animals. Hitherto Bernhart had never questioned the Were-wolf upon any matter, neither had the latter manifested a desire to learn any thing more precise concerning his young scholar; as yet he did not even know his name. Notwithstanding this, Bernhart felt himself drawn toward his benefactor with a feeling of love and gratitude. Frequently already had he shed bitter tears at the thought of how many pains the Were-wolf must needs endure without its being permitted him to seek for consolation or alleviation for his suffering. His grateful sympathy was increased yet more, when, after the lapse of a

year, he remarked that the Were-wolf grew visibly
thinner and thinner, and was evidently sinking by
degrees into the grave. With deeper grief still,
Bernhart soon saw that it was only with painful
effort that the old man could leave the hut in order
to repair to the tree, that his eyes had lost their
brilliancy, and his voice had become dull and almost unintelligible.

Once, as the Were-wolf was striving to explain
to him a passage in the large book, he suddenly
lost the power of utterance, and heaved a sigh,
which showed that his breast was now too weak to
be able to endure the fatigue of continued speaking. Bernhart's feelings here overpowered him,
and he exclaimed, in a flood of tears, —

" Oh, master! thou art ill, and thou doest nothing
to restore thyself. Thou dost then wish to die?"

Instead of answering, the Were-wolf lifted up his
book from the ground, and turned slowly toward
the hut, saying, in a melancholy voice, "Until to-
morrow, my son."

Bernhart saw him depart with fainting steps.
When he had wept a long while in the same spot,
he returned full of grief and anxiety, to the open
heath. During that entire day he thought of the
illness of his benefactor, and poured out many a
secret tear over his unhappy fate. When the day
was declining he took his way homeward, and as
they passed into the field he counted over, in presence of the farmer, the sheep of his flock. Five
of the sheep were wanting. Thereupon the long·

suppressed indignation of the farmer found vent;
in stern language he upbraided the shepherd with
his negligence, and loaded him with invectives. At
the same time he ordered him to tie up his knap-
sack, and without further delay drove him from
his house.

When evening had wrapped the earth in gloom,
the young shepherd lay weeping on the heath, not
far from the well-known bramble-brake. The unhappy youth knew not whither to bend his steps,
and had laid his head down upon his bundle in
order to wait for the morning, and then to acquaint
the Were-wolf with his misfortunes.

In spite of his deep trouble, he at length closed
his eyes in sleep. Scarcely had he slept two hours
when the heavy, sultry air began to weigh upon
him like a covering of lead. His breathing became oppressed, perspiration covered his body,
and from time to time he would draw his hand
unconsciously toward his chest as though to fan
himself. All, even the inanimate things of nature,
seemed in anxious expectancy; not the smallest
breeze, or a sighing zephyr, stirred the leaves; the
heath seemed one illimitable grave. Only from
afar one might hear the croaking of the frogs as
they sent forth their greeting to the approaching
rain.

Shortly there showed in the far horizon a sombre
veil, which slowly lifted itself higher and higher,
and spread itself out wider, like a mourning crape
which the hand of God was stretching over the

anguished earth. Ever and anon from behind the
horizon there flamed forth a light gleam: the
silence of night became more awful, the air more
oppressive — until at length the threatening vol-
cano sent forth a messenger, as though to say, "I
come!"

The harbinger breeze murmured caressingly
through the leaves, and gently swayed the tops of
the tender plants; but soon after the storm rapidly
developed itself: a fiery arrow flew athwart the
broad expanse; a dreadful thunder-clap shook the
lowly couch of the young shepherd. Awakened
and still deafened with the sound, he started from
his slumber, opened his eyes, and gazed upward.
At that moment twenty flashes shot from the
heaped-up clouds, and directly after a hurricane
swept howling over the wild heath, bowing or
snapping the strongest trees, and bearing the torn-
off leaves in rapid whirl toward the heavens. The
clouds broke; the rain burst down in torrents, like
a second deluge. Alarmed and terror-stricken,
Bernhart fell down upon his knees and prayed.
Then he rose up and hurried toward a large beech,
in order to find shelter from the storm; but before
he could reach it a serpent-like flame ran down
the trunk of the tree, and broke it like a straw,
while its splendid crest was hurled to the earth
with a fearful crash. The lightning hissed without intermission over the heath; Bernhart's terror
increased with each moment, and, whether it was
that he expected help from the Were-wolf, or that

he was spurred onward by the destiny that ruled him, he crept under the bramble - brake, and hastened, all distracted, to the hut. As soon as he had reached the oak-tree he uttered, despairingly, the accustomed cry; but no reply reached his ear, nor, though the lightning lit up the heath with its dazzling splendor, could he see the old man approach. At first it occurred to him that the Were-wolf, in pursuance of God's chastisement, was to wander about that night as a wolf, and that he would perchance return under that guise. The hut he dared not approach, for that would have been to break his plighted word. He went back therefore by the path he had come, and threw himself down upon the ground at some distance from the brake. The storm went on careering toward the north, and presently an awful calm sank down upon the earth.

CHAPTER IV.

THE EXPLANATION.

ON the following morning the sun rose clear and resplendent in the blue horizon, throwing its beneficent light upon Bernhart, and quickly drying his wet garments. He took his bundle from the ground, and repaired again to the oak-tree in the wood, and uttered his usual cry; but the call remained unanswered as before: no one emerged from the hut. Bernhart repeated it several times, but in vain. Terrible forebodings now filled his breast: he thought of the possible death of the Were-wolf; then, perhaps, that he was only ill; but how, then, could he help himself? — he who was only able to walk a few steps. This thought quickened Bernhart's resolution to go to the very hut, and, if necessary, to fall a sacrifice even to his own generosity.

He advanced toward the hut; but scarcely had he looked within, when a cry of alarm burst from his lips, and, quaking with affright, he remained standing like one rooted to the spot.

In front of the cross lay the Were-wolf, half-naked, and stretched out like a corpse; blood gushed in thick drops from his bared back, and his fainting hand still grasped convulsively a dis-

cipline, wherewith he had scourged himself thus
pitilessly.

After Bernhart had gazed in mute horror at
this fearful spectacle, he sprang into the hut, encircled the Were-wolf with his arms, and cried
out, weeping, "Master, master, awake! it is I, thy
scholar: oh, do not thus die!"

The Were-wolf opened his eyes, and looked at
the young shepherd unsteadily, and with a sad
smile.

"My son," he said, "I forgive thee for having
broken thy word. Thou hast now discovered a
secret of my bitter life. To-day, alas! I shall not
die; but I hope that God will soon grant to me a
resting-place in the grave."

At these words he rose up, drew on his hairy
garment, and seated himself on the edge of the
bed; he looked unusually pale, his lips were livid,
and his eyes fixed and glazed.

Bernhart could no longer bear the sight.

"Oh, master!" he exclaimed, with doleful voice,
"wherefore dost thou punish thyself thus? That
cannot be God's pleasure! If thou hast indeed
committed a deadly sin, it cannot be so grievous
as the punishment thou dost inflict upon thyself."

A disdainful smile hovered over the Were-wolf's
features. "Not grievous!" he exclaimed. "Listen,
young man: since death is now near to me, and
thou wilt never guess who thy benefactor is, I will
confide to thee the secret of my crime. Thou hast

7

read in the book which I gave thee how Cain
killed his brother Abel, and how he was therefore
cursed by God in his posterity. Well, then, my
son, the Were-wolf likewise hath murdered his
brother, and God hath cursed him till his death!
Behold this sword: it is the very one that slew
my brother; on this garment his innocent blood
still remains."

A painful silence followed these words. Soon,
however, the Were-wolf gazed anew at the affrighted Bernhart, and in a broken voice continued his recital:

"My son, I will reveal to thee in a few words
my misdeeds: the history of my life will be the
last instruction I can impart to thee. I had a
brother, and we loved one another with the
deepest attachment. We also had a sister, whose
features are very like thine; therefore am I gladdened by thy presence. We lived long together
happy and content, till a woman excited jealousy
in our hearts. I loved her with a burning ardor;
my brother not less earnestly: but he was hand-
somer than I, and seemed to be rewarded with a
return of love.

"Jealousy burned like poison in my veins, but
could not prevail over brotherly love; I concealed
my affliction, and suffered in silence. As I was
returning one day with my brother and an old
domestic from a visit to this lady, he began to jeer
and scoff at my unrequited love. The long pent-up
rage began to burn in my breast. He still went

on with his scoffings. I lost all reason, and
indignation made me blind; involuntarily I
seized the sword which hung from my saddle, and
cleaving the head of my brother, he dropped down
dead upon the ground. I sprang from my horse
and threw myself upon his body; his blood spurted
out upon my surcoat; I tore my hair in despair;
with heart-rending tears I called him by his name,
but all was in vain; no answer was returned."

The Were-wolf here paused to recover breath.
Bernhart stood motionless before him; he shuddered visibly, and his whole bearing betrayed his
impatience to learn the continuation of his narrative.

The Were-wolf continued:

"It was not long permitted to me to bewail my
crime over the dead body of my brother. The old
domestic soon came with a travelling-bag, which
he attached to my steed; he then tore me away
from the body, compelled me, by an irresistible
power, to mount my horse, and urged me to fly,
that our house might not be covered with eternal
shame.

"Blindly, and bereft of consciousness, I gave
spurs to my horse, and let it gallop on the whole
night long. Two years I wandered about in
foreign lands, and after their expiration I made
my confession, and the penance appointed me
was, to pass my whole life in solitude and in prac-
tices of penitence. I chose this wood for that
purpose. I am not a Were-wolf, my son; but, in

order the better to conceal my secret, I submitted to this appellation, which the country-people had given me. Now thou knowest thy benefactor."

Bernhart would fain have spoken, but his surprise was so great, that for some time he could not utter a word; at length his bosom became lighter, and he cried out, like one distracted:

"Abulfaragus! Aleidis! Arnold! Oh, master! thou art no murderer; thy name is Hugo Van Craenhove!"

Who could describe the expression which came over the features of Hugo at these words? His eyes flashed suddenly with new fire; he leaned his head toward Bernhart, as if he would fain crave a clearer explanation of his words.

The youth, however, again cried out:

"No, Count Hugo, thou art no murderer! thy brother lives!"

With a loud cry and a flood of tears, Hugo sank from the bedside to the ground, dragged himself toward Bernhart, seized his hand, and sighed out these words:

"What sayest thou? Oh, speak! Have I not slain my brother? Am I not then a murderer? Does he live, and hast thou seen him alive since that dreadful night? O God! could I but believe this! But thou dost err; I have certainly killed him; there, there hang the tokens of his blood!"

"No, master!" exclaimed Bernhart; "I mistake not. Arnold Van Craenhove lives, I repeat it:

he it was that gave me the sweet Aleidis for my
sister. I have spent eight years of my life in
the 'Lanteernenhof,' and am acquainted with the
events of that dreadful night. The blow thou
didst deal thy brother was not mortal: he only
bears a deep scar upon his forehead. Now has it
become clear to me why Abulfaragus banished
me: it was that I might lead back thee, my master, to Count Arnold."

Hugo now no longer doubted the truth of Bernhart's words. He cast himself down before the
cross, and poured forth with loud voice a fervent
thanksgiving to the Almighty. When he rose up
again, a blissful smile beamed over his countenance,
and with unspeakable joy he repeated:

"So, then, I am no murderer! Heaven be
praised for its mercy!"

Then he sat down fainting upon the couch, and
tears of joy coursed unrestrained down his cheeks,
where a settled smile still continued to linger.

Bernhart stood silent awhile, and held his hands
before his face, as though given over to deep emotion. After a few moments he drew near to Hugo,
and said, earnestly:

"The all-beneficent God hath made me unhappy
for a short time, in order to use me as the instru-
ment of his inscrutable designs: my mission is
now half accomplished. As Abulfaragus formerly
predicted, I shall now quickly return to the 'Lanteernenhof,' in order to change, by one single
word, the suffering of thy brother into joy."

7 *

An expression of deep pain glanced darkly over Hugo's features:

"My brother," said he, thoughtfully, — "my brother! shall I ever dare to appear before him? Will he not load me with reproaches? And yet, oh God! I must see him, crave his forgiveness, feel his brotherly kiss upon my cheek, and press my sister Aleidis to my bosom. And then — then will I give up my spirit beneath the shadow of the towers of my ancestral castle."

"Thy brother?" said Bernhart, interrupting him; "thy brother will receive thee as an angel sent by the Lord to bring him pardon. He hath suffered as grievously as thou; he also is worn with sorrow, and droops his head under the bitter weight of remorse. The intelligence that thou art living will restore to him all his vigor and joy; and he will bless me as his deliverer!"

A fresh pause followed these words. Count Hugo was the first to break the silence; he bent forward, grasped Bernhart's hand, and said, in a sorrowful voice:

"My good son, thou wilt perchance marvel at the request I am about to make thee: it is probably the last service which thou wilt have to render me."

"Any thing, every thing," exclaimed Bernhart; "I have never yet been able to do any thing for my benefactor who taught me to read."

"Well, then, good youth, I wish to accompany thee to the 'Lanteernenhof!' Hast thou strength

and courage enough to support my fainting
limbs?"

"Thou art then so feeble!" sighed Bernhart.
"We have two good leagues to go from this spot!
Will thy strength sustain thee? If it be agree-
able to thee to stay here till to-morrow evening,
I will return with some wagon to convey thee
hence."

"My impatience is too great," returned Hugo;
"and dost thou not comprehend, my son, that servants and men-at-arms would accompany me? In
this wise I never will return."

"I will do as thou wishest," said Bernhart: "I
am ready."

Count Hugo gratefully pressed the hand of
the youth, and said, while he pointed before
him:

"My son, this abode of the Were-wolf must not
remain standing here, like a leaf in the unhappy
history of his life. Take from the couch both
moss and leaves, tear up the stakes from the
ground and lay them thereon, and cast the reading-
desk also upon the heap."

When this was accomplished, Hugo seized the
blood-stained garment and laid it upon the pile.
Bernhart followed his movements without venturing to utter a word, although the greatest astonishment was depicted on his countenance. He
laid the cross down at some distance. Hugo was
busied with a flint in striking sparks from the
sword, which he caused to fall upon the heap of

dry grass. Now for the first time Bernhart understood his intention. He ran quickly back, seized
the large book and took it under his arm, as an
old frien1 whom he would fain rescue from the
flames. Pointing to the travelling-bag, he inquired :

"But this gold, master ? "

" If thou wouldst take some with thee," returned Hugo, " do so."

Bernhart took two of the golden coins, and put
them with his little book into the leathern scrip.
The expression of his countenance made it evident
that he was not taking the money without some
peculiar design.

Suddenly the **dry** grass took fire and blazed
around the hut. The old man seized Bernhart
by the hand, bade him take the cross with him,
and walked before him to the oak-tree. When
they looked around, they beheld dense clouds of
smoke ascending into the air; tongues of flame
mounted over the roof, and quickly encircled the
hut.

" Now, my child," sighed Hugo, " let us with
united hearts pray to God yet once more in this
wood."

With these words he knelt down slowly, and
lifted his hands in prayer. Bernhart imitated his
example, and while the hut became a prey to the
flames, they both sent up a heartfelt prayer to
God, amid the silence of the forest, and bade a
last farewell to the solitary spot which had so

long been watered by the tears of Count Hugo.
After the hut was reduced to ashes, they rose up,
planted as a remembrance before the oak the
wooden cross, and with slow steps entered the
footpath. A moment later they stood upon the
open heath.

CHAPTER V.

THE REUNION.

COUNT HUGO had relied too much upon his strength. Scarcely were they both out of the wood, when he felt a trembling in his limbs. He sat down exhausted, and let his head droop dejectedly upon his breast. Bernhart meantime broke an oaken staff from the thicket and returned to Hugo.

"Be of good heart now, master," he said; "I will become thy prop, and carry thee, if need be. We will journey on slowly; only take courage!"

He helped the feeble Hugo to stand up, and then placed his shoulder under the count's arm, and obliged him to lean upon it. With sinking steps they toiled on over the heath, interrupting their journey with frequent pauses to take rest.

For a little while there was a silence between the two; but by degrees they began to hold comforting discourse with each other. Bernhart was doubtless relating the history of his changeful life, for his eyes now shown with unwonted fire; the name of Aleidis resounded amid the lonely trees, and the fields assuredly heard the thrilling avowal of the secret feeling of his heart. Although Hugo

experienced great fatigue, there nevertheless shone
from time to time a smile upon his features, when
he learned the noble birth of his young companion, and felt assured that reciprocal love had
bound together the hearts of Bernhart and Aleidis.
The young man's account convinced him that
Arnold bewailed his scoffing, and had never ceased
to love him in spite of the deadly wound which
Hugo had inflicted. This comforting assurance
inspired him with new strength; he struggled
manfully against his weakness, and thus about
two hours after mid-day they reached a little wood
near Wyneghem.

There the strength of the count abandoned him.
He sank down by a tree, and lay fainting on the
ground, like one dead; yet his features were lighted
up with a blissful smile, his eyes sparkled, and a
color rose upon his hollow cheeks. The energetic
spirit rose triumphant over the exhausted body,
and he believed that after a kindly repose he would
again be able to proceed with his journey.

Wonderful was the tender solicitude of Bernhart. He looked anxiously about, and his eyes
sought for some object which might serve as a
pillow for the feeble head of the old man. As he
found none, he let himself down upon the ground,
drew Hugo's head gently toward him, and leaned
it on his breast, and there he remained sitting
motionless.

Not a sigh was to be heard under that tree, not
a motion revealed life in those two forms, until at

length Count Hugo, after he had rested half an hour, said to Bernhart:

" My son, I am thirsty."

The youth, thus released, turned himself round heedfully, and replied, while he rose up:

" Remain lying quietly here, master; I will look about for some drink."

And with these words Bernhart passed on between the trees, and as soon as he could no longer be seen by Hugo, he ran with all his might to the village of Wyneghem. There he changed one of his gold-pieces for a pitcher of beer, a piece of boiled meat, with some butter and bread. Laden with these provisions, he returned in haste to Hugo, who was sitting upright against the tree, and seemed to be somewhat rested from his fatigue. He ate and drank of all that Bernhart offered him, and rejoiced his young companion by an appearance of restored strength and courage.

Two hours after sunset they beheld from afar the towers of " Lanteernenhof." The same feeling possessed both; their hearts beat faster they trembled, and fixed their eyes earnestly on the distant battlements without revealing their emotion by a single word.

One might think that they would now have hastened with redoubled steps and heightened impatience toward the end of their wanderings.

But it was just the contrary. Overpowered by their feelings, both sank to the ground, and were for some time lost in silence at the sight of the towers, while tears rolled over their cheeks in silvery pearls.

Hugo first broke the silence.

"Oh, my son, couldst thou look into my heart! Couldst thou know what endless joy possesses and seizes me! Yonder they are, those towers of my ancestral home! After thirteen years of suffering — thirteen years, during which remorse has gnawed at my heart — I behold them again with the blessed feeling that I am no murderer. Ah! the leaves of the trees that overshadowed the sports of my childhood will yet once more rustle over the gray head of the feeble, sinking Hugo. I shall find anew rich remembrances of my forefathers, and fold my brother, my Aleidis, my faithful Abulfaragus, with ecstasy in my arms. Ah! may the all-beneficent God accord me yet a few days — and then, then will I gratefully and cheerfully —"

A singular cry from Bernhart interrupted him in his speech.

"Look! look!" exclaimed the young man, while he pointed in the distance. "Dost thou see under those trees an old man who is gathering herbs? Yes, yes, it is he!"

Before Hugo could follow with his eye the direction in which Bernhart pointed, the latter had already risen in impetuous haste, and was now running forward as fast as he could between the trees toward the old man. Hugo, without recognizing the stranger in the distance, saw him press

8

Bernhart to his breast three times, and kiss him
fervently. They soon advanced rapidly to the spot
where Hugo was sitting, and as they approached
him he first recognized his faithful Abulfaragus.
He rose with a cry of joy, and sank into the arms
of the astrologer. The latter could not speak for
emotion, and his tongue only muttered unintelligible words; he sat himself down upon the grass,
and a stream of tranquil tears flowed from his eyes.
Hugo sat down by his side and took his hand;
Bernhart sat on the other side in the like position.
After a few moments Abulfaragus dried the tears
from his cheeks; with wonder and love he con-
templated the countenance of Hugo, and with
eyes gazing heavenward, exclaimed:

"I thank, I thank thee, O God, that I behold
him once again before I die!"

Then he fixed his eyes again upon Hugo, and
said:

"Thou art weak and ill, master, but fear not
that death shall tear thee from us; more than once
have I combated him, and, besides, the noble blood
of Craenhove flows in iron frames. Courage and
hope, Count Hugo! happiness and joy await us
all."

"So it is then true, Abulfaragus, that my brother Arnold hates me not?"

"Hate thee?" said Abulfaragus, amazed; "hate
thee, Count Hugo? Thy face betrays how much
thou hast suffered, but I can scarce believe that
thy life has been more wretched than that **of**

Arnold. Thou didst believe thou hadst killed
thy brother; Arnold holds himself, on account of
his mocking words, as the cause of the misdeed,
and, perhaps, of a self-murder. After he had
travelled about for two years, and had sought
during that time for some token of thy being still
alive, he buried himself as one dead in the walls
of the ' Lanteernenhof,' under the conviction that
he himself had taken away thy life. Thou mayest
easily conceive how this double sting of conscience must have irrecoverably troubled his repose. Thou art thin and worn, he is still more
so; thou art happy to behold him again, and he
will perchance lose his senses for joy at the sight
of thee."

"Well, then, let us hasten to him," cried Hugo,
" so that I may behold him again, and receive his
pardon!"

"My lord count!" returned Abulfaragus, quickly,
"thy wish neither can nor ought at once to be fulfilled; thy sudden appearance might easily have a
fatal issue. Besides, thou knowest that the greater
part of our life has been spent in tears and affliction, in order to conceal the dreadful secret. It
ought not yet to be unveiled. Should Count
Hugo Van Craenhove enter the ' Lanteernenhof '
in this poor guise by day, the servants and retainers would seek for the solution of the enigma;
and who knows whether they might not succeed
in discovering it? Remain here till evening; I
will return to the castle, and there give orders that

no one go forth. Meanwhile I will send thee
Aleidis, and will myself return betimes to fetch
thee. Have patience yet a little while; it is but a
few minutes added to thirteen long years. It is
the last sacrifice thou offerest to the honor of thy
house!"

With these words he pressed the hand of the
count, and with hasty steps entered the path to
the "Lanteernenhof." Filled with hope and joy,
Hugo began to hold happy converse with Bernhart, and so shortened the delay. Suddenly they
beheld in the distance a noble dame, who seemed
to approach them. She was of a tall and slender
figure, and wore black robes, and a transparent
veil which half concealed her countenance. Although Bernhart knew her not, he listened, nevertheless, to the voice of his heart, sprang up quickly,
and ran toward her with all his might, while he
called out, with ecstasy:

"Sister, dear sister,—Aleidis, Aleidis!"

With outstretched arms he rushed toward her,
but at a little distance stood suddenly still, as
though paralyzed; he let his arms sink down,
while, all abashed and embarrassed, he bent down
his weeping eyes. Poor Bernhart! he had thought
to find again his sister, the little Aleidis; but instead of her, he now saw standing before him a
tall damsel of surpassing beauty. She looked
upon him without even the smallest semblance of
easy, unconstrained friendship; on the contrary,
a blush covered her alabaster forehead at his first

glance. Then Bernhart first felt in what coarse
and unseemly garments he was clothed; how his
hair was all in disorder, and his face grown pale.
Confusion filled his breast; and at that instant,
perhaps, he discovered for the first time that some
other feeling besides that of brotherly love was
unwittingly striking root in his heart. It must be
that the eye of love penetrateŝ into the depths of
the heart; for Aleidis understood at one glance
the young man's pain, and, instead of saluting
him with the brotherly name of Bernhart, she said
to him, with her silvery voice :
  "Burgrave Van Reedale, art thou pained in beholding thy sister again?"
  The young man raised his head and smiled
gratefully upon her for these comforting words;
and while he, thrilling and ravished, allowed his
eyes to rest upon her, she said, in a low, and as it
were, anxious voice:
  "Bernhart, I have thought of thee alone during
the long and sorrowful separation; but hast thou
not forgotten Aleidis?"
  This avowal drew from Bernhart's breast an exclamation of wonder, and from his eyes a flood of
joyous tears.
  "Forgotten! oh, heavens!" he exclaimed; "forgotten thee, Aleidis! utter not such words, for my
heart is almost bursting at beholding again my
sister and my friend."
  And he clasped her hands in his, and bedewed
them with tears of love and gratitude. Hand in

hand, all trembling with emotion, they both approached Count Hugo; and now began a touching struggle of sisterly affection. Aleidis sat near
her brother without uttering a word, her arms
twined about his neck, and her glistening blue
eyes fast fixed upon him. From time to time
Bernhart's shy and furtive glances wandered toward the beautiful Aleidis; for her graceful at-
tractions agitated his sensitive soul too keenly,
and inspired a feeling in his heart which astonished and abashed him. This feeling was still
heightened when Aleidis's eyes met his own, and
rested softly and mildly upon him. Meantime the
sun was disappearing under the horizon, and twi-
light was beginning to steal over the fields. Abulfaragus now came back to them.

As soon as Bernhart perceived the old man, he
ran to him, and threw himself with wild joy upon
his neck, exclaiming:

"Oh, thanks, thanks, good and noble Abulfaragus! thou hast done for me what a father does for
his son: thou hast kept for me a beautiful and
loving sister. May Heaven prolong thy days for
this, and bestow upon thee —— "

Abulfaragus tapped the young man on the
shoulder, and replied, with joyous pleasantry:

"Young friend, thou seest that what joy now
bestows upon thee might formerly have proved a
misfortune to this noble house, and thy own ruin.
Abulfaragus hath not persecuted and banished
thee without design. Now all danger is passed

away: my happy child, I have not only kept a
sister for thee —— "

He approached his mouth to Bernhart's ear, and
went on mysteriously :

" For the sacristan of Deurne has received orders to deck the church for the celebration of a
splendid wedding.   Dost thou know the bride-
groom?"

With these words he quitted the astonished
Bernhart, and went on to Hugo.   He apprised
him of his brother's condition; and as soon as he
perceived that the darkness favored their entrance
into the castle, he urged his departure.   During
this short journey, all observed a strict silence;
the approaching meeting kept their minds on the
rack and in anxious thought.   Hugo trembled
in every limb; his heart beat with irregular
throbs.   He was now to appear before his brother, whom he had almost slain.   At length they
proceeded over the bridge, and entered the court-
yard.   Hugo could no longer hold himself upright, but begged for some support.   Bernhart
took his right arm, and Aleidis his left, and thus
they advanced slowly to Arnold's room.   The
door opened, and then, in wondrous tones, there
resounded the words, " Brother! brother! Pardon! pardon!"

Both brothers sank weeping into each other's
arms.   One long kiss — a few unintelligible words
followed — and then the worn-out frames gave way
together, and dropped with heavy fall to the

ground. As they held each other fast embraced,
those present believed that over-excitement had
thrown them into a momentary swoon. Abulfaragus was the only one from whose lips burst
forth a piercing cry, which resounded through the
whole castle; he threw himself sobbing upon the
bodies of the brothers.

Alas! thirteen years of suffering had not been
able to break down their vital powers. One
single moment of joy had done this. They were
dead, and their souls had mounted upward together to the judgment-seat of God.

Had any one, ten years later, cast a glance into
the solitary castle, he would have found it in no
way altered.

Were it permitted him, at the same time, to
wander in the evening under the over-arching
trees of the court-yard, a small thicket of oaks
would soon have arrested his attention, in the
midst of which stood a gravestone, with the following inscription:

D. O. M.

WALTER VAN CRAENHOVE

AND

HIS SPOUSE

MARIA,

And their Children

HUGO AND ARNOLD.

May God have mercy upon their souls.

Before the gravestone he might have seen five
persons kneeling : an old man, who tottered like
a child under the weight of years ; a man with
fair hair and blue eyes ; a most beautiful matron
with fair hair and blue eyes ; and two children, a
little boy and a little maiden, with hair and eyes
of the same color as their father Bernhart and
their mother Aleidis.

CHAPTER VI.

THE STORY OF ABULFARAGUS.

ON a winter evening, in the year 1374, most of
the occupants of the "Lanteernenhof" were
assembled in the large hall of the castle.

Abulfaragus, now eighty years of age, was seated
in an easy elbow-chair by the fireside, and looking
silently at the dancing flames. On a footstool near
him sat a boy of some five years, who, with his
little head pressed against the knee of the old
man, slumbered peacefully. A little farther on, at
a heavy oaken table, might be seen the beautiful
Aleidis Van Craenhove, with a little daughter on
her bosom, in earnest conversation with the Burgrave Bernhart Van Reedale, her husband.

Outside the castle the weather was apparently
very stormy, for the window-frames rattled fearfully in their leaden fastenings, and occasionally
there came such violent gusts of wind, that Aleidis
more than once turned round her head in anxious
alarm. Still more vehement was the howling of
the storm on the castle roof. In the chimney it
blew back the flames of the hearth-fire with irresistible force; its sharp whistlings played around
the turrets, and the rapidly-revolving weathercock
creaked wildly on its hinges.

94

Painful thoughts kept possession of the hearts of Bernhart and Abulfaragus, not perhaps because either of them dreaded any thing, or had any occasion for alarm: it was simply the natural effect of the storm. Aleidis, on the contrary, sat there in inexplicable anxiety; the loud voice of the storm and its wailing tones affected her feeble nerves, and caused her to remain trembling and agitated on her seat. The paleness of her face alarmed her spouse not a little, and with all thoughtful effort he strove by kindly words to turn her attention to other subjects. It might easily be seen that he was suffering anxiety on her account, for every feature betrayed his emotion. Suddenly a smile played about his mouth, as though some happy thought had occurred to him, and, turning to Abulfaragus, he said:

"Abulfaragus, my old friend, is it then well to be disconsolate, so long as one dwells not under the same roof with adversity?"

"No, my lord," answered the old man, without looking up; "the hours of pain and misfortune are but too numerous without this; but man is a part of creation, and therefore I marvel not that his spirit should be overclouded, when the face of heaven is shrouded in tempest."

The hollow voice of the old man terrified Bernhart not a little, and scared away from his mind the thought which had caused him to smile. He inquired:

"Doth this hour tell thee any thing sorrowful,

Abulfaragus, that thy words sound thus mournfully?"

The old man turned his gaze upon Bernhart, and said, in still more doleful tones:

"The storm, my lord, exercises an irresistible power over the hearts of men: it compels the soul to self-contemplation; it awakens the memory, unrolling before it pictures out of the distant past, and showing us the most awful moments of our life. Thus it is that it overclouds the spirit."

"It is so, indeed," replied Bernhart; "before me also, during the last half-hour, the most terrible moments of my life have been passing. I was thinking, Aleidis my beloved, how fearfully I suffered when destiny so suddenly and so cruelly tore me from thy side; again I fancied myself overwhelmed by that old grief."

Whether it was that the noble lady wished to reward Bernhart for these loving expressions, or that his words had rendered her deaf to the fearful noise of the storm, she smiled, and pressed his hand with warm affection. Bernhart inquired of the old man:

"But of what art thou thinking, Abulfaragus? Thou seemest to me as if overpowered by some deep affliction."

"I!" sighed the old man; "I am thinking of my father, and my mother, and my sister."

"Of thy father and mother?" cried Bernhart and Aleidis in one breath, and with a look of surprise. "Hast thou not always told us thou didst never know them?"

"I held it to be unadvisable to cause discomfort by the recital of the mishaps and evil fortune which befel them; and even now, I pray you question me no further: your hearts would be too deeply filled with sorrow and compassion."

"And were it even so," replied Bernhart, "could we pass the evening more profitably? Permit us to weep with thee over the sad fate of thy parents; tears of sympathy are sweet, and help to relieve the burdened spirit. Is it not so, Aleidis?"

"Ay, truly, Abulfaragus," said the noble lady. "Thou hast awakened our curiosity and our interest; and however sad thy history may be, I pray thee to share it with us. I long to know the fate of the parents of our friend and guardian."

"Their fate, noble dame?" cried Abulfaragus, with trembling voice. "That of my father, torn to pieces by wolves, — is that sufficiently dreadful?"

"Oh God!" sighed Aleidis, "what an awful secret hast thou always kept from us!"

"Is it not so?" continued the old man. "Such remembrances are too dreadful for one to be able to share them with others. It is better that they be still buried in my breast."

"Oh, no!" interrupted Aleidis; "recount to us thy history; thou hast already so often promised, and we have just now a long evening. It will hinder the storm from alarming us any further."

9   G

Bernhart joined his request with that of his spouse; and both entreated so long and so earnestly, that at length Abulfaragus consented. Thus he began:

THE STORY OF ABULFARAGUS.

" In the year 1308, there dwelt at Damascus a Jewish physician, by name Ab-el-Farach, who had acquired among the Arabs much knowledge of various kinds, and who was renowned throughout all Syria for his learning and skill. Persons came to him from Aleppo, Jerusalem, and Bagdad; yea, even the inhabitants of Scanderon and Bassora did not hesitate to undertake perilous journeys in order to consult him. This Ab-el-Farach was my father. I can yet remember that we dwelt in a sumptuous house, to which a spacious garden was attached, in which I played every day with my good mother Abigail and my sister Rebecca. We possessed slaves and servants in great number; and every one, Jew, Christian, and Saracen, esteemed and loved us.

" At that time, the Christian band of nobles, who were called Knights of St. John of Jerusalem, undertook a crusade against the Saracens, in order to wrest it from the Mohammedans, and lay with their fleet before the island of Rhodes. Universal terror spread itself over the Saracen land, for all dreaded the invasion of Syria and Palestine by the Christians. How it came to pass I know not; but suddenly a rumor was spread abroad that the

Christians and Jews were in secret league with
the European host, and were prepared to deliver
up the towns of Syria, by treachery, to the Knights
of St. John. All the inhabitants of Jerusalem who
did not believe in Mohammed were assassinated;
in still larger streams ran the blood of Jews and
Christians at Aleppo; and already, in the streets
of Damascus, men incited one another to follow
this example.

"On the evening of this day I was sitting with
my mother and sister on the flat roof of our house.
I was just ten, and my sister seven years old; and
we took little notice of the silent affliction of our
mother, so much the less because we knew not its
cause. We played together, inhaling the balmy
fragrance which the wind wafted toward us from
the west, and pointing out to one another the
most beautiful stars in the heavens; when suddenly we remarked in the court-yard underneath
our house a man who was secretly leading a
horse and a camel, and was endeavoring to conceal the animals from view. Then the house-
door was opened with violence, and again shut.
A scarce audible cry escaped from the breast of
my mother, and our attention being thus drawn
to her, we then first perceived that she trembled.

"With anxious hurry she took us by the hand,
and drew us silently on with her to the lower
apartments, into which my father was just entering. Without leaving time to my mother to speak,

he closed the door cautiously, and said, with agitated voice:

"'Abigail, if we remain here until the morning sun returns, its first beams will shine upon our dead bodies. We must away hence with all possible speed. Togrul Almahadi tells me that the slaughter of the Christians and Jews is to begin to-morrow, and that we, as the richest, are destined to fall the first victims. Ask no further now, but take these garments of our slaves and put them on, that you may be taken for a Turkish woman. Let the children also be attired in like manner. I am going to pack up some gold and pearls. A horse and a camel stand ready in the court-yard. Hasten, and say nothing to the slaves; they would betray us.'

"Toward midnight we set out. Our mother was seated on the camel, and each of us on either side of her in a kind of pannier; my father, well armed, rode forward on horseback, in order to show the way. Assuredly the anxiety of our parents must have been great, for we frequently passed by groups of Saracens; but we always made our way through them unnoticed, or else my father contrived to avoid suspicion by making them suppose that we were Turks travelling to Aleppo. After proceeding on our journey for some nights, — for during the day we kept ourselves concealed, — we came to Scanderon, and thence to Simta, not far from Rhodes. At last my father succeeded in reaching secretly the Christian

ships; there he offered his services, and very soon
gave such proof of his ability and knowledge as a
physician, that the Knights of St. John gladly consented to his proposals. On the following night,
a small galley cruised along the coast, and took us
in. Under cover of the darkness we reached the
ship in safety, and soon found ourselves in a commodious cabin.

"The siege of Rhodes lasted more than a year.
Day by day the most sanguinary conflicts took
place, and many of the knights were wounded. My
father, by his skill and attention, saved so many
of them from death, that the Christians felt themselves under the deepest obligations to him, and
honored him as their greatest benefactor. Our condition was sufficiently endurable; for our galley,
being set apart for the reception of the sick, never
took part in the conflict, and we soon felt ourselves at home with the sea and its storms. It
happened that there was in the fleet a knight of
Brabant, whose eagerness in the pursuit of knowledge soon led him to form a cordial friendship
with my father. Their mutual attachment increased from day to day, and at length became so
intimate, that the two friends scarcely ever quitted
each other, and at times they would watch together, the whole night through, the course of the
stars. The affection of this good knight extended
likewise itself to us: he often played with Rebecca and myself for hours upon the deck of the
ship, and made himself a child again, in order to

9 *

join our amusements, and render our sojourn at sea as agreeable to us as possible.

"My mother loved us with the greatest tenderness, and her heart glowed with gratitude toward the noble-minded Christian knight, who showed himself so friendly to us poor Jewish fugitives. From our earliest years the Christians had been pictured to us as cruel and detestable — as the sworn enemies and persecutors of our race.   The behavior of this knight, however, awakened our gratitude to such a degree, that every evening, as we sat alone with our father, we spoke with increasing admiration of our benefactor and protector.   The Christian religion awakened our interest and excited our astonishment more and more.   We conversed with each other on the prowess and magnanimity which the Christian faith had infused into the souls of these knights, and of that sublimity of Christian love which alone had induced our protector to transform into a paradise of friendship and brotherly love our former melancholy existence.

"Our father must certainly have often talked with his Christian friend on the subject of religion; for at times, when he returned to us, he was full of thought, and would say, 'It is not, after all, so utterly impossible that the "Crucified One" may have been the Messiah!' By-and-by he went still further, and even took pains to convince us that no other Messiah was to be looked for, since the God-man of the Christians was the promised

One. But in truth our father's exhortations were superfluous: we had long been Christians at heart; and for three months we had possessed a little image of the Saviour, and had prayed secretly before it that the 'Crucified One' would preserve the life of his servant, the Brabantine knight.

"One day, while we were yet at our morning repast, my father came into our chamber, and sat down upon a couch without uttering a word. On his features there shone a remarkable expression of happiness and joy; his eyes sparkled, a smile played around his lips, his whole countenance seemed illumined with a mysterious glow; it was as if a sunbeam had pierced through the deck and was playing upon his forehead.

"After a moment's silence he rose up, and said to us, in a glad and solemn tone:

"'Abigail, thou faithful companion of my fortunes, and you, my children, listen attentively to what I have to communicate; but think not, from what I am about to say to you, that I shall compel you to follow my example. Come hither, my son, and thou also, Rebecca, that I may kiss you once more before I proceed further.'

"However much the joyous expression of my father's countenance was calculated to inspire us with confidence, we were nevertheless possessed by a certain feeling of anxiety. Tremblingly we received the fervent kiss, and my mother wept in his embrace. We could not explain to ourselves what we had to hope or to fear.

"Suddenly my father exclaimed, in a tone of exalted enthusiasm :

"'Oh, my children! there is only one Messiah, and that Messiah is JESUS, and I am his servant! His voice hath spoken to my heart, his mercy hath filled me with light and joy!'

"With these words he drew forth a silver crucifix from under his garment, hung it on the wall, and said :

"'Jesus is my Saviour and my God!'

"My father evidently expected to be met with expressions of grief and lamentation, on account of his change of faith, and for this reason he had given the explanation thus cautiously; but to his great joy he found it far otherwise. My mother's eyes were suddenly lighted up with the same fire; like a Christian, she threw herself down before the image of the Crucified, and my sister and I knelt beside her. She lifted her hands to heaven, and prayed thus to the Incarnate One :

"'Jesus, Son of David, Thou art He of whom Esaias spoke : " Therefore the Lord shall give you a sign; behold, a virgin shall conceive and bring forth a son, and shall call his name Emmanuel!" May thy name, O Messiah! be honored by all that have breath and life! Thou art the Son of God and the Saviour of the world, the God of my husband and my own!' And we answered joyfully, 'Amen, Amen!'

"Tears of emotion and joy streamed from my father's eyes; he knelt down behind us, encircled

us with his arms, and prayed silently for a few
minutes, as though he were beseeching the Lord
mercifully to accept the offering of our common
prayer. Then he raised us all from the ground,
embraced us again and again, and exclaimed, with
ecstasy:

"'WE ARE CHRISTIANS!'

" This was the most glorious day of our life.
We experienced an inward and unforeseen gladness of the soul, and we burst into tears, while we
felt within us a foretaste of the bliss of heaven.
Toward mid-day the Brabantine knight came into
our room and shared our joy; nay, he was still
more joyful than we, for in our conversion he recognized the highest blessing which his friendship
had procured for us.

" Much time was not required to make us acquainted with the mysteries of our new faith; our
hearts received with joy the doctrine of Christ,
and we were soon prepared for the reception of
baptism. The Brabantine knight was to be my
godfather, and other noble lords were to stand
sponsors for my mother, my father, and sister.
On the appointed day a bishop arrived at our ship
with a numerous retinue, and we received at his
hands the holy rite. All the noblemen who were
present at the solemnity wished us happiness; but
the Brabantine knight especially was filled with
the greatest joy; he kissed me a hundred times
and called me his son Walter, for that was the
new name I had received. My father was called

Joseph, my mother Susanna, and my sister Maria;
Ab-el-Farach became Abulfaragus.

"While they were congratulating us on every
side, and the knights were joyfully celebrating
our conversion, we suddenly perceived on the
coast of Rhodes a large number of Turkish gal-
leys putting to sea and steering their course toward us.

"Rapidly through the whole Christian fleet re
sounded the cry, 'To arms! To arms!' The
knights hastened away each to his own vessel; all
was got ready for the combat, and our ships at
once made sail toward the enemy. As we were
ordered to go below, however, and our galley did
not take part in the engagement, we scarcely heard
anything of the conflict.

"After the fight had lasted about an hour, intelligence was brought to us that the Christians
had been victorious, that four Turkish vessels had
been destroyed, and that the rest of the fleet had
put back to shore. We heartily rejoiced at the
good tidings, and thanked God with fervent prayer
Suddenly we heard the sound of heavy footsteps
overhead; with anxious foreboding we hurried up
the gangway, and there we saw a wounded knight
borne upon the deck of the vessel.

"A sudden outburst of tears from my father at
once told us who it was they were carrying along
all bloody and lifeless. A cry of agony arose from
our breasts, and my sister fell weeping into the
arms of my mother. Springing forward, I cast

myself on my knees near the pallid face of the knight; I called him by his name, kissed his blue lips, and bedewed his pale forehead with my tears. Alas! my sponsor, our noble benefactor, had received a deadly wound: an arrow had pierced obliquely through his neck.

" The wounded man was placed upon my mother's bed, and my father then entreated all present to withdraw, and leave him alone with the knight. When this was done, he said to us:

" ' Let us cease to weep and lament, for we cannot save him thus. Let the women kneel down and pray; as for thee, Walter, run quickly for ,some water.'

" My mother and sister threw themselves upon their knees; I hurried up the gangway, and soon returned with a pitcher full of water.

" Without speaking a word, my father began to wash the wound, in order to discover whether any of the larger vessels in the neck had been injured. His forehead glowed with feverish anxiety during this examination; I saw him tear his hair with anguish, and at length sink down on the edge of the bed as if in utter despair. My tears broke out afresh; for now I could no longer doubt of my benefactor's death.

" After some moments my father raised his head, and began to examine the wound afresh. Soon after his features assumed an expression of hope, and with a calmer voice he said to my mother and sister:

" 'Oh, pray, pray earnestly; for with God's help he may yet recover!'

"A cry of joy was their only answer, while their heads bent lower still in fervent supplication. All the afternoon I assisted my father in the preparation of salves and cooling drinks; during the night we both remained beside the still motionless body, anxiously watching for the least symptom of returning life.

"The third day was at length a day of happiness and joy for us; a slight sound had been audible in the throat of the wounded man, and my father said:

" 'He will live!

"From that moment the condition of the invalid visibly improved; on the twelfth day he was able to fix his eyes upon us, and to reward us for our solicitude with his kindly looks. During fourteen nights my mother and sister watched by his bedside alternately. His wound had meanwhile closed, and before a month was over he had regained his former health and strength. His affection for us after this knew no bounds; my father had become to him as a brother, and he never after called me anything else but his son Walter.

"In the year 1310, on the 16th day of May, the Christians at length captured the island of Rhodes, and expelled the Turks. Many knights then returned to their own country, and we resolved, in like manner, to quit the fleet, and seek somewhere in Europe a fixed abode. Our friend besought us

to accompany him to Brabant. As we possessed
but little in the world, and needed a protector,
and as we felt it almost impossible to part from
our benefactor, we consented to his proposal with
grateful hearts. Soon after, we set out under the
escort of our friend *Walter Van Craenhove.*"

"Heavens! my father!" exclaimed Aleidis,
amazed. "Abulfaragus, why hast thou so long
kept this name secret from us?"

"Noble lady," replied the old man, half smiling, "yes, it was thy father, my sponsor, and the
bosom friend of my parents. Thou canst not believe how deeply I loved that most valiant of all
Christian knights! Oh, the blood which flows in
thy veins is the noblest which the sun shines upon
in the three parts of the world! If I have not
named his dear name to thee sooner, it was only
that I might not torture thee with the description
of his dreadful illness, or make thee a partaker in
that anguish which filled our breasts at his bed of
sickness."

Aleidis was silent; her glistening eyes and
parted lips showed with what unwonted curiosity her heart was beating. Abulfaragus remarked this, and presently continued his narrative.

10

CHAPTER VII.

THE PLAGUE.

A FTER a long journey, we arrived at the town of Luttich, on the Maes. My father found there so many of his former fellow-believers who spoke our mother-tongue, that he took the resolution of settling in the town as a physician. The good Count Van Craenhove obliged us to accept a considerable sum of money from him, with which we purchased a house in the street of the Jewish money-changers, and there took up our abode. Walter Van Craenhove meanwhile proceeded to his castle of 'Lanteernenhof,' accompanied by our fervent prayers and heartfelt gratitude.

"We resided in Luttich for more than a year, in happiness and peace. My father in this interval initiated me into the sciences of the Arabs, particularly in the art of healing, and in astrology, or the knowledge of the stars. He soon acquired in the Luttich territory the same celebrity which he had formerly enjoyed in Syria. Both nobles and ecclesiastics were daily cured by his means, and he gained, moreover, considerable sums by the prediction of future events. He was called the rich astrologer Abulfaragus. His prosperity, doubtless, excited ill-will and jealousy in the hearts

of many, and more than once we heard that people were secretly endeavoring to throw suspicion
upon him as a magician; added to which, the
Jews calumniated and slandered him on account
of his conversion to the Christian faith. We possessed, however, powerful friends, and so many
sick knights and prelates were constantly in need
of my father's aid, that we were amply secured
against all danger.

"About this period, there was promulgated
throughout Christendom a brief from the Pope,
calling on both knights and citizens to arm themselves for battle against the Turks. In all the
public squares, in the market-places and streets,
the papal envoys preached a universal crusade.
In their enthusiasm, they described, with the most
touching pictures, and with tears in their eyes,
how the blood of the Christians of Palestine was
poured out in torrents; how the Saracens dese-
crated, every day with fresh and blasphemous
insults, the tomb of the Saviour. Often they
spoke, too, of the sufferings of the Messias; and
related how, by that wicked and execrable race, —
for so they called the Jews, — he had been condemned and crucified. It may easily be supposed
that the adherents of our former creed would be
ready to murmur at hearing such discourse.
Slowly, in fact, there grew up a deep hatred between the people of Luttich and the Jews who
resided among them; and this aversion became
by degrees more intense and alarming. It was

commonly asserted and believed that the Jews had been guilty of all kinds of wickedness, so that whenever an assassination was committed, the people invariably ascribed the crime to their agency. However unjust it is that the innocent should suffer with the guilty, I cannot help acknowledging that many Jews were led by their fanaticism to commit crimes that fully justified this open and general aversion.

"In this conjuncture, and while the crusade was still preached, there suddenly appeared throughout Europe a fearful malady. It was called the 'Leprosy.' Whoever was seized with it felt his heart beat impetuously, and a cold sweat break out on every part of his body; his face and hands assumed a dull yellow color; and two hours after, they were sown all over, as it were, with large blue spots. These, on the following day, changed into hard tumors, which soon became so many running and incurable sores.

"Most of those who were seized by this awful pestilence died in a few days; others held out longer, and lived whole months, to the great terror of their fellow-townsmen. The most fearful thing in this malady was its infectious character; whoever pressed the hand of a friend who had been attacked, with that single touch received death; whoever went into an infected house, or handled the clothing of the leprous, on the following day was covered with the fatal spots; even money became a vehicle of contagion.

" An indescribable terror seized the hearts of all
at the breaking out of this fearful malady; doors
and windows were closed, and not a living soul
was to be seen in the streets. Luttich, during the
first days of the plague, seemed like an abode of
the dead. My father was almost the whole day
from home, occupied in the labors of his profession. Having carefully anointed himself with the
extract of certain herbs of which he knew the
qualities, he was able to carry help and consolation
into the dwellings both of Christians and Jews,
and he succeeded in rescuing from death about ten,
perhaps, in every thousand. The scenes which he
described to us on his return home at night were
truly awful. Children might be seen pitilessly
driving their sick fathers down the stairs with long
staves, and thrusting them into the street; mothers
would cautiously throw from a distance a rope round
the neck of their infected children, and drag them
out of the house; brothers would keep their sisters
away from them, and would fiercely threaten them
with uplifted axe if they approached. Scarcely
could one believe it. The dearest ties of blood
and family were rent asunder; every one hated
and mistrusted his neighbor; people fled into
holes and cellars, and prepared to slay any one
who ventured near them, were it father, spouse,
or child. And if an infected creature was seen
in the streets in search of food, or who had
been driven forth by his own family, scarcely
could he take a step without an arrow shot from

10 *   H

some neighboring window piercing his miserable frame.

"After six or seven days of this terrible death-like life, a sudden frost came on, and everything indicated a severe winter. This change of the weather brought about a favorable change in the disease; only a few fresh cases were remarked; the patients no longer died as before, and the ulcers appeared to spread no farther.

"The town council and the cathedral chapter ventured once more to assemble; here and there people began to resume their work, and the town gradually recovered an appearance of life. Forthwith stringent but necessary laws were promulgated with regard to the lepers, and every possible measure was taken by the authorities to stay the infection. Whoever was attacked by the disease was to bear about with him a white wand, and whoever killed a leper not bearing this mark received a fixed reward from the mombour or burgomaster. Persons were forbidden to approach a leper within ten paces; an infected person was not allowed to go into either churches or houses, or to cast anything into the street, or even to give an animal a crust of bread; and any one infringing these regulations was liable to be put to death. In short, the poor lepers dared not show themselves; the sword of the 'man-slayers,' appointed for this purpose, quickly terminated their wretched existence.

"As the greater part of the infected consisted

of the poor, a very great number of them died of
hunger and cold; others, urged by necessity,
entered forcibly by night into the shops of the
bakers and corn-dealers, and carried off their contents, so that the trade in provisions became actu-
ally dangerous.

"Partly through compassion, partly also to prevent the spread of the contagion, the bishop re-
commended some houses to be purchased outside
the walls, and fitted up as hospitals or pest-houses.

"The towns-people, who saw in this a means of
ridding themselves of the dreaded presence of the
lepers, willingly brought their offerings of money,
and in a short time a certain number of houses in
the vicinity of the town were ready to receive the
sick.

"In these no change had been made, except that
the windows were walled up, and a large square
space behind the houses was surrounded by a lofty
wall; the doors, too, were strengthened, and in the
front gable, at about a man's height from the
ground, a large hole had been pierced, which was
secured by heavy iron bars in the fashion of a prison window. All lepers found in the street after
the first order was given to repair to these recep-
tacles, and who did not immediately follow the
'man-slayers' to one of these lazar-houses, were
put to death. In less than eight days all these
houses were crowded with miserable beings, who,
pressed by hunger, had been compelled to let
themselves be seen in the streets. The more

wealthy lepers, however, found people willing for a large bribe to procure food for them and throw it to them from a distance.

"Awful and heart-rending was the fate of the poor imprisoned lepers. When the door of the pest-house once opened to receive them, it only unclosed again to receive some new inmate and companion in suffering. Their food was conveyed to them on the point of a long pole through the iron grating; the unfortunate beings might then be seen casting themselves half naked and with trembling hands upon the scanty nourishment; while their tears and lamentations were enough to soften a heart of stone. It was a hideous sepulchre, peopled by living beings. And when one of their number came to expire, what a fearful task was it for the survivors to be condemned to dig his grave with their own hands in that square enclosure!"

Abulfaragus now began to fear that his narrative was producing an injurious effect on the mind of Aleidis. He therefore asked:

"Were it not better, noble lady, that I should delay the remainder of my history until to-morrow? thou weepest so bitterly, and yet thou hast not heard the most dreadful part of my narrative. Night and darkness render the nerves more susceptible; in the clear sunlight one listens to awful things with less fear."

"I have not heard the most dreadful part of thy history?" sighed the noble dame. "Alas! what can be more dreadful than the suffering of these unfortunate lepers?"

"The fate of my father!" cried Abulfaragus, while a flood of tears burst from his arid eyes. "Oh that I might bury it in oblivion!"

All sat still awhile, sunk in painful thought. At length Bernhart said:

"Yes; relate to us to-morrow the remainder of thy painful narrative. We should be unable to sleep after listening to so dreadful a tale; and thou thyself art, moreover, too much excited."

Soon after, the three friends quitted the hall and betook themselves to their apartments.

CHAPTER VIII.

THE LAZAR-HOUSE.

STATELY and resplendent rose the sun next day in the clear blue heavens. Very early Bernhart and Aleidis were present in the hall, expecting from Abulfaragus the continuation of his history. Mid-day, however, approached, and their old friend had not yet appeared. At last a domestic entered with a message that Abulfaragus was unwell.

Much troubled at this intelligence, they both repaired to the apartment of the old man, and there found him lying on his bed. They saw, or fancied they saw, that he was only suffering from a passing indisposition, and they endeavored to cheer him with affectionate words.

"Abulfaragus," said Aleidis, after awhile, "I take blame to myself for having caused you all this suffering. My thoughtless curiosity made me ask from thee a history which has awakened many harrowing recollections in thy mind, and has thus painfully affected thy nerves."

"In truth, noble lady," answered Abulfaragus, "this history has deeply affected me; not so much on account of what I have already related, as of

118

that which still remains to be told. When I promised this narration, I calculated, indeed, too much upon my own strength; I feel that it will be impossible for me to finish it. Alas! little do you know what fearful events remain behind."

"Thus, then, we shall not know the history of thy life. My curiosity is not satisfied, Abulfaragus, for the name of my father is inseparably interwoven with thy lot. I do not wish, however, that thou shouldst proceed with thy narrative at once; that this would be imprudent, I can well understand; but wilt thou not at some future time make us acquainted with what yet remains of thy story?"

"My lips, noble lady, will never be able to recount the cruel fate of my parents; I feel that I should sink under the recital."

With these words he put his hand under the pillow and brought forth a manuscript, which he gave to Aleidis, saying:

"Behold here, noble lady, the entire history of my life down to the death of thy father, my sponsor and benefactor. Thy husband will read it to thee, and then thou wilt know more than I could relate. Meanwhile, be not solicitous about my health; I am not ill, and only require a little rest to be once again re-established."

Bernhart and Aleidis repaired with the manuscript to the hall, and there the Burgrave read as follows:

"During the continuance of the frost, the violence of the dreadful malady was checked; it ap-

peared to make no farther progress, and already
the severity of the enactments began to be relaxed.
Scarcely, however, had the frost given way, when
the plague began to spread again like a devouring
fire. Within a few days the newly infected num-
bered more than a hundred; men began as before
to avoid each other; additional ' man-slayers ' were
appointed, and whoever did not repair to the lazar-
house at the first signal from these legalized execu-
tioners, fell under the stroke of their hatchets or
were pierced through with their long lances. Even
the citizens undertook this cruel office with wil-
lingness; wherever they met with a leper, they
believed that they fulfilled a duty in pursuing and
killing him as they would a rabid dog.

" My father persisted in generously waiting upon
any one who required his assistance; and he was
sometimes absent from his home the whole day,
employed in comforting the sick and saving life
wherever it was possible. However much he
loved us, our tears and entreaties could not prevent him from visiting the houses of the infected ;
he considered it a sacred duty to continue his offi-
ces of mercy toward his suffering fellow-men, and
for this he was ready to brave every danger. He
believed, moreover, that he was sufficiently protected from infection by the precautions he had
adopted, and so he continued his visits and his
journeys daily without the least fear of the consequences.

" One evening, the usual hour of his return had

ıong past without our seeing him. My mother trembled with anxiety, fearing that some evil had befallen him, but she kept these apprehensions to herself, in order not to alarm us needlessly.

" I was just then occupied in teaching my sister to read, and being both intent upon our book, we did not remark how pale our mother's face had become, nor with what anxious attention she listened to every noise in the street. After some time Maria shut the book, and looking around her with alarm, she inquired :

" ' But, mother, where is our father then ? '

" Our poor mother made no answer ; tears rolled down her cheeks ; she looked sorrowfully upon my sister, and without saying a word drew her to her bosom. I, who for my part thought that my father was probably spending the night at the death-bed of some rich person, did not comprehend the anxiety of my mother, although her tears involuntarily called forth mine. All the words of consolation I could use were without any effect upon their minds ; a secret misgiving caused them both to anticipate some terrible misfortune, and both continued weeping until morning. The sun arose higher and higher in the heavens, but, alas ! our father came not.

" The lamentations of my mother and sister filled the house ; they tore their hair and rent their garments in the intensity of their grief; and I, who thought myself so courageous, could only stand near them and weep helplessly ; not a word of

11

consolation now escaped from my lips. At last I
awoke out of this state of unconsciousness, and
told them I would go and seek my father, or endeavor at least to learn something of his fate. My
mother kissed me with unusual tenderness, as
though she feared that I also might not return,
and cast herself, together with my sister, in prayer
before a crucifix. I sought to comfort my sister
and inspire her with some hope, although all the
while I was but trying to deceive myself; at last
I quitted the room with a breaking heart.

"No one of our friends could tell me where my
father was; no one had seen him on the preceding day. In vain I wandered through the town
with drooping head and silent tears; no one could
give any answer to my questions. At midnight I
was standing on a bridge, a prey to the most painful feelings, and with my eyes despairingly fixed
upon the water that rolled beneath. Presently I
was aroused by the noise of many voices near me;
and turning round, I saw a leper driven forward
by the 'man-slayers' at the point of their lances.
The piercing cries of the unfortunate being found
a deep echo in my heart, and I followed him compassionately for some time, without even knowing
whither I was going or what I was doing, until at
last I reached the gate and passed into the open
country. There I saw them open the door of the
pest-house, drive the leper in, and shut the door
again; an awful stillness reigned during the whole
scene. Overpowered by the most bitter grief, I

seated myself upon the grass before this yawning
sepulchre, and saw in imagination the whole life
of these lepers pass before me.   I saw them wander
on, a company of living corpses, united in a fellow-
ship of death, shrinking from each other at the
sight of their horrible sores, and wasting away in
loathsome disease and mutual hatred.   Oh, with
what death-like torture did the thought oppress me,
that within these walls there were mortals who
with fury in their every feature gazed down upon
their already dying limbs, while their heart still
possessed sufficient strength to feel the whole
horror of their fate !

"In such horrible thoughts I lay sunk, when
suddenly my own name broke upon my ear. A cry
of joy burst from my lips, for I had heard the voice
of my father.   I stood up and looked around me ;
but, O God what did I see !   I was struck as with
a thunderbolt, and with a wild mocking laugh I
fell senseless to the ground.

"Oh, could I but express what I suffered at that
moment !   The sight which presented itself was
so terrible, that the strongest expression of bound-
less grief, a jeering laugh, was my only utterance.
I had seen my father behind the iron grating !
He who gave me life lay entombed, forever entombed, in that devouring whirlpool !   O God !
in thy mercy Thou didst stand by me in that hour;
how otherwise should I have survived that crushing blow ?

"As soon as my consciousness returned, I sprang

up with a loud cry, and rushed against the iron
grating; but five or six 'man-slayers' immediately
held me back, threatening me with death if I persisted. But once again my bewildered gaze rested
on the revered head of my father, and then a flood
of hot tears rolled down my cheeks. Only five
paces removed from my poor father, I leaned upon
the cross-bar which stood in front. Nearer I dared
not approach, for four ' man-slayers ' stood ready
with bent cross-bows to pierce me through with
their iron shafts as soon as I put hand or foot
through those bars. After I had relieved my
oppressed heart with abundant tears, I raised my
head and remained standing speechless, and with
clasped hands, my eyes fast fixed upon my father.
His beloved voice penetrated distinctly to my
ear, while he said, in accents of heavenly patience:

" ' Walter, my son, take courage ! the Lord hath
called his servant home. I endure the blow with
resignation, how hard soever it may be. Weep
not thus, my son; preserve rather the strength of
thy soul in order to support and console thy mother and thy sister.'

" ' Oh, my unhappy father ! ' I exclaimed, with
choking voice, ' can I not then save thee ? Must
our science remain powerless before this fearful
malady ? '

" ' My child, what would art avail ? ' he replied;
' were I cured here a hundred times in an hour, I
should be a hundred times infected anew. I will

tell thee the whole truth, Walter, so that thou
mayest prepare thy mother and thy sister beforehand for the painful shock. Be courageous, my
son ; I conjure thee too, by the deep affection thou
bearest me, to prepare thy mother slowly and
warily for these tidings ; I belong to the dead, and
soon ——— '

" He still continued to speak in this heart-rending language, but anguish had made me deaf
and blind. I no longer understood his words ;
everything swam before my eyes, and a deafen-
ing ' rush ' filled my ears ; only from time to
time I could still distinguish the voice of my father
saying :

" ' Walter ! Walter ! my son ! '

" I know not how long I remained thus with
my head leaning on the cross-bar. When I awoke
out of this stupor, the ' man-slayers ' were still
standing there with their bows bent, and my father's face still smiled upon me from behind the
iron grating. With a forced calm, proceeding
from exhaustion, I sighed :

" ' Alas, father ! what ill fortune, then, hath
brought thee to this loathsome prison ? '

" Upon this he related to me, in a few words,
how, on the morning of the preceding day, he had
passed over the Maes in a boat, for the purpose
of visiting some rich lepers ; how his confidence
in the infallible strength of the remedies had deceived him, and his face after mid-day had become
covered with blue spots. In this state some ' man-

11 *

slayers' had perceived him, and, without listening
to argument, had driven him, like any other leper,
to the pest-house.

" The sun was already sinking in the horizon,
and more than once had my father urged me to go
home and console my mother and sister. I remained, however, with my head leaning upon the
cross-bar, and my eyes fast fixed upon the iron
grating. I should doubtless have passed the whole
night thus, had not one of the ' man-slayers ' compelled me by force to quit this position. He drove
me forth toward the road to Luttich, and said, as
he quitted me:

" ' Shall I tell thee what to do, instead of weeping like a woman about a misfortune which cannot be avoided ? '

" I looked at him with hopeful eyes, as he continued :

" ' Bring thy father to-morrow wherewith to eat
and drink ; for the greatest torment in this lazar-
house is hunger and thirst. Forget not, however,
the feeding-pole, ten feet long, otherwise thou wilt
be compelled to throw the food a great distance,
and that does not answer well. Good-evening.'

" How these words made me thrill! I felt them
glowing in my heart like burning coals. As
wretched as it was possible for man to be, I went
back to the town with heavy, toilsome steps.
There an idea occurred to me which brought consolation to my mind : I had thought of a way of
gaining admittance to my father. Laughing joy-

ously in the midst of my misfortune, I hastened
on toward a house where I knew that a leper
dwelt, who had been befriended by my father.
When I was on the point of entering, however, I
thought once more of my mother and sister. I
held back, wept again, and then quickly withdrew. For a moment I had made the resolution
to betake myself to the leper; to beg from him,
as a boon, a share in the contagion, and then to
let myself be shut in by the ' man-slayers ' with
my father; but, happily for us all, the picture of
my mother and sister rose up before me, and prevented the fatal step.

"Alas! what was I now to say to these unhappy women ? I was as a messenger whom
death had deputed to announce his coming, and,
like a murderer, I was about to crush, as between
two stones, the hearts of those dear ones who still
remained to me. This, in truth, was my fearful
errand. The overpowering feeling of my utter
misery threw me into a kind of unconscious stupor,
otherwise, perchance, I should not have ventured
to approach our dwelling, though all the while it
was as if my feet were hurrying me rapidly onward.
On arriving at the door, my consciousness again
returned in all its clearness. I traced my misfortunes over anew with terrible distinctness, even to
the minutest detail, and again arose before me the
thought of my terrible mission. I trembled so
violently that my knees bent under me, and I sank
down before the threshold of the house. At last,

summoning up courage, I proceeded with unsteady steps to the apartment of my mother and sister, where a scene of indescribable anguish awaited me. There, in the farthest end of the room, sat my mother with her head buried in both hands; her eyes red with weeping, even as though some of the vessels had burst; her mouth convulsively distorted, and allowing her fast-set teeth to be seen. Near her sat my sister, in a similar state. Both looked steadfastly but with rigid gaze upon me, as upon some indifferent stranger.

"Deeply moved at this terrible spectacle, I paused for a moment in the same state of insensibility; then casting myself upon my knees before my mother, I kissed her with wild fervor. Every other utterance failed me. I received no answer; passively she allowed me to clasp her again and again in my arms. My sister, too, remained like one utterly insensible. At last, with rending voice, I cried:

"'My heart is breaking! Mother, sister, let me hear your voice, or I die!'

"'Alas, Walter!' sighed my mother, gently.

"'Poor brother!' murmured my sister.

"These tokens of life in some measure calmed the despair which had seized upon my heart; they imparted to me a certain strength, and I bethought me of my errand.

"'What new misfortune, then, had occurred during my absence?' I inquired. 'Be not thus overwhelmed with sorrow, be not so utterly dis-

consolate ! I have seen our father; perhaps he
will be restored to us in a few days.'

" ' Thou hast seen him !' exclaimed my mother,
with a wild cry.

" ' I have seen him; be assured of this,' I
replied.

" ' Then hath thy guardian angel protected thee,
Walter, since God hath left thee thy reason.'

" These words were an enigma to me; but they
caused my sister to burst into tears, while she
said :

" ' Ah, brother, speak not falsely, speak not
falsely ! Our father is in the pest-house; we
know this already : the Jew Borach has seen him
there ! '

" I threw myself once again upon my knees before my mother, and embraced her and my sister
at the same time. Our tears streamed down together; but not a sigh, not a whispered breath,
disturbed the awful stillness of the night which
reigned around us. Lamentations are ordinarily
the interpreters of grief; but here words were too
weak to express our immeasurable woe.

" Why should I attempt to describe our condition during that fearful night ? The endeavor
to comfort our fainting mother alone effected any
change in our unhappy state.

" The next morning found me busied in pre-
paring the dreadful implement with which I was
to reach my father his food. This was a pole to
which was attached a long bar, at the end of which

I

was fastened an iron bowl. When this was ready, I packed up a quantity of roasted meat, a flask of Cyprus wine, bread and salt, and a few linen bandages, and then repaired to my mother and sister to take leave of them. Earnestly, however, as I strove, prayed, and entreated, they were absolutely determined to go with me, and to see once more our unhappy father. I knew too well that such a spectacle would only renew and augment their grief, and I employed every argument I could think of to dissuade them. All my efforts, however, were in vain: they resolutely insisted upon accompanying me.

" Thus, then, we wandered through the streets with drooping head, like so many mourners accompanying a body to its last resting-place. Our dejected looks, and the implements which I carried, served only to excite the attention of the passers-by so far as to keep every one away from us. Such a spectacle was nothing new, and produced no further impression; it merely told the spectator that we belonged to a family in which the pestilence had found a victim.

" Outside the gate, I turned round to my mother, and was not a little astonished when I perceived in her features an expression of comfort, nay, even of joy. I slackened my pace to allow her to come up to me, and said, in an earnest tone:

" ' Ah, mother, I see well that thy heart is courageous; may it remain so ! '

" She continued standing for some time in the
open fields, and we with her. At last she said,
with a voice which had in it something of a holy
and heavenly character :

" ' My children, during the journey I have been
praying fervently to our dear Lord and Saviour,
and I felt, as it were, a beam of light penetrate
into my soul, infusing into me new strength for
the fulfilment of our painful task. Wherefore do
we go to our father ? Is it to rend his heart with
the sight of our suffering ? — to double his anguish
by our own ? No, truly : the unhappy should be
comforted by those who are less so than themselves. Well, then, my children, let us force back
our bitter tears into our oppressed bosoms, and let
us manifest to our father not so much our affliction as our love; and if it should prove that we
are weaker than our resolution, and our tears
should nevertheless spring forth, yet let a gentle
smile beam through them all in the presence of our
unhappy father.'

" These words exercised a wonderful influence
on our minds, as they dropped from our mother's
lips. New life and strength arose in our breasts,
and we became full of courage for the accomplish-
ment of our duty, which now appeared in the
light of a sacred mission. Thus comforting and
supporting one another, we approached the house
of the lepers. Already at some distance we perceived the ' man-slayers' bend their bows, and
heard them call to us, in threatening tones ;

" ' Remain before the cross-bar, under pain of death ! '

" However much we felt ourselves strengthened, we could not avoid trembling very much as we approached the cross-bar. Fortunately we had some time to recover ourselves, for we perceived no one before the iron grating. Meanwhile one of the ' man-slayers ' advanced toward us, and inquired whom we wanted to see. After we had mentioned my father's name, he cried out, with a strong voice :

" ' Abulfaragus ! Abulfaragus ! '

" Thereupon my father's head appeared before the iron grating. Unhappy as he was, he smiled lovingly upon us. Silent tears rolled down our cheeks, but through them there beamed an expression of sweet affection, and we saw clearly how great was the consolation my father derived from our tranquil frame. While I prepared to reach him the food and drink which I had brought, my mother comforted him with such words as her womanly heart alone knew. Oh, wonderful effect of love ! all were unspeakably miserable, and yet at this moment a feeling of blessed joy found its way into our hearts. We submitted ourselves wholly to the will of the Lord, and cheerfully embraced the destiny which He had prepared for us. The very strings of grief seemed as if torn from our hearts ; for had we not in the preceding night twice emptied the chalice of suffering to the very dregs ?

" When I placed the feeding-pole upon the iron
grating, and saw with what avidity my father
seized the food, there ran through my whole frame
an ice-cold shudder. My mother and sister, too,
became deadly pale; but soon the consoling words
of my father again restored us to calm.

" What further need I say of this visit?   We
remained standing for some time before the
grating, anxiously considering whether any means
could be adopted by which our father might be
cured. This deliberation, however, could not possibly lead to any result, as his recovery was not
to be thought of so long as he remained in the
lazar-house.   At last, prevailed upon by his entreaties, and urged, moreover, by the threats of
the ' man-slayers,' we withdrew, and returned
silently home.

" On the three following days we repeated our
journey in the same manner, and at each visit
lingered a long time before the doors of the fearful prison.

" Meantime the pestilence, favored by the continuance of the mild weather, spread again more
and more; during the last two days it had regained all its former virulence, and everywhere
one was met with the intelligence of new cases
and sudden deaths.

" At this awful period an outcry suddenly arose
among the populace that the lepers were poison-
ing the fountains and conduits by washing their
bandages in them; and it was asserted, moreover,

12

that they were bribed to do so by the Jews, in order to bring about the destruction of the Christians, and thus prevent them from following the call of the Pope to go to war with the infidels.

"In France, people called Pastoureaux wandered about, in bands of four or five thousand men, seeking out Jews and lepers, and slaughtering them without mercy. Doubtless the rumor of these disturbances in France had reached Luttich, and given rise to the outcry. Whether the imputation of so infamous a conspiracy had any foundation in truth, I know not: this much is certain, that the sanguinary hatred which existed between the Jews and Christians was sufficiently great to excite the ignorant rabble on either side to the most horrible outrages.

CHAPTER IX.

THE FLIGHT.

ONE evening a woman of our neighborhood came to tell us that large assemblages of people had been wandering about through the town without any one knowing for what purpose; she also told us, that in the vicinity of the town-walls some ten Jewish houses had been plundered, and she even pointed out the blazing of the flames which were reducing the houses to ashes. After many long and painful reflections upon the fate of our former companions, we were about to betake ourselves to rest, when suddenly a mysterious knock was heard at the door. Terror-stricken, I hastened to a window which overlooked the house-door, and opened it; through the darkness I could distinguish a man leaning close against the door, and who was, therefore, scarcely visible.

" ' What dost thou want, friend ? ' I inquired.

" ' Does not the physician Abulfaragus live here ? '

" ' Yes.'

" ' I have something to say to you, upon which his own life and that of his family depends.'

" ' Speak, then ; what evil tidings hast thou to tell us ? '

" ' I must not speak so loud, lest I be overheard.'

" ' Thou knowest that we dare not open our house to a stranger at so late an hour of the night.'

" ' I know it, and I commend thy prudence ; there is no need, however, to open the house ; only come and place thyself behind the door, and I will tell thee my message.'

" I closed the window immediately, and after acquainting my mother with what had happened, I went down and placed myself behind the door. Upon this the stranger said, with a stifled voice :

" ' A band of Pastoureaux has arrived from France, and the populace have joined them ; already they have plundered many of the houses of the Jews, and to-morrow they have resolved to demolish every one that remains, and to slay all the lepers in the town. I have just come from the assembly they have been holding on the Cornillon. Abulfaragus once cured me of the leprosy, and gratitude for his kindness urges me to bring him this warning. Listen carefully, then, to what I have to say. Wicked men have asserted that Abulfaragus is only a Christian by outward profession, and that he is still a Jew at heart. They denounce him, moreover, as a God-despising magician, who by his devilish art has amassed unheard-of treasures.   This last accusation was sufficient to condemn him; to-morrow, therefore, at sunrise, they will demolish his dwelling, and will assuredly murder him, and those of his family who do not escape by timely flight. Tell him this.   Farewell.'

"And with these words the unknown went his way.   His communication had so deeply shocked me, that I remained in the entrance-hall for a long time, trembling, and unable to come to any resolution.   By degrees, however, I summoned up my energies to struggle against this new misfortune. I knew what a heavy task had been laid upon me, and how my mother and sister depended for their safety solely upon my courage.   I was not yet more than twenty years of age, but the blow which the fearful visitation of my father's illness had inflicted upon me had steeled my heart against fate; besides, I considered that I had nothing more to fear, and that I might endeavor to effect the deliverance of my father without the apprehension that his flight would be revenged upon my mother and sister.

"With my head full of confused, torturing thoughts, I rushed up the stairs and related to my mother all that the stranger had told me.   My sister wept bitterly; my mother, on the contrary, endeavored to bear patiently this new affliction. This awful announcement affected them both (which, indeed, I had foreseen) less deeply than that of my father's malady.

12 *

"In the greatest haste, I gathered together every thing which I thought necessary and useful for our flight. My mother and sister followed me like children; by my advice they put on three suits of clothing one above the other, and took with them a supply of food, a knife, a tinder-box, a flask of wine, a crucifix, a quantity of money, and other portable things. I took only a hunting-knife and a sharp hand-axe. As soon as we were all ready to leave our dwelling, I wrote the following words in Arabic on a small piece of parchment:

"'Pursued by the Pastoureaux, we have fled and concealed ourselves in a cavern. To-morrow at midnight I will stand with a ladder at the northern side of the wall. Come and save thyself. Removed from thy companions in misfortune, our science may yet be able to restore thee to health.'

"I folded this missive, and attached to it a small piece of lead, fastened it about me, and took my departure with the two women.

"With the greatest circumspection, and favored by the impenetrable darkness, we hastened onward without a word escaping our lips. At the gate of Amercœur we encountered the sentinels, who refused to let us out of the town; and it was only by means of a handful of gold-pieces that we were enabled to make our escape. Once outside the gate, we took the road to Germany.

"The neighboring mountains were all well known to me, as I had visited them weekly for

many years in order to collect herbs for my father.
About a league from the town, in a very solitary
place, I knew of a secret cave with a narrow entrance, extending far under the mountain; the
ground was level like the floor of a chamber, and
here and there might be seen stalactites of various
forms.   Into this cavern I conducted my mother
and sister; the opening was so small that we were
compelled to crawl in upon our hands and feet.
After a few encouraging words, I made them
acquainted with my plan for saving our poor
father, and told them I had resolved at once to
go to the lazar-house and convey to him my letter.
Both joyfully approved of my undertaking, and
begged me even to hasten my departure, so that
I might return before sunrise.

" In order to defend them from the attacks of
the wolves, which, in consequence of the hard
frost, had begun to traverse the forest of Ardennes
in large numbers, I rolled, by dint of great exertion, two heavy stones to the mouth of the cave.
This done, I set off for the town.   Near the foot
of the mountain I turned off to the right and
journeyed on for a considerable time, until I
found myself approaching the lazar-house.   I
then crept with the greatest precaution between the
trees and bushes, in order to avoid being noticed
by the ' man-slayers,' till at last I reached the foot
of the wall.   I threw the letter over.   I could
distinctly perceive the white parchment as it flew
along, and I was fully convinced that it had

reached its destination. I knew that it was almost
certain to fall into my father's hands, for he was
the only one there acquainted with the Arabic characters, and whoever found it would be sure to
show it to him in order to learn its meaning. Rejoiced at the success of my enterprise so far, I
returned speedily to the cave.

"Before sunset I gathered a bundle of herbs and
plants, with which I prepared a couch for my mother and sister; on this was spread a portion of
their clothes, and at my request they composed
themselves to sleep. When I found that both
were asleep, (it was now about nine o'clock,) I
took some of the money which we had brought
with us, and left the cavern, after having rolled
the stone again before the entrance.

"I had already passed the greater part of the
day in creeping about the farm-yards like a spy,
but I had nowhere found what I was in search of.
I saw ladders enough, but they were all fastened
with chains and locks to the walls, so that there
seemed no hope of my being able to procure one.
In this state of disappointment and dejection, I
was on the point of returning to the cave, when
all at once I saw a chimney smoking in the distance. Hurrying through the thicket in the direction of the smoke, I found a solitary peasant's hut
with the doors standing wide open; and how did
my heart beat with joy, when I perceived a long
ladder lying on the ground behind the house, and
within my reach!

" This was enough. I immediately withdrew, marking carefully the situation of the house, and the road which led to it. With the smile of hope upon my countenance I now retraced my steps, and speedily found myself at the cave, where I consoled my mother and my sister with the happy prospect of my father's liberation. A refreshing sleep had invigorated them, and blissful hope beamed forth in their reanimated hearts. We ate a little, and then waited with impatience for the approach of night.

" Toward evening the heavens were covered with dark clouds; rain fell in torrents, and soon the deepest darkness overspread the scene. I interpreted this change of the weather as a good omen; it seemed to me as if God evidently favored my perilous undertaking. At last the wished-for hour of midnight approached. My mother and sister had already been long on their knees before the crucifix; I kissed them both, closed up the opening, and quickly set off on my journey. I had already left behind me a great part of the road, and was still hastening forward through the darkness, when I suddenly perceived behind me between the bushes two eyes, which gleamed like torches, and were steadfastly fixed upon me. I was not a little alarmed at this apparition, and so much the more because at the first glance I could not guess whether it was a man or an animal; I did not stop, however, but courageously pursued my way. From time to time I looked anxiously round, and each time I found the two glaring eyes at the same distance from me. Passing through an oak-copse, I heard upon the dry rustling leaves the footsteps of the creature, which was still following me; a scarcely-perceptible gurgling sound told me that I had a wolf for my companion. As I knew that these animals seldom attack a man unless he stumble or make some sudden movement, I took care not to make a trip, and held my hunting-knife in one hand and my hatchet in the other, ready for defence. Trembling, and full of anxious suspense, I proceeded thus for more than a quarter of a league. The wolf had by this time ventured to approach nearer to me, and I became awfully certain that the danger was now imminent.

"Suddenly there resounded from afar in the wood a hollow cry, like the howl of wolves when they spring upon a horse, and, being too few in number to bear it down, call to their fellows for aid. Upon this my pursuer turned round, and I heard him speed like a dart through the copse to his howling companions. For a moment I slackened my pace and breathed more freely; then I clasped my hands and thanked God fervently for my deliverance.

"I now continued my journey with renewed courage. Arrived at the lonely cottage, I saw with joy that the ladder was still lying in the same spot. I raised it up, left upon the ground a sum of money ten times its value, and ran off stealthily like a thief.

"About midnight I reached the house of the lepers. I carefully measured my pace, in order, as I approached, to place the ladder against the wall without noise. Now I took it on my shoulder, now crawled on hands and feet, then drew it after me on the ground, until at last I felt the stones of the wall. Doubtless the 'man-slayers' were slumbering at their post; for although I was almost close to their guard-house, I heard no movement whatever within. At last I mounted the ladder, and seated myself astride upon the wall. I trembled like a reed, and was so overcome with fear that my heart scarce continued to beat. I looked anxiously round the yard, and imagined I descried in the deep gloom the movement of a dark shadow. I inquired, with stifled voice:

"'Is it thou, father?'

"'It is I, Walter!' was the whispered answer.

"'Wait until I draw the ladder over and come down to help thee.'

"'But listen, Walter,' said my father. 'If thou comest down, and dost not keep thyself at the distance of ten feet from me, I shall return to my fellow-sufferers, even were I distant from them a league. If thou desirest my deliverance, obey me in this.'

"While he was speaking I drew the ladder over the wall, and let it down into the court-yard. My father ascended, but he had scarcely reached the top of the wall when he obliged me to withdraw some distance from the ladder. Then he sat upon

the wall, drew the ladder to the outer side, descended, and stood upon the free earth. We were
soon at a distance from the place of misery; and
now that there was no 'man-slayer' to stand in
dread of, I would willingly have approached my
father; but however much I insisted, he always
kept me unflinchingly at a distance.

"How painful this was to me I need not relate:
I was, in truth, upon the point of approaching and
touching him even against his will. When he
perceived this, he said, but with a voice which
caused a cold shudder in my veins, so different was
it from the sweet voice of my father, that hollow
and harsh sound which disease and suffering had
given him:

"'My good Walter, I understand how it must
grieve thy loving heart that we should not be able
to fold each other in sweet embrace.'

"'Alas, I am drinking a bitter chalice!' I replied, weeping.

"'But, my child, dost thou not then know that
the slightest contact would give thee the infection?
Thou wouldst die, my poor son.'

"'Alas, father,' I cried, 'let me embrace thee,
for God's sake! Die, sayest thou? Dost thou
then believe that it would appear to me other than
a happiness to share the sufferings and death of
my father? besides, it is not certain that I should
catch the contagion.'

"My father's voice became more doleful as he
thus spoke to me:

"Couldst thou behold my face and my body, then, my child, thou wouldst gladly fly me. Alas! thou hast perchance already inhaled with thy breath the dreadful plague. On my knees I beseech thee, keep far from me.'

"In spite of the darkness, I saw my father in fact kneeling down, stretching out his arms toward me, and craving my obedience. Deeply moved and agitated, I remained standing, while he thus continued:

"'Walter, cherish not deceitful hopes; I am doomed to death, for the contagion has struck deep root into my vitals. What would it then avail that thou shouldst offer thyself as another victim, and leave behind thy mother and sister alone in the wide world? It is not the expectation of an impossible cure that has urged me to quit the lazar-house; only my love for you, and the desire to behold you once again from a distance, has impelled me to this step. Dost thou wish that the thought should gall me that I have brought infection into my own family? and this simply that I might be able to feast my eyes once again upon my children? Walter, I must suffer and die without any hand to press mine, without any sweet embrace to console me, without its being permitted thee to close the eyes of thy dying father: thus runs the sentence which the Lord hath pronounced against his servant.'

"During these heart-rending words a stream of bitter tears rolled down my cheeks; sobs and sighs

13   K

were my only answer. A strange emotion suddenly came over me; my blood boiled in my veins, and rushed with terrible fury to my oppressed brain. I bit my clenched hand till it ran blood, and my soul was filled with dark and desperate thoughts.

" ' Is it not so, Walter ? ' asked my father, entreatingly. ' Thou wilt be obedient, and not touch me ? '

" ' Father,' I exclaimed, ' life is then to me a burden which I can no longer endure. Should I have saved thee in order to see thee die helpless ? Must I fly thee as a poisoned adder ? Must I not embrace thee, nor close thy eyes, when the Lord calls thee to himself ? Ah! thy son bends not his neck so low; he embraces and kisses his father in spite of the contagion ! A share in thy malady — no other life, no other death, than thine, my father!'

" And with these words I threw myself upon his bosom, while my lips pressed his cheeks. For a moment he opposed me with all his might; but he soon felt how irresistibly I had clasped him in my embrace, and his head sank powerless on my breast. I felt the hot tears rolling from his eyes upon my hands, and soon my own were mingled abundantly with his.

" ' Oh, my child,' he exclaimed, with deep emotion, ' what hast thou done ? I blame thee not for thy ardent love toward me; it is a blessing to me in my misfortune; but, alas, how is my heart torn with the certainty that disease and death are now thy inevitable portion ! I am old, Walter, and there remain to me therefore but a few burdensome years; but thou, still so young, dost sacrifice a whole life!'

"Elevated and strengthened by what I had done, I exclaimed:

"'I shall not be infected; I shall not die! Knowest thou not what the howling storm uttered to me through the trees: "Honor thy father and thy mother, that thy days may be long in the land"?'

"'God grant that the spirit of the prophets may have spoken to thee at that moment, my child! But is it not in like manner written, "Thou shalt not tempt the Lord thy God"?'

"'Let him do with me according to his ever-blessed will. If there still remains gall in the chalice, I am ready to drink it. I have already enjoyed a sweet earnest of my reward; thy kiss hath given me strength and courage. Come, let us hasten to our mother.'

"With these words I seized his hand, and we proceeded together to the cave. When we had advanced some distance, my father said, in a dejected tone:

"'Walter, I bewail my deliverance as the greatest of our misfortunes. I marvel at thy love and courage, for they will surely destroy the thread of thy life. But how will it be with thy mother and thy sister? Do they love me less than thou, and will they also sacrifice themselves on the altar of their affection? I am in a terrible strait, and would gladly, if thou wouldst consent to it, return to the pest-house.'

"'No, to that I will not consent,' I replied, firmly. 'Listen, father, to what I have to say. I have for thy sake followed the voice of my affection, and have perhaps on that account delivered myself up to the contagion. But I am conscious that, if my own life be at my disposal, I am sacredly bound to prevent my mother from imitating my example. Trust me, misfortune has within these few days brought me to the full growth of manhood. Neither of the women shall touch thee, and their love shall bend before my will, even should I have recourse to force and severity.'

"'I thank thee, my child,' sighed my father; 'but whither art thou leading me, and how wilt thou keep thy mother and sister at a distance from me?'

"'I have already considered this carefully, and I believe that I have found a means. About ten paces from the cave there is a smaller one. Dost thou not remember where we once found a plant unknown to us?'

"'The *aconitum* of the Latins, with its blood-red leaf?'

"'Ay, there. In that cave thou must remain. I will take care that my mother and sister do not quit theirs. In the daytime I will permit them to approach thee within a certain distance, so that you may be able to see and console one another

without danger. Then will we again joyously
and eagerly consult our science. Have only good
courage ; thou wilt again recover thy health.'

" ' Oh, my son,' cried my father, amazed, ' thy
love for me has inspired thee with wisdom ! Do
as thou hast said : I abandon myself to thy guid-
ance.'

18 *

CHAPTER X.

THE CATASTROPHE.

MEANWHILE we had arrived at the cave which I had fixed upon for the dwelling-place of my father. I there prepared for him a bed of dried branches and leaves, and laid him down; then I repaired to the other cave, and without entering, called out, with a loud voice:

"'Mother, sister, are you there?'

"'Ay, Walter!' exclaimed the two voices.

"'My enterprise has succeeded; our father is free, but he cannot come to this place until it is day. I am going back to him; be at ease, therefore, until I bring him.'

"The tone of their voices showed me with what joy they received these tidings. Once again I repeated my request, and then returned to my father. During the remainder of the night I consulted with him on the means to be employed for his recovery.

"At first he gave no heed to my proposal, so entirely had he given up all hope; at last he could no longer withstand my entreaties, and said, to my great joy:

"'Walter, my instructor bestowed upon me at parting a small silver box, telling me that it contained a little salve, which infallibly cures the plague, and even stays impending death. It contains only what suffices for one man, and holds no more.'

"'Where is this precious life-giving remedy?' cried I, trembling with joy.

"'Hast thou not remarked,' continued my father, 'that on one of the walls in our cellar there are graven many crosses in the stone, one of which is larger than the others?'

"'Assuredly; and I often asked thee what that signified, yet thou wouldst never tell me.'

"'Well, then, underneath that large cross there is a hole in the wall; a few strokes of the hammer will remove the stones, and in the hole is to be found a lump of asphaltum, in which the silver box is fixed.'

"'I will go at once!' I cried, with exultation; 'I will go and bring thee health!'

"And I was on the point of rushing forth, when my father held me back, and exhorted me to defer my journey until the following night, as already a slight glimmering appeared in the east, and I could not possibly reach the town before sunrise. I submitted impatiently to necessity, and postponed my journey.

"Some time before sunrise I led my father to a recess, in which some rain-water had collected, and there I washed his body with pieces of linen.

Notwithstanding the excessive cold, this ablution eased his pains in a wonderful manner. The nearer the sun approached the horizon, the more clearly I saw his countenance; alas! it was seamed with cancerous wounds, and full of livid spots. His eyes were deeply sunk in their sockets; his cheeks were hollow, and his mouth convulsively distorted. I wept aloud at this terrible sight, and as often as my eyes fell upon his countenance, a cold shudder ran through my whole frame.

" Scarcely had the sun shone upon the horizon, when I led my father a little distance in front of the larger cave, and made him sit down while I rolled away the stone from the entrance.

" ' Mother, and thou, Maria,' I cried, 'listen to what I have to say. Our father is not far from here, and I have come to seek you, that you may benold him. Be not troubled, however; come not within ten feet of him, otherwise he will return to the lazar-house, and I myself will lead him thither in spite of all your entreaties, nay, even if you should weep tears of blood in order to detain us. The same will happen if you touch me, for I also am infected.'

" Both women shuddered at these terrible words; instead of the joy which they thought awaited them, anguish now filled their hearts, and a flood of tears streamed from their eyes.

" ' Not touch, not embrace him ! ' exclaimed my sister, in despair.

" In as calm a voice as I could command, I said, ' Maria, tell me, dost thou wish the death of thy mother? Thou tremblest at the very thought. Well, then, if thou dost not follow punctually my directions, thy mother, as well as thyself, will be infected and die. And thou, mother, dost thou desire the death of thy child?'

"'I understand thee, Walter,' sighed my mother; ' but fear not, we will submit like the slaves of inexorable misfortune.'

" Tranquillized by this promise, I led both the women to the spot where my father was seated. A cry burst from their bosom, and both sank senseless to the earth. There lay the two dear ones stretched out lifeless before me, and it was not in my power either to touch or to help them.

" My sister was the first to come to herself; she raised up my mother's head from the ground, and began rubbing her face and hands, until at last both recovered sufficiently to be able to speak to my father, though with a flood of tears. It now occurred to me what danger we were in if any one should perceive us; I, therefore, left the women with my father, and ascended a neighboring height, in order to reconnoitre the surrounding country.

" I remained there a whole hour without perceiving a living thing; then, however, I descried in the distance two men advancing from behind a hill, and directing their steps toward the path which led to our hiding-place. I soon discovered that they were not enemies, for they bore no arms, and their clothing betokened poverty and negligence. I rapidly descended from the height, however, and led back my father at once to his cave, and the women to theirs. I then rolled the stone before the entrance, and withdrew in another direction, while I bent myself down to the ground, as if I were gathering herbs and roots. I remarked that the two individuals advanced very hurriedly, and turned their heads around continually, as if they feared pursuit. As soon as they observed me, they held back, and appeared to consult with each other as to what they should do, for they were evidently alarmed at my presence. A moment after, however, they came up to me, and then I at once saw that they were lepers. They looked at me very distrustfully, and one of them inquired :

" ' Young man, hast thou seen any men-at-arms or " man-slayers " hereabouts ? '

" ' No,' I replied; ' why should they come hither ? '

" ' Hast thou not then come from the town to-day ? '

" ' No; I live in one of the neighboring villages.'

" ' Are there any lepers in thy village ? '

" ' Yes, a few.'

" ' Hasten, then, and advise them to fly immediately from this district ; for the Pastoureaux are scouring the country, and killing all the lepers they can find.'

"'But if they have taken refuge in secret dens and caves?'

"'Ah, that will be of little avail! Is it not possible to discover these hiding-places? and does not every one know that they are the usual resort of such as wish to conceal themselves? If thou hast a little money, young man, thou wouldst be doing a work of mercy in giving it to two unfortunate lepers.'

"I was not sufficiently aware of the new danger which threatened us, and I therefore answered:

"'I have two gold-pieces, and will gladly bestow them upon thee, if thou wilt tell me what the lepers of my village have to fear, and what can be the motive of this fresh persecution.'

"The other leper, who had not yet spoken, replied:

"'Oh! that is easily told. During the last night the lepers have broken out of the lazar-house, and have fled, to the number of a hundred and eighty. The Pastoureaux and the "man-slayers" are pursuing them through the open country, and wherever they light upon them they slay them without mercy.'

"I gave them the two gold-pieces, and, returning quickly to my father, related what I had heard. As we did not dare to quit our asylum during the day, — more especially as our faces bore

the unmistakable impress of our Jewish origin, —
I bade the two women hide themselves in the
large cavern, while I crept with my father into the
smaller. We spent the whole day in the greatest
stillness, and in momentary fear of the arrival of
the Pastoureaux; but happily no one came near
us. After mid-day a heavy snow-storm came on,
which lasted till far in the night; and this cir-
cumstance probably prevented them from extending their search so far.

"When thick darkness had at length settled
down upon the earth, we crept out of our cave,
and I proceeded to the other hiding-place to seek
my mother and sister. Poor women! they were
utterly cast down, worn out with weeping, languid,
and almost paralyzed in body and mind. With
difficulty could I draw one word from their lips,
and then the tone in which it was spoken sounded
so trembling and hopeless, that it cut me to the
very heart.

"Whither should we bend our steps? First of
all, it was absolutely necessary that we should go
away as far as possible from Luttich. In the
other towns of the bishopric, owing to the disease
being less prevalent, the laws were not so severe;
if, therefore, we could descend the Maes, and get
as far as Maestricht, we should be in comparative
safety, as the leprosy scarcely existed in that
quarter, and there were no Pastoureaux. Ac-
cordingly we resolved to set out without delay,
and even that very night to travel as far as our

strength would carry us. My mother and sister spoke not a word; they followed us through the snow like shadows.

"After we had left some two leagues behind us, my father no longer answered any of my questions. I felt that fatigue was overpowering him, for he leaned himself more and more heavily upon my shoulder. I was well aware that this violent exertion inflamed his wounds and caused him much suffering; but I could not stay to speak of this, for fear of retarding our flight. We were, moreover, in a region little known to us, and where it was impossible to find, amid the darkness, any secure place of refuge. I therefore held my father up, so as to bear nearly the whole weight of his body; and I comforted the two speechless women with words of love and hope.

"After some time, we advanced between two high hills, through a wild and desert region; when all at once my father's limbs became paralyzed, and he fell like a weight of lead upon my shoulder. I tried to advance, but his legs slipped upon the snow. A cry of horror escaped from my lips, and he sank down powerless upon the earth.

"My mother and sister threw themselves upon their knees; they dared not approach us. Scarcely was a heavy sob wrung at intervals from their breast; they were as if petrified by their immeasurable woe. My father was not entirely deprived of speech; for while I was rubbing his forehead with snow, he sighed out, with feeble voice:

14

" ' Walter, my child, my hour is come! I am going to God! Listen well now. Go for the silver salve-box as soon as thou canst. If thou art not seized with the contagion, then preserve this precious remedy for another occasion; it may prove the means of thy restoration. Thou wilt close my eyes like a loving son; and when my soul shall abandon its loathsome habitation, thou wilt dig me a grave with thy hatchet, wilt thou not? '

" A heart-rending cry of grief was my only answer. Like one bereft of reason, I dragged my father over the snow to an eminence, while, in broken accents, I exclaimed:

" ' No; Death shall not stand between us to-day! I go — the silver salve-box — Luttich — patience — I come — pray — pray! '

" And, rapid as an arrow, I flew in the direction of Luttich. It was a little after midnight. I ran faster and faster, until my heart beat so impetuously in my breast that I thought it would burst in pieces. When I came to Luttich, I found the gate open, and a great number of armed men going in and out. From their speech I at once knew them to be Pastoureaux; but the importance of my errand urged me to pass boldly through them, and penetrate into the town. Arriving at our abode, I found the house-door lying in the street, all the window-panes dashed into fragments, and the entrance blocked up, with the household furniture broken into atoms. The

warning of the stranger had thus been verified;
they had pillaged everything.   I crept as quickly
as I could into the cellar, beat with a heavy stone
against the large cross, and made an opening in
the wall.

"In joyful haste I seized the piece of asphaltum,
made my way back, and soon arrived with my
precious treasure in the open country.   I ran with
such speed that the sweat ran down my forehead
in streams.   What strength and courage did that
joy which filled my heart bestow! Did I not hold
my father's life in my hands? Soon should I reach
the spot where I had left him, and be able to say,
'Here is health for thee; live long with us still!
The disease is conquered!   Embrace now my mother and sister also!'

"With these happy thoughts I pressed the
packet to my lips, and kissed it with earnest fervor.   Thus I approached the spot where my father
was lying, and was on the point of calling aloud
to him the happy tidings from a distance, when
all at once I beheld upon the snow, in my very
path, three wolves, apparently occupied in rending
to pieces their prey.   I was afraid to pass the
wolves, and yet it was necessary, for I found myself in a narrow defile between two mountains;
and if I had turned back and taken another path,
I should have delayed myself more than half an
hour.

"Upon this, it occurred to me that wolves are
terrified at the clashing of steel; and drawing

forth my hatchet from under my garment, I struck it with my hunting-knife, and made as much noise as possible. The wolves looked up, and ran off scared through the bushes. Overjoyed at this speedy victory, I hastened onward, and was about to pass by the remains of their prey without stopping, when the shining of the blood upon the snow compelled me to cast a glance upon the ground. A body was lying there, and, O God! I recognized it, — it was that of my father!

CHAPTER XI.

HENCEFORWARD I no longer relate what I myself heard or knew. That which follows was told me many years later by my sister.

"During my absence from Luttich my mother and sister saw plainly that my father was breathing forth his last sigh; they approached him, and found that, in fact, his soul had already gone to God. They then retired to some distance and prayed fervently for the departed. At length, overpowered by their feelings, and worn out by their painful journey, they sank into a state of dreamy stupor. After awhile they suddenly heard near them a dreadful howling of wild beasts, and to their horror saw three wolves dragging the inanimate body up the mountain! My mother uttered a last cry of anguish: this terrible sight had broken the feeble thread of life; she sank down, and rose not again from that bed of death.

"My sister lost all consciousness, and remained lying on the ground until break of day. Her bewildered eyes first fell upon her mother; she lifted up her ice-cold hand, and let it drop again in terror. A cry escaped her when she saw me sitting cowering at the foot of the mountain; she rushed toward me, and threw herself on my breast. I returned her kiss, and wished to keep her back; but she held me convulsively in her embrace, like a shipwrecked mariner clinging to the last plank. At last, unloosing her arms, she said:

" ' Walter, let us go quickly to the nearest habitation, that we may get our parents buried in consecrated ground. Come, I see a church-tower yonder in the distance.'

" I laughed, however, like a lunatic, and leaped round about in a phrensy of delirious joy.

" ' Ha, ha ! ' I cried, ' our father is cured; I have brought him the salve-box; he has anointed himself. See, there he lies ! He is cured, is he not ? Wolves — blood ! — Look how beautiful the sun is ! '

" And I played like a child with the lump of asphaltum. My poor sister threw her arms round my neck, forced me to sit down, placed herself near me, and said:

" ' Poor Walter, be calm ! be still ! Thy reason is bewildered ! Pray to God, if thou canst ! We also shall soon die here. Heaven will unite us all four in its bosom.'

" The series of our woes was at length accomplished.

" On the next day a body of knights on horseback halted beside us. They all looked at us with deep compassion. They had doubtless observed us

from the high-road sitting on the snow, and had
been induced by curiosity to come near.

"'Walter, my godson, is it thou?' inquired one
of the knights, leaping from his horse.

"His voice affected me powerfully; I ran toward him with the asphaltum, and called out with
a laugh:

"'Ha, ha! Father, here is the silver salve-box!
There! anoint thy wounds — quick — before the
wolves come.'

"Count Walter Van Craenhove — for he it was
— clasped me in his arms. My raving, and, still
more, the horrible spectacle which he saw before
him, made him quiver with anguish.

"In my delirium I still continued to treat him
as my father, and as he could gain no further information from my incoherent speech, my sister
recounted to him the tale of misery. All the
knights alighted from their horses, and began to
show us many tokens of their sympathy; but
Count Walter left them little time for this. He
called to his attendants, who were behind, made
each of us mount a horse which a servant was leading by the bridle, and then gave orders to repair
to the nearest village.

"When he had conveyed us thither, he caused
the bodies of our parents to be brought to the
village, and buried with the solemn rites of the
church. On the following day he bade his companions farewell, and did not proceed to Luttich,
as he had before intended, but remained in the

village with us until nourishing food and kindly
attention had somewhat restored my sister's
strength.   He then purchased a commodious vehicle, and conveyed us to his castle, the 'Lanteernenhof,' from which we never again departed.

"There we lived in peace and joy.   My sister
followed each one of my steps with anxious concern; I was the object of her constant care; she
lived only for my sake, and to ward off from me
everything that might be injurious.   My madness
was not of a violent kind; I laughed incessantly,
and although I did not know my sister, I loved
her nevertheless, because I felt that she loved me.
My chief occupation consisted in making wolves;
whatever fell under my hand — clay, wax, paste, or
anything of the like—was straightway transformed
into a four-footed animal resembling a wolf.
Sometimes I would place perhaps a hundred of
these objects before me, and laugh and dance
with the utmost mirth.   My sister had striven to
turn me from this practice, but as soon as she
remarked that she caused me grief in consequence,
she left me to do as I liked.

"Count Walter was not less attached to me; he
provided us with all that could make life agreeable.
When I in my delirium called him father, I gave
him the right appellation; he was indeed a father
to us.

"After we had thus spent seven months at the
'Lanteernenhof,' the count appeared one day in
the room in which I happened to be with my

sister. I had crowned myself with flowers, and upon the ground before me stood a whole line of wolves modelled in clay. The count took a chair, seated himself by my sister, and said :

" ' Maria, thy generous and loving nature has filled me with the greatest wonder; it seems to me, in plain terms, that thy virtues have awakened in my heart another and more fervent sentiment toward thee. In the presence, however, of this being, for whom thou hast sacrificed thyself so entirely, I will not speak to thee in the name of an earthly passion. Thou canst not any longer live, Maria, without family and without parents, thus absolutely dependent on thy friend Walter. Often, when sleep flies my couch, do I reflect upon the lot which awaits thee when the Lord, according to the decree of his inscrutable will, shall call me to himself. Thy father, Maria, snatched me from the jaws of death ; his friendship was of still greater worth to me than the life which he gave me back. I know that God hath chosen me for the consolation and protection of his children, and I would wish that the soul of thy father may rejoice in heaven at the manner in which I accomplish the sacred mission. Hitherto I have done but little ; I feel that I possess the power to protect thee and thy brother from fresh sufferings. A voice from above, and a secret feeling in my heart, tell me that I ought to bind my lot with thine in the most sacred bond, and bestow upon thee a protection for life. Wilt thou, then, be my spouse ? '

" My sister listened to the count with amazement; instead of answering, she pointed to me,
and sighed:

" ' Who then will remain with the poor lunatic?'

" ' Thou, Maria,' said the count. ' My prayer is
not a selfish one; thy love for thy brother has,
indeed, kindled love in my heart for thee. The
more thou continuest in such self-sacrifice, the
more fervent will my attachment become.'

" However earnestly the count spoke to my sister, she did not seem inclined to adopt any other
name than the one which bound her to me. This
noble and unselfish refusal excited the love and
admiration of the count to a still higher degree;
and as his intentions were of the purest kind, he
made many endeavors at a later period to obtain
my sister's consent. Her determination, however,
was unalterable.

" In the following winter the snow fell in abundance, and wolves from the Ardennes again in-
fested the whole country. One evening, when my
sister had left me alone for the purpose of seeking
some plaything for me, I ran out of the castle into
the fields. What happened to me I know not;
but the men who had gone, at the entreaties of
my afflicted sister, to seek for me with torches,
found me stretched to all appearance lifeless upon
the snow.

" I was seized with a mortal illness; for eight
whole days I lay speechless, with fevered head,
upon the couch, without the physician being able

to decide what was to be hoped or feared on my account.

"I now began gradually to waste away; but when this had reached its height a new life seemed to flow into my frame; my health daily improved, and with it soundness of mind and memory returned. Three months later, I was in the full possession of all my faculties.

"After this my sister became Countess Van Craenhove. She presented her husband with three children — two sons, Hugo and Arnold, and a wondrously fair daughter, who received the name of Aleidis.

"A few years later she died with a celestial smile upon her countenance, and in fervent prayer, like a very saint; the good Count Walter soon followed her.

"Both lie buried under the elms, and near them their sons Hugo and Arnold.

"I, Walter Abulfaragus, became the guardian of the children of my benefactor and my sister.

"When God, to whom be honor and praise forever, hath permitted me to accomplish this mission as I ought, then will I joyfully lay my head upon the bed of death, and resign my soul into the hands of my Creator."

Here ended the manuscript.

For the full understanding of the history of Abulfaragus, a few words are subjoined.

When the old man had attained the age of a hundred and two years, he breathed out his soul in the arms of Bernhart and Aleidis.   Such a departure could not be called death; there was no pain, no feebleness of spirit.   Before he closed his eyes, he looked round once more upon the numerous children of Bernhart and Aleidis, who surrounded his bed, and said to them, in thrilling accents:

"Children, honor your father and mother, that like your friend Abulfaragus your days may be long in the land!"

Then he added gently:

"Farewell! farewell!" and slowly closed his eyes.

His pure soul had winged its way to heaven!

THE END.

The Curse of the Village.

THE

CURSE OF THE VILLAGE.

By Hendrik Conscience,

AUTHOR OF "THE VILLAGE INNKEEPER," "THE HAPPINESS OF BEING RICH," "VEVA,"
"THE LION OF FLANDERS," "COUNT HUGO OF CRAENHOVE," "WOODEN CLARA,"
"RICKETICKETACK," "THE DEMON OF GOLD," "THE POOR GENTLEMAN,"
"THE CONSCRIPT," "BLIND ROSA," "THE AMULET," "THE MISER,"
"THE FISHERMAN'S DAUGHTER," ETC.

Translated Expressly for this Edition.

BALTIMORE:
PUBLISHED BY JOHN MURPHY & CO.,
44 W. BALTIMORE STREET.

Preface to the American Edition.

THE "CURSE OF THE VILLAGE" is a bold description of the ravages of intemperance,—that bane of villages in the Old World as well as the New. This tale is one of his latest additions to the charming sketches of Flemish life, for which the author is so celebrated.

We are not anxious to forestall public opinion of M. Conscience; but we must observe that both in his subjects and style he unites many of the peculiarities of Scott, Dickens, and Hans Christian Andersen. His romances possess the varied interest, the rapid narrative, and the bold grouping of the first of these distinguished writers; while his everyday stories are full of the nature, simplicity, humor, and pathos that have made Boz and Andersen, household names throughout our country. A British writer has well remarked that the characteristics of his works "are a hearty, sincere appreciation and love of the simple life of the poor in all its forms; a genial sympathy with its occupations, its joys and sorrows; a recognition of its dignity, and an earnest, reverent treatment of all conditions."

CURSE OF THE VILLAGE.

𝔄 𝔗𝔞𝔩𝔢.

CHAPTER I.

It was afternoon, and two peasants were slowly
wending their way homeward from a neighboring town. Their path lay through one of the
loveliest landscapes of Hageland.* It was near
the crest of a hill, and was hewn out of the brown
ironstone, and then it wound along in numberless
gentle curves over hills and through quiet dells to
their village, which lay below them in the distance, there where a little spire, surmounted by a
gilded cross, gleamed amidst the dusky foliage.
On one side of the way rose the massive wall of
ironstone,—its dark hue relieved and adorned
with the exquisite green and purple of brambles

---

* Hageland is a tract of Belgium, beginning at the foot of the
hills at Aerschot and Diest, and stretching away beyond S. Tron
and Tirlemont, in the direction of the Limbourgeois. The most
beautiful part of it is above Aerschot.

and thorns, and other climbing shrubs and flowers.   Above these, rose stern and inaccessible
peaks of mountains, which shut in the view in
that direction; but at intervals the ground sank
down into a graceful valley, and then the eye of
the traveller could range unobstructed over the
whole landscape, and watch the low lines of dark
firs which marked the undulating ridge of the
distant hills, and, now expanding, now contract-
ing their masses of green, but ever quieter and
softer in tone, died away at length into the blue
mist which curtained the horizon.

On the other side of the road, the torrents
which rush down the mountain-side in winter had
cloven for themselves a broad channel in the ironstone; and beyond this noisy stream stretched a
vast expanse of cultivated land, the well-defined
patches of which ran up the sides of a farther
range of hills, and seemed to hang like variegated
tapestry from their rugged shoulders.

It was autumn.   The sun of the waning year
shone with fervid glow in the clear blue sky, and
played in countless changeful tints among the
half-decayed foliage.   Although its rays were yet
powerful, there lay beneath the distant woods the
purple hue which shows that the air is cooler than
the earth, and the mist of evening was creeping
slowly up the hill-side.

From the eminence to which their path had
conducted them, our two travellers might have

seen the whole country for leagues around, and enjoyed the magnificent picture that nature, in her peaceful autumn mood, had spread out before them; but they seemed to take but small notice of it, and continued their journey in unbroken silence.

The one was an old man with gray hair and a countenance set with deep wrinkles. Although his back was slightly bent by the pressure of years, he stepped out lightly along the road, and apparently did not lean upon the medlar-tree staff, which was attached to his wrist by a thong of leather. His eyes, too, were still clear and bright, and the calm, earnest expression of his whole face betokened great courage and a firm will.

An ample felt hat of antique fashion partially concealed his white hairs, while a brown cloak, equally old-fashioned in shape, hung down almost to his heels. These clothes the good man had worn as he knelt before the altar when he and his Elizabeth were made one in holy wedlock. He had kept them with scrupulous care, for they had cost him much;—it was now six-and-twenty years ago, and even yet they came to the light only when he was going to church or betaking himself to the town on business.

The companion who stepped out by his side was a young fellow on whose merry face beamed health and vigor. A gay cloth cap hung over his left ear, and allowed his brown hair to fall in

clustering curls upon his shoulders; the ends of a
variegated neckerchief fell gracefully on his
breast over his fine blue blouse. His black eyes
shone with quiet gladness; a sweet half-smile
played about his mouth; and the rapid glances
which he cast around him from time to time were
full of simple innocence and gentle trust in life.
A walking-stick, from which hung a well-filled
basket, rested on his right shoulder, and the hand
which grasped the stick was unusually broad and
strong; his fingers seemed hardened and stiff
with labor, and so this young peasant, though
scarcely a man grown, had already toiled and
slaved much.

For some time the old man walked on with his
head sunk lower upon his breast than was his
wont. Apparently some profound emotion had
touched his heart, for his face changed its expression from moment to moment, and he seemed as
if he were trying to digest some cause of vexation
or anger.

His companion looked at him in silence, and
endeavored to read in his countenance the cause
of his disquietude; and there was in the look
which the youth kept fixed upon the face of
the old man, as they walked on, a quiet, modest
sympathy, which betokened deep respect and
veneration.

At length, as if the thoughts of the old man had
led him to some conclusion, he said, in an energetic tone of voice—

"Yes, Luke, my son, it is just what our old pastor says sometimes, with a smile:—when the devil saw that he could no longer catch souls fast enough, he turned himself into gin. And since then, hell has been too small."

"Why do you say so, father?" asked the youth, in astonishment.

But the old man followed on undisturbed the thread of his meditation, and continued, with a contemptuous smile—

"What more despicable creature is there on earth than a drunkard? Indolent and careless, he leaves his fields unsown and overrun with weeds; he sees, without a blush of shame, his purse gradually waste, and consumes, like a silly sot, the little that he has earned. His wife and children live in sorrow and misery; they suffer hunger, and see the bitterest wretchedness stand threatening at their door. He, meanwhile, dances, sings, shouts, and swears, to the scandal of the whole village; he tries to stifle the gnawing reproaches of his conscience by yet wilder excesses, and he stifles nothing but his soul and his common sense. And so he goes on, from bad to worse; until he and his wretched family are forced to go out and beg, perhaps at the gate of the very farmyard which his father had rendered productive with the bitter sweat of his brow, in order to leave his thankless son in a decent position. Look you: when I think of it, my blood boils in my veins. Base spendthrifts!"

2

The youth looked up at him with an expression of inquiring amazement.

"Look at my hands, look at my face and my bent back!" continued the old man, with increasing emotion. "I am old in years, and worn out by fatigue. I was early left an orphan; my parents perished in the flames which consumed their dwelling. I had an uncle, and the worthy man sent me to school until I was thirteen years old; then he died. I became a servant at the great farm behind the Crossberg. When I married your good mother, we had nothing but one goat and a few florins we had saved from our wages. We have worked and slaved, and been thrifty and saving. God always blesses honest labor. Now we have a horse, four cows, land enough for us to cultivate, and, besides, a little bit of money laid up for a rainy day. One day a humble cross will stand over my grave in the churchyard — that is in the course of nature: but, Luke, you will then remember—won't you?—that all that I have saved and scraped together for you,—that your little inheritance is the sweat of your father's toil; that he, that your mother, have suffered want and have worn themselves to death that they might not leave you on the world? You will keep it together, you will increase it by your own labor, you will treasure it as a memorial of our love, won't you?"

The deep and unusually solemn tone of the old man's words had affected the youth so much that

the tears glistened in his eyes. With sorrow, yet
with sweetness in his voice, he sobbed—

"Oh, father dear, what are you talking about?
you are deceiving yourself. I drank only one
glass of Flemish beer in the town at Master An-
toon's house; one glass only, and no more."

Pressing his hand, the old man resumed:

"Oh, it is not about you, Luke, that I am
speaking; you are honest and hard-working. I
thank God that, in reward of all my toils, he has
enabled you to be good and virtuous. Whenever
you shall stoop under the weight of years, old and
worn out, then will you feel, my son, what a comfort it is to know that the fruit of your labors will
not be squandered after you are dead!"

"But, father, I don't understand you," said the
son; "there is something still upon your heart.
Why don't you explain your meaning to me?"

"It would sadden you too much, Luke."

"Sadden me! what can it be, then?"

"Come, you shall hear all about it at once. Do
you know what our landlord's lawyer told me in
the town? Farmer Staers is to be turned out of
his farm by the bailiffs to-morrow, or the day after
to-morrow!"

"Good heavens! and Clara?" cried the young
man, in a tone of grief.

"Yes, Clara, poor Clara!" answered the old
man. "She has not deserved this miserable lot;
but she must follow her father wherever he goes."

"Farmer Staers turned out of his farm!" repeated Luke, with a shudder; "but it is impossible, father; what reasons can there be for it?"

"It is because he has not paid his last year's rent; we are now in October?"

"But he has still a good piece of land, all his own?"

"That was mortgaged two years ago, and so came to nothing," answered the old man.

"But he was left rich?"

"Not rich; tolerably well off: and if he had taken care of things, he might perhaps have become rich, for he has lived through many very good years for farmers."

"I am quite bewildered. Where can the inheritance of his father have gone? one man could never waste so much as that in drink!"

"Do you think so, Luke? The throat of a drunkard is a cask without a bottom, and it does not take fifteen years to pour through it much more than Farmer Staers ever possessed. I will tell you the whole affair, how things have gone with him; it will shorten the road, and at the same time it may be a useful lesson to you, my son."

Luke, agitated by very different feelings, wanted to make some further observations and inquiries, but his father beckoned him to be silent, and continued:

"Listen, and don't interrupt me. The parents of Jan Staers were very comfortably off; they farmed well, and were not afraid of hard work;

but they lived too high, and gave themselves more airs than are becoming in country-people. Their only son, they said, should never run behind the plough; he should live in the town and be *Mynheer* Staers. So they sent him to a school where lawyers and doctors are made; but at the end of two years Jan got tired of learning, and wished to be a farmer; thinking, I suppose, that it was much more comfortable to be master of a large farm than to have to seek an uncertain livelihood in the wide world. So far, it might have been worse; but instead of accustoming their son to work, his parents let him do just what he liked, and gave him plenty of money in his pocket. 'Opportunity makes the thief,' says the proverb; and 'Idleness is the fountain-head of all vice,' says our old pastor. Jan did not know what to do with himself the whole day long. He went to the inn, at first to amuse himself, then from habit; he drank first one dram, then two, then several. The innkeeper treated him with great attention, and flattered his pride; the toadeaters, who, unhappily, are everywhere to be found in our villages, followed him wherever he went, and praised every thing he did or said, to get a drink at his expense. In short, Jan Staers had become a drunkard before either he or his parents were aware of it. About this time he struck up an acquaintance with the daughter of the landlord of the Blind Horse, a small inn which stood at that time behind there on the hill. He was married the same

B   2*

day that I was, and that is the only time I ever
felt vexed at another's good fortune. The bride
of Staers was clothed in silk and velvet; he had
got a fine new cloak made in the town, and his
hat quite shone against the light. They looked
like the lords of the village. And there stood I
by them, with the same clothes I have on now;
and my poor Betsy, your mother, so humble, with
her cotton jacket and striped frock, that we looked
just like the servant and the maid of Farmer Staers.
Then, before the altar, I vowed to God that I
would slave and work until my good Betsy too
should go to church in better clothes. And I
have kept my vow. But I am forgetting the
adventures of Jan Staers. You see, Luke, when
once a man becomes the slave of drink, he has
made over his soul to the devil. Very few ever
get out of his clutches again.

"For a little while after his marriage, Jan behaved tolerably well, and worked in his fields by
fits and starts. Everybody thought, and I thought
too, that all his folly and wildness had vanished
with his youth; but by degrees he was to be seen
again in the inn, and though he did not drink as
freely as he used to do, his cheeks were now and
then flushed, and his eyes wandering and bloodshot. His father and mother died in the same
year, very near together. Jan became tenant of
the stone farm-house, and because he found his
father's coffers well lined, he thought himself
above toil and carefulness. From that time he

took to drinking more freely, and neglected his
work more and more. His poor wife—whether
he treated her ill I don't know, but somehow she
pined away visibly, and every one could guess that
it was not from happiness. Jan still went to church
now and then; and one Sunday the curé said
something in his sermon—a sort of parable—
about a clay cottage which had devoured up a
farm-house of stone. The cottage, said he, was
inhabited by an industrious man; while the occu-
pant of the stone house was, on the contrary, a
drunkard. And because our house, which was at
that time built of clay, stood not far from his farm,
Jan Staen took it into his head that the pastor
had him and me in his mind's eye. This made
him so angry with me, that from that time he has
looked on me with an evil eye. Among his boon
companions he called me all manner of names
—scrape-farthing, hair-splitter, pin-collector, and
such like—but I only laughed at his silly jests;
and I think, indeed, that it is a bad thing to have
the good word of wicked people.

"But I am always running away from my story.
And so, Luke, I need not take long in telling you
what your own eyes have seen, in part at least.
When Jan Staers saw that his affairs were going
down hill a little too fast, he tried to push them
up again by a few vigorous strokes. He tried to
do something as a dealer in grain; but as he had
the glass in his hand a great deal oftener than the
pen, that all went wrong, and in a very little while

he had made a clean sweep of his fortune In
about six years his wife died, and since then Jan
Staers has been running headlong to ruin. Man-
servant and maid must troop from the farm-house
one after another; the fields were left always
fallow, or just one half-starved lad hired to set in
the potatoes; his cows were sold one after another,
so that he has only one left. His last horse has
gone the same way. Fancy—only one wretched
cow in a farmyard like that! You see, Luke, it
vexes me as if it were my own property that was
wasted in this way. We, who are toiling and digging our dry sandy patch of land from morning to
night to wring a moderate harvest out of it, we
must look on and see such rich heavy fields as
these devoured by weeds, and of no use to anybody! Ah, it is a shame, I say—a shame in the
sight of God and man. Well, now, Jan Staers has
not been able to make up his last year's rent; our
landlord, who has borne with him a long time out
of respect for the memory of his excellent father,—
our landlord, I say, has lost all patience with him.
He is going to make very short work with Jan
Staers; for to-morrow morning the bailiffs will put
an execution into the farm, and sell every thing he
has, and turn the lazy scoundrel into the street.
So it goes with all drunkards, my son; the beginning is *a little dram*, but the end is the beggar's
wallet, or theft, or—or yet worse still."

THE CURSE OF THE VILLAGE. 21

CHAPTER II.

THE youth had listened to this long story with much sorrow and many distractions; and, now the old man had ceased speaking, he asked—

"Have you finished, father?"

"Yes, Luke, I have finished. Now you will understand what put me out of humor."

"But, father, does Farmer Staers know the misfortune that threatens him?"

"To be sure he does; there has been a writ out against him, and he was allowed till yesterday to get the money together. Yesterday and the day before he was reeling about from one public-house to another, and turning the whole village upside down. That is not the way to find money to pay one's rent."

Both were now silent for some time, and walked on, lost in thought. A little in advance, on the top of a hill near the road, there was a stone cross, just such as are set up in places where some foul deed has been perpetrated. The father looked at it, and said, in a kind of reverie, as if talking to himself—

"On that cross it says that one Peter Darinckx

was barbarously killed just here. The barbarous murderer was—gin! That happened before this road was cut out of the hill-side. Down there, there were great heaps of stones; in the inn yonder behind the hill, Darinckx had been drinking till he lost his senses, and in the darkness he lost his footing and fell down this precipice, with his forehead on the stones. God is merciful; but for all that, I fear for his poor soul."

The lad was walking on by his father's side, with his head bent down on his breast, and without seeming to be listening to what he said. The old man saw that his heart was filled with bitter sorrow, and looked at him with deep and tender compassion. Suddenly raising his head, the young peasant exclaimed, with suppressed energy,—

"But Clara, the poor helpless Clara,—what will become of her?"

"I was thinking of her, too, my son; but I see nothing before the poor lass except misfortune and sorrow."

"Nothing but misfortune and sorrow!" repeated Luke, in a dejected tone. "Oh, father, may I tell you what is in my heart? But you would be so angry that I dare not."

"I can well guess what it is; and it gives me pain enough on your account, my poor Luke; but God has so decreed it, and you must bow meekly beneath his will."

"You can guess it?" stammered the youth, his face suffused with a blush of modest shame "Nobody on earth knows it, nobody but—mother only, and she did not scold me, but the contrary."

A few wrinkles began to throw their gloom over the old man's forehead.

"No, father, don't vex yourself," said the youth, imploringly. "It is a feeling that has grown up in me so gradually, without my knowledge, without my will. First of all, it was only pity and sympathy; I could not bear to see that luckless lamb, so tender and so beautiful, working alone in the farmyard, hoeing and manuring the ground, and from morning to night toiling and slaving so hard that a man would break down under it. So, when her father was away, and our own work was slack, I helped her a little now and then, and did some of the hardest of her work for her. But out of her gratitude and my pity, another feeling sprang up in both of us. I have kept it a secret from everybody, except mother. But the thought that they are going to drive Clara out of the farm-house and turn her into the street, and that in all probability she will have to beg her bread, oh, this thought half kills me—it makes me beside myself —it makes me bold enough to say to you now, father, what otherwise would never have crossed my lips."

And in a low voice, and with his head hung down, he murmured, or rather allowed to escape, as it were, on the breath of a deep-drawn sigh, the words—

"Father, I love Clara!"

After a little pause, the old man asked, as if his thoughts were wandering—

"Have you ever told her this, Luke?"

"Oh, no, never!" said the youth.

"But how do you know, then, whether she has any inclination toward you?"

"I don't know it at all, father," answered Luke with his eyes fixed on the ground, and a very visible tremor; "but her eyes, her voice, something that I can't explain, something mysterious, as if our two souls were but one soul—"

"Don't worry yourself about it, Luke," said the old man, with a tender voice; "I knew all this long ago; and if I had been displeased about it, I should have stopped it all at first. The weed, if weed it is, must be rooted out betimes, or else it is not easy to get the upper hand of it."

"Ah, thank you, thank you, father, for your goodness!" cried the young man. "Now you can well understand my grief, my anguish. Clara turned out of doors—Clara driven to beg, like a mere vagrant! But it cannot be, father; and it shall not be. It will make me ill;—I shall pine away, and most likely die outright!"

"No, no, Luke, not quite so bad as that; but still, I feel your sorrow very deeply. Clara is a good and industrious child, and if it were possible to do any thing for her, I,—the hair-splitter, the screw, the lick-penny,—I would not let her beg or starve; she should have a few crowns out of your mother's hoard; but if I were to give her

money, her father would get hold of it and be off
with it to the public-house."

"An alms to her!" sobbed the youth, in a tone
of despair.

"My toil, and the toil of your mother, shall
never go to pay for gin—never!"

"There is another plan, father."

"Another plan, Luke? let us hear it, then."

The young man was silent, and kept his eyes
fixed bashfully on the ground, and it seemed to
his father that his legs trembled as he walked,
and that he was suffering from some unwonted
perturbation.

"Is the plan, then, so very dreadful, my
son," asked he, "that you are afraid to tell it
to me?"

"Well, then, it must come out!" exclaimed the
young farmer, as though he had taken a desperate
resolution. He then relapsed a while into silence,
and at length said, in a voice very low and tremulous with emotion—

"Oh, do not be angry with me, father; I will
submit myself entirely to your will, even if my
obedience to you carries me to the churchyard. I
had a sort of dream—I dreamed—in the night—
it was a month ago last night—I had dug a few
roods of land for Clara the evening before, and
my work had quite tired me out—"

"Come, come, don't go such a way round about.
What was it you dreamed?"

"It was beautiful enough! Methought I saw

3

you, father, in the chimney-corner, with your pipe
in your mouth, sitting quite at your ease, laughing
and making merry, just like a rich man; and mother was singing at her wheel, '*Where can one
better be?*' It was so beautiful and so much like
heaven, that I should like to dream on so till—forever; but you, father, must be there, and mother
too, and—and—and Clara, too."

"Ho, ho! Clara was there, was she?" said the
old man, with a smile. "I had a notion she
would be."

His countenance assumed a more serious expression, and he remarked—

"But, Luke, my boy, take care what you say.
You would like to dream like that forever; would
you really give up heaven for a dream?"

"Oh, forgive me, father; it is only a way of
speaking; I don't mean that; I mean to say only
that my dream was so very lovely—"

"Now, then, Luke," said the old man, impatiently, "are you going on with your dream? or,
rather, let us talk of something else."

"No, no, father, keep in a good temper," said
the youth, in a beseeching tone; "I will take
courage and out with all; you may be angry with
me, but I cannot help it now. Listen to what I
saw in my dream;—We had eight cows and two
horses, ploughed land and meadow-land in abundance. Methought I was as strong as a giant;
my hands had grown broad and thick; I felt in
myself a continually increasing energy and a

wonderful courage. We worked—I mean, I
worked—from break of day to the late evening.
My labor made me so happy, that I could have
nailed the sun fast in the sky, to have more hours
to work in. Every thing went well with us;
God's blessing was on our dwelling; our orchards
and our fields all looked bright with beauty and
with abundance. You must not work any more,
father;—yes, you have already slaved too much in
your life: is it not so? But, however increased
our property was, yet the work was all too little
for us—for me, I mean. You, father, you sat in
the chimney smoking your pipe, or you just strolled
out into the fields to give me your advice. That
is just as it should be, for you know every thing
about farming from your long experience; but
you must not work any more. And mother was
waited on, and tended, and cared for, by Clara, out
of pure love and affection—oh, we were all the
while so happy and blithe,—and Clara, too. And
you, father, and my good mother, you loved Clara
as if she had been your own child; for she it was
who, by her sweet affection, made our home a
heaven of peace and of love!"

The youth here paused, and watched for his
father's answer, with downcast look.

After a while, the old man asked drily—

"So, in your dream, Clara lived with us; as a
servant, I suppose?"

Trembling in every limb, and with a deep sigh,
Luke whispered—

"No, father, she was my wife!"

The old man gave his son a gentle slap on the face, and said, good-humoredly—

"Well, that beats all! why, you ought to be a lawyer, Luke. There is a horrible word to bring out!—your wife, indeed! This is a serious matter, my lad; let us talk it over soberly; let us have it out plainly and frankly, like two friends. I will tell you something that will put you quite at your ease. For more than five years your good mother and I have had our dreams too, and we had a notion that Clara would make you a very good wife. It is quite as long as that, I fancy, Luke, since you have taken to wander round about the stone house whenever you found the way clear? Would you believe, Luke, that our slaving and scraping together was not quite unconnected with our wish to see you married to Clara? Her father was, or seemed to be, a well-to-do tenant farmer, and so he carried his head uncommonly high. He would never have consented to his daughter's marriage with the son of a poor cattle-driver, such as I was at that time."

"But now, father, now he will give his consent joyfully!"

"I haven't a doubt of that! But that does not make all square. Then he had plenty, now he has little—"

Luke raised his hand with a deprecating gesture toward his father, as though he would check the chilling decision that was coming.

"That is to say, now he has nothing left," concluded the old man.

"Oh, father!" exclaimed the youth, "you yourself have said that you had nothing when you married my mother, and you have assured me that you have always been quite contented with your lot. Oh, do not render me miserable for the sake of a little money."

"Money!" repeated the old man; "it is not the money that makes the difficulty. They call me scrape-farthing — they think I am a miser; but money is worth nothing to me, except so far as it is the fruit of my own labor. If anybody were to offer me a treasure, I should not care to take it, unless I thought that you, Luke, might perhaps be the better for it. For myself, I should not care for money that I did not earn; I should not be able to eat or drink more than before; and if I were to give up work, idleness would soon make me ill, and I should pine away."

"But, father, you are an extraordinary person! why won't you give your consent?" cried the youth, in an agony of impatience; "or do you think that I shall not follow your example? Be very sure that my horny hands will not have time to grow soft, any more than yours have. Have you ever heard me say of any work, It is difficult; or, It is too much?"

"No, Luke; it is right good blood that flows in your veins, I know that. But you interrupt

3*

me, and I don't like it; it leads us away from
the matter in hand. There is something, my son,
which you have not taken into your calculation.
When farmer Staers was well off, if Clara had
become your wife she might have lived with us,
or you could have hired a little cottage; but now
her father has no home over his head. He
would, of course, live with you, drink the pro-
duce of your toil, and perhaps help to bring you
to ruin."

The young man stood still a moment; a sudden thrill of anguish convulsed his heart, and, at
length, a cry of bitter disappointment relieved his
laboring breast. The father continued:

"It is a solemn duty—I think it even stands
written in the Law—that children should support
their parents whenever they are no longer able to
earn their own bread. To be a drunkard is a
much worse thing than to be a cripple or lame;
for a drunkard not only earns nothing, but he
wastes and consumes every thing he can lay hands
on. Think for a moment, Luke; you will toil
like a slave; he will roam about, and be every
where; he will defile your house with unseemly
words, with curses, and blasphemy; perhaps he
will ill-use your poor wife if she will not give
him money enough to satisfy his contemptible
craving. And then, God may grant you children;
they will have this example before their eyes from
their cradle; they will hear cursing and swearing;
they must say 'grandfather' to a wretch who will

hear nothing of church or clergyman, and who, with his eyes wide open, gives his soul to the devil! No, my son, that can never be: you see, now, it never can be, and you will bow in humility beneath the cross which God gives you to bear. Is it not so, Luke? You will be good and sensible, and not sacrifice your life and your well-being to a passion which, after a brief moment of anguish, will die away of itself?"

The young man spoke not a word; only a dry, hoarse sound was heard in his throat, and he insensibly quickened his pace, as though urged on by keen suffering, or distracted by grief. He pressed his arms in silence close to his body, and his every muscle quivered with his agony.

His father fixed his eyes on him with profound sympathy and compassion; after a while he said, in a sorrowful tone—

"Do not imagine, Luke, that I inflict this sorrow on you without keen pain. I dare not neglect my duty as a father. Oh, be sure, I would give the half of my little possessions to be able to gratify your wish; it is my own wish, too, and the wish of your mother; but it must not be!"

CHAPTER III.

THESE last words of his father smote on the heart of the youth as an irrevocable decree of fate; a faint, shrill cry burst from his lips; he thrust his hand into his bosom, and his fingers moved convulsively, as though, in the extremity of his despair, they were tearing his breast; but he spoke not a word.

The old man, too, walked on rapidly, without uttering a word. After a while he turned his face toward his son, and pressed his hand on his forehead. He was buried in deep meditation; making a violent effort to discover something to console his poor son.

And now they were drawing near their home— at the end of an avenue of lofty pines they could already see the houses at the entrance of their village.

Suddenly the old man raised his head, a cry of joy escaped him, and he said: "Ah! Luke, I have found it!"

The youth stood still as a statue; his eyes, suffused with tears, glistened with eager expectation; trembling, and with both hands stretched out toward his father, he looked as if he would see the words issue from his mouth.

"No, not so fast, Luke," said the old man, moderating his own joy. "It is a serious project, and I must sleep over it first."

"For God's sake, father, tell me, tell me, what have you found?" implored the distracted youth.

The old man took his son's hand, and said, with a restrained gladness of tone—

"Luke, suppose I were to go to Jan Staers, and propose to him to take his lease, and to let him remain still at the stone house with your mother and me? I would show you, old as I am, whether the land would not, with some toil and sweat, amply pay the yearly rent. The example of Jan Staers cannot hurt me; continual work has given me a tolerably thick skin on my body. Then you and Clara might go and live in our cottage; we should be able to see one another every day, and help each other—and you and your wife, and your children, when they come, you at least might live in peace. If the night does not bring any change of plan, I shall go over in the morning and break the matter to Jan Staers."

Luke let his basket drop on the ground, threw his arms round his father's neck, and, overpowered by emotion, burst into tears on the old man's breast, while he murmured, with a voice choked and interrupted by sobs—

"Father, you are too good! May God recompense you in his heaven—and I will never forget
c

it as long as I live—I shall love you and honor
you—Oh, I don't know where I am—my brain is
reeling—Clara, the sweet Clara, she shall—"

"Look, yonder comes Clara!" said his father.

Along a side-path between the pine-trees, and
at some little distance, the young maiden was
coming toward them; she was walking steadily
on, with her eyes bent on the ground, slowly, and
with an air of distraction.

At the first word of his father, the youth had
released himself from his embrace, and was about
to run toward the damsel, in the fulness of his joy,
when the old man detained him, and, with solemn
voice, charged him—

"Luke, not a word of this plan to Clara, do you
hear? I must first sleep over it, and know what
her father thinks about it."

The young man made a sign with his head that
he would keep silence about the good news, and
then sprang forward to Clara, who had by this
time come several steps nearer to them. Luke
was so overjoyed that he threw his cap into the
air, and sang and danced like a child, and filled
the wood with cries of joy. But that he had any
good news to tell, and had good reason to be glad
—of this he said not a word.

He seized the maiden by the hand, and drew
her toward the spot from which his father was
watching him with a look of reproach.

"Come, Clara, come!" exclaimed the young
man, quite wild with joy. "Oh, if I could tell

you all!—Father won't let me—to-morrow! to-morrow!—Come, Clara; laugh, sing, be merry;—but I must not speak of it—I am ready to burst, but I must not speak. I would give five francs—that is, if I had them—if you could guess it your-self.—It sticks like a great ball in my throat—Oh, it is so lovely—so lovely!—"

The old man had meanwhile advanced several steps, and now seized his son's wrist in his still powerful grasp.

"Luke, Luke," said he, reproachfully, "this is not manly of you!"

As though the pressure of his father's hand, and the severe tone of his voice, had aroused him from a dream, the youth bowed his head in shame, but soon raised it again boldly, and with a sweet smile playing on his face.

"It was time, father," murmured he; "I can't help it; but it was on the tip of my tongue."

The damsel looked at them both with a quiet astonishment, and seemed to ask what had hap-pened, or what it was that they were so anxious to conceal from her. Her features were beautiful, and her figure slender and graceful; there was something of earnestness and patient endurance in the slow, cautious gaze of her dark eyes. Although her cheeks, embrowned by exposure, betokened a degree of thinness, continuous toil had made her limbs firm and strong. She carried her head erect, and there was an expression about her fine mouth which might have been construed into pride, had not the whole village known that it was impossible to find a damsel more tender-hearted and humble than she was. Constant reflection and thought, the bearing her melancholy burden without hopě, without alleviation, had graven two delicate wrinkles around her lips. Although her clothes had well-nigh lost their original color, and here and there a patch or a seam showed that much care had been expended to conceal the ravages of time, they were so clean, and were worn with so becoming a grace, that, at the first glance, she seemed more richly dressed than other peasant girls.

After a few quiet words of greeting had passed between her and the old man, the latter took the basket on his shoulder, placed himself in the middle between the two young people, and so all three went on toward the village.

Luke began to talk of the beautiful weather, of the approaching procession, and of the Kermes on the Crossberg, and of all kinds of bright and joyous things; but, every now and then, he mixed with his remarks some words of double meaning, which more than once compelled his father to make him a sign to remember the prohibition laid on him.

Clara seemed out of sympathy with all their demonstrations of joy, and she walked on with a downcast and melancholy look.

They were now only two or three bowshots from the first house of the village, when Luke addressed to Clara a direct question, which compelled her to turn her face toward him.

"Clara, you are crying! your tears are flow-ing!" exclaimed he, suddenly leaving his father's side and planting himself directly in front of the maiden. "Oh, comfort yourself, comfort yourself —there will be an end of all this; we will—oh, no—you shall be so very happy—to-morrow you shall—"

But a glance from his father cut short his revela-tions.

"Oh, tell me, Clara, tell me, why you are weeping so bitterly!" asked he, in anguish; and, all of a sudden disenchanted, he raised his hand to his eyes, and brushed away from each a pearly tear.

"Oh, dear friend," sobbed Clara, "I have suf-fered so much! my heart is breaking in my bosom Since the morning I have been wandering in the wood, and weeping in solitude over my bitter lot. I dare not return home; it will be henceforward so desert and lonely to me—"

"Good heavens! has any misfortune happened?" groaned Luke. "Your father?—"

"My father is gone to the town," answered the maiden.

"But you distress me, Clara. Tell me, then, why your tears are flowing."

With increased melancholy, the damsel replied:

"You know, well, Father Torfs, our cow—the last of all—that Luke used to call 'white mammy.' Alas! I have fed it and cared for it ever since it was a poor little calf—my only companion in the

4

world, my last possession on earth—to whom I
used to tell every thing that made me suffer and
feel sad. She had as much sense as a human
being; she could see in my eyes what I wanted to
tell her. Whenever I was crying, and my tears
would fall as I rested my head on her neck, the
grateful beast would lick my hands to console
me. Yes, Luke, you might well call her 'white
mammy,' for she has fed us a long time, and has
been my only resource. But for her, and but—
but for you, Luke, I should long ere this have been
laid to rest beneath the grass in the churchyard.
Oh, I did not know that a human being could ever
feel so much love for a beast; but if I had a sister,
and she were, unhappily, to die, it seems to me it
would not pierce my heart more deeply. I shall
become quite ill with it. Oh, poor creature, poor
creature, my good beast!"

"Is the cow dead, Clara?" asked the old
man.

"Worse, worse than dead!" sobbed the poor
maiden; "father sold her this morning to our
neighbor, the butcher, Thomas ——." And with
a flood of tears she ended with the words—"And
I saw her white skin, all stained with blood, hanging at his door. Oh, God! it is enough to kill me
with grief!"

The old father, overcome by the tone of Clara's
voice, had covered his eyes with his hands; Luke
wept aloud; all three stood melted into tears over
the death of a cow! Marvellous sentiment of grati-

tude, which retains so deep and living a memory of benefits, even when conferred on us by a beast of the field!

The weeping of the aged father changed very rapidly into anger; he stamped his foot on the ground with vexation, and murmured between his lips biting words, of which enough was heard to show that Clara's father was their object.

"And why did your father sell the cow?" said he; "as usual, to—"

"To pay his arrears of rent," interposed the damsel.

"Ah, he is gone to pay his rent!" exclaimed Luke, with joy.

"And do not blame my poor father," said Clara, in a tone of entreaty; "you cannot know all; but he is so unfortunate! Oh, rather have a little sympathy with him, and pray God to look mercifully on him!"

The old man felt his eyes becoming moist again. The last words of the maiden, spoken with a voice so beseeching and so full of love, had deeply affected him; and he looked at her thoughtfully and with beaming eyes, as though he were on the point of saying something very important to her.

The young man divined what was working in his father's mind, and with his hands upraised to him he seemed to implore a favorable decision. The old father seized Clara's hand with deep emotion, and while he led her hastily toward the vil-
he said—

"Clara, I love you right well; you are a noble child. But be of good comfort: the God above us tries and proves even virtuous men; but at length he rewards steadfastness in goodness, and patient endurance in suffering. Come, we will have some coffee, and talk with mother about good things. Be of good courage, my child; whatever may happen, look you, in us you will always find friends in need."

"Oh, father, tell her *it* now!" implored the youth. "Tell *it* to her: all her grief will be suddenly changed into gladness."

"I shall tell Clara in the house all that she ought to know," answered the old man, in a tone of severe rebuke. "If you will not obey me, and cannot keep silence to-day, I shall cease henceforward to tell you of my projects and intentions."

At this moment they turned a corner in the village path, and stood before the humble dwelling of old Torfs.

Clara pointed with her finger in the distance toward the house of the butcher, before whose door, sure enough, there hung the bloody hide of a recently slaughtered beast.

"Poor mammy! Oh, my helpless cow!" sobbed she. "Look! look! her skin! all bedabbled with blood!"

But Luke put an end to her lamentations, by seizing her arm and pushing her before him into the cottage.

CHAPTER IV.

THE morning after these occurrences, Clara **was** sitting in a lower room of the stone farm-house. On her lap lay a garment of her father's, and she was trying, with needle and thread, to mend its numerous rents.

All around her was unusually still and lonely; not a noise, not a sound, either within or without, broke the deep repose which brooded over the spacious apartment. Even the pendulum of the clock hung motionless; and it was easy to see that the wheels had been long doomed to inaction, for both the hands had fallen by their own weight and pointed to the number six.

Very little furniture adorned this best room of the stone farm; its scantiness revealed that poverty had her dwelling here. From the wretched condition of the few things that remained, one might conjecture that decay and slow ruin had prevented the inhabitants from replacing gradually what was worn out and mending what was broken.

Thus in the farther corner stood two chairs, but their rush bottoms were broken and stuck up in the air like the bristles of a hedge-hog; a little farther off were two others, each with one or two

4*

of its legs broken. Yes, one could see that the
leaf of the table and the corners of the great ward
robe had been injured by violence; for the miss-
ing pieces could not have been broken off except
by a great effort and on purpose.

On the dresser—where our farm-houses usually
make a very brilliant display of pewter plates,
dishes, and spoons—stood only two or three tin
trenchers, the crushed and bent edges of which
also indicated violence. The rest of the things
were nothing but fragments: plates with pieces
out of their rims, jugs without lip or handle,
spoons with broken handles, forks with their
prongs dislocated or wanting.

And yet, withal, every thing in this room was
neat and clean. The tin trenchers shone like
silver, not a speck dimmed the brightness of the
well-scoured plates, the woodwork of the chairs
was well washed, and on the floor of red tiles,
sadly injured here and there, glittering sand had
been sprinkled in fantastic patterns. No one
could doubt that in this house there was some
one who exerted every effort to conceal as far as
possible the tokens of approaching poverty.

Clara continued her work in silence, although
her countenance gave indication of manifold and
varied meditations. A smile of gentle gladness
played restlessly about her mouth, her dark eyes
glowed with a soft light, her bosom rose and fell
more quickly than usual, and her very lips kept
moving, as though she were whispering words of

hope to herself. From time to time she paused
and turned her head in the direction of a small
door, and hearkened whether any sound came
from behind it.

After having kept her eyes fixed for a long time
on her work, she raised her head and said, half
aloud, as if talking to herself:

"Ah, won't father be glad?—Now I know what
has made him unhappy for so long a time. It
was the being forced to leave his farm! It was
shame that was gnawing at his heart; it was to
drown his bitter grief that he——wandered about
so dejectedly from morning to night. But now
Farmer Torfs will help us, and set us up again;
the good man—he says that he will raise my father
out of his poverty, and make his life calm and
peaceful. Oh, my God! may this come to pass!
Perhaps then he will be cured of the horrid vice;—
but what could Luke want to make me understand
with his extraordinary gestures and grimaces?
There is a secret I must not know. I am sure it
must be a merry secret, for Luke could scarcely
contain himself for joy. He turned and wriggled
about on his chair, then he jumped up as if he had
something to tell me, then he sat down again in a
hurry, and looked deep into my eyes—I am quite
dying of curiosity. What can it be?"

The maiden bowed her head, and, while a quiet
smile lingered on her countenance, she tried to
guess what it could be that they were so anxious
to keep from her. At last her expression relapsed

into its ordinary cast of seriousness, and, resuming the thread of her former musings, she said—

"Really, I do think father is a little better now! He went yesterday to pay off a part of his arrears of rent. This must have given him great comfort, and he will rise this morning with a lighter heart. Yes, yes, he will talk in a friendly way with Farmer Torfs: my poor white mammy will, after all, have helped to make us very happy by her death. But father stays too long in bed. Eight o'clock already! Anyhow, it was very late when he came home. Perhaps he may be sick. Ah, if he should have one of his wretched head-aches, and be quite distracted with pain! I wish I could go into his room and see. No, no; he would only be angry with me, perhaps. And Farmer Torfs, who may come any moment—I don't know—I am quite at a loss. Father cannot endure old Torfs. Suppose he should begin to abuse him or treat him ill!"

She raised her eyes beseechingly to heaven, and her lips moved in deep though quiet prayer.

At this moment a man's head appeared at the window which looked out into the street. It was Luke, who, with his neck stretched out at full length, and his face all smiles, was looking into the room from the street.

But no sooner did his eye fall on the young maiden, who with folded hands gazed steadfastly toward heaven, than he was struck with wonder and admiration; an expression of surprise banished the smile from his countenance, and he stood, with his mouth open, gazing fixedly on the praying girl.

How charming did she now appear in his eyes, now when her moistened eyes were uplifted in trustful prayer to God, now that the glow of her eager petition and the sweet smile of her entreaty irradiated her graceful form with a beauty super-human!

The young man might have lingered long in utter forgetfulness of all but the lovely vision before him; but the maiden's prayer ceased, her head had sunk on her bosom, and she had begun again to talk aloud to herself, in a sort of half distraction.

Luke suddenly disappeared from the window; a moment after, Clara was surprised to hear a gentle knock at the outer door. She turned round and saw her friend Luke, who nodded to her and gave her a sign that she should make no noise. When the maiden had come near him, he asked, in a low voice—

"Clara, is your father up yet?"

"No, he is still asleep," was the answer.

"Haven't you heard him stirring yet?"

"Not yet."

"My father has sent me to see whether he can come now to speak to Farmer Staers."

He then raised the damsel's hand, and with an air of joyful mystery he drew her into the corner near the door, and then he whispered—

"Clara, do you think you know what my father

has to propose to yours? Ha! ha! you know nothing at all about it. It is the most beautiful, altogether the most beautiful thing you could ever imagine!"

"Oh, Luke," said the maiden, in a coaxing tone, while her eyes glistened with eager curiosity, "do tell me what it is; I haven't slept all night long for thinking about it; the secret was every moment before me; I could not close my eyes: I can't imagine what it can be."

"Ah, if you had known what it is, Clara, you would have had better reason for lying awake. I haven't slept a wink all the night either—at least, so far as I know. Oh, it is something, something so—I can't tell you what—it is just the thing to make you jump ten feet into the air for joy. I have already cut more capers this morning than in a whole Kermes day."

Clara looked at him with entreaty in her eyes, and as if she would draw the reluctant words out of his mouth, when he suddenly changed his tone, and said—

"Oh, lassie, lassie, you would like to know what it is; wouldn't you, now? yes, I know that right well. If you could only half guess what it is, you might get me to tell you the rest, but that you can't do. Father has forbidden me—and so you see clearly, I can't tell you. Beautiful! and so blissful! this news! when you hear it, and it can't be more than two hours more, you won't know what to do with yourself for joy."

"Won't you tell me?" asked the maiden, with a little vexation on her face, and a slight accent of threatening in her tone of voice.

"Don't be sulky, Clara; I must not. Else!— You may fancy I have been ready to burst ever since I knew it. Last evening and this morning, as soon as I was alone, I have been telling you all about it out aloud more than twenty times—but I couldn't tell it to you as you stand there now—no, not for the world. But if you did know it, oh, oh,—how you would laugh!"

"Get along with you!" muttered Clara, turning away from him. "You have come here only to tease me and vex me! my father may get up any moment, and he would be very angry if he surprised you here."

"But why? my father has sent me —-and besides, as soon as I hear any thing, I shall be off like a shot."

"A likely thing, indeed, that I should be sulky! if you would only stay away—"

"Come here, Clara," said the youth, "I will tell you all about it—I can't keep it in any longer. Will you hold your tongue about it? you won't tell your father?"

"Lasses know how to keep secrets better than lads," answered Clara, again coming close to Luke.

"So! that means that I ought to keep my secret—and now, a plague on my face!—it won't keep still—I can't say a word for laughing."

" Well, now, are you going to tel. me ? torment that you are !''

" Oh, yes, yes ; wait a bit, Clara."

He cast his eyes on the ground, and seemed to ne meditating.

" Have you forgotten it ?" said the girl, in a mocking and impatient tone.

" Forgotten ! oh, yes ; it isn't so easy to forget things like this," stammered Luke; " but you see I don't know what ails me ; I can't tell how to set about it. I had thought it all over and over; but it is not so easy to say things like this right out in the face of—of a young girl—Clara, I am so ashamed."

" What a baby you are, Luke ! It is beautiful, and happy, and all that, you say; there is no great mischief, then. How can you be ashamed about it ?"

" Yes, I am very anxious to know how you will take it !"

" Look you, Luke; if you are not going to speak right out, I shall run away !"

" Listen, then ; but don't be too glad, Clara, and try to restrain yourself, else you may forget yourself in your joy, and make a disturbance. My father is coming here to make a proposal to yours."

" Well, I knew that before."

" Yes, but there is another proposal—how shall I get it out ? Clara, you have always wished me well, haven't you ?"

"But why do you ask such stupid questions?"

"And if you had to choose among all the lads of the village, which would you choose?"

"Oh, you have lost your senses!" muttered Clara, impatiently.

"Come, come," sighed Luke, "I will try to bring it out better somehow. My father is coming to see your father to—to—"

"To!—to!—to what?"

"To ask whether Luke may marry Clara!"

The maiden, as if petrified with astonishment, gazed incredulously at him.

"Whether we may go and live in a little cottage, and be man and wife," repeated the young man, with joy in every gesture.

Clara trembled; a sudden paleness drove the color from her cheek, and then cheek and forehead glowed with fiery crimson, and she bent her eyes on the ground in violent emotion.

Accusing himself as the cause of her perturbation, Luke sighed sorrowfully:

"Yes, didn't I tell you, Clara, that you would be ashamed? It is your own fault: you forced me to tell you."

The girl remained silent, and from each eye dropped a glistening tear.

"Oh, Clara," said Luke, imploringly, "don't be vexed about it. Think, now, my father will help yours to pay all his debts, and stand by him as a friend and adviser. We shall go away, and live in our little cottage, and work together, and save,

D 5

and live in tranquil happiness. Too long have you endured pain and grief, and sat weeping in dreary loneliness. I shall hold nothing so dear as your happiness; I will slave from morning to night to provide for you; I shall love you, and make every thing around you smile on you. My mother will be your mother,—she loves you so dearly already. And, do you know, last evening she took out of her box her gold chain with the large golden heart, and she said, 'This is for Clara, my daughter!' But why do you weep so bitterly, Clara? Your father, when he sees happiness open all around him, and all cares are removed from his mind,—when he meets with nothing but friendship and affection,—ah, then he will be cured of his dreadful malady, and his old age will yet be peaceful and happy!"

While Luke was speaking, the damsel had covered her face with her hands, and was sobbing aloud.

"Oh, God!" said Luke, with bitter disappointment, "I thought you would have jumped for joy like me, and there you stand crying as if something very bad had happened. But you have only to say, Clara, that you won't have me, —I will go home—and I shall fall sick—and—"

Suddenly a loud noise was heard behind the door of a small chamber, as of something that fell to the ground with a crash and was broken in pieces.

"My father,—my father is coming," sobbed

the girl, with terror depicted on her countenance.
Luke made a step toward the door, folded his
hands in a gesture of earnest entreaty, pleaded—

" Clara, Clara, you will consent after all, won't
you? oh, don't let me die of sorrow! I will do
any thing you wish; I will be obedient to you, and
surround you with love—"

" Hold your tongue! be off with you!" said the
maiden, with a confused and faltering voice. " My
tears are tears of joy; I never dared to hope for
so much happiness on earth—"

"Ah! thank God, it was all for joy!" shouted
the youth, in an ecstacy, and at the top of his
voice, as he ran toward the door.

Then he turned back again a step or two, and
said:—

"Clara, don't say a word to anybody! I shall
go and tell my father. Good-by! and won't we
laugh and be merry with mother? Ha! ha! it
was all for joy!"

He darted out at the door—and when he was
fairly out in the farmyard he threw up his cap in
the air with a loud shout:

" The lassie, the lassie! it was all for joy! it was
all for joy!"

Clara fixed her eyes a while on the door of her
father's bedroom, and, hearing no further sound,
her thoughts reverted to the intelligence which
had so deeply moved her. She wiped away her
tears and sighed, as she turned her eyes to heaven
with a look of gratitude, and said—

"O God, how good thou art to me! Dame Torfs will be my mother! my poor father will be quite cured! yes, he will be quite right again, and be happy in his old age! Luke and I will toil and be careful now, to make his life pleasant to him, to tend him, to give him all he needs. Alas! I have from my childhood pined and sighed within these four walls; and now I shall live with friends who love me dearly; I shall be always merry, and work and sing—O my God, I thank thee! it is a heaven on earth!"

Again she heard a slight noise,—the door was opened, and Jan Staers, her father, entered the room.

CHAPTER V.

Jan STAERS was a man above the middle size; but although his frame indicated great muscular power, his limbs hung loose and disjointed, and his dull inanimate countenance was bloated and pallid.

The bright light of the sun had taken him by surprise as he entered the room, and he was obliged to close his weak and bloodshot eyes. His hair hung negligently over his forehead, and his clothes were soiled and disordered.

He stood a while at the door, pressing his hand heavily on his head, like one who is suffering from a violent headache. In the mean time, Clara, after

a word of affectionate greeting, had run to the
hearth, placed on the table a coffee-pot, a loaf and
some butter, and set a chair for him.

With downcast eyes, and without speaking a
word, his legs trembling under him as he moved,
Jan Staers drew near the table and let himself
drop into his chair. The sunlight seemed still to
annoy him a great deal, for he looked fiercely out
of the window, and then said to Clara, in a tone
of great irritation—

"Shut the window, can't you?"

Clara obeyed his command, and then remained
standing in silence at a little distance. Meanwhile
Jan Staers took the loaf and tried to cut off a
corner of the crust, but his hand trembled and
shook so violently, that he found it utterly impossible to help himself. He threw down the loaf
sulkily, with such violence that he broke another
piece out of the plate that contained the butter.
He growled some words that sounded like an oath,
but restrained himself when he saw that Clara,
anticipating his wish, was cutting some slices of
bread and butter for him.

"Father dear!" said the girl, with an insinua-
ting tone, "don't be vexed. I will do all that you
wish; only keep in a good temper and don't worry
yourself. Our neighbor Torfs is coming directly
to speak to you about something."

"The hypocritical old hunks! He dare to come
into my house, will he? But you have been cry
ing—always at your old tricks!"

"Oh, father, Farmer Torfs means to make you such a nice proposal; he will save us from ruin, and make us so happy—"

"I won't see him, I tell you. Don't mention it; it only vexes me."

The girl retired two or three steps behind her father's chair, and there remained standing, with her troubled look bent on the floor. Jan Staers took the bread and butter, and began to eat; then he threw it down in disgust, and said—

"It is dry as sand. A bit of wood has more taste in it. Why haven't you got fresh bread?"

Clara was silent.

"Why is there no fresh bread in the house?" repeated he, still louder.

"The baker will not trust us any longer," stammered the poor girl.

An expression of anger clouded her father's countenance. Without further remark, he buried his head in his hands, and remained for some time thus without moving.

The damsel looked at him in silent sorrow, and exerted herself to restrain the tears that were starting from her eyes. After a while she went close to him, stroked his hand coaxingly with hers, and said, in a tone of entreaty—

"Don't fret yourself, father; things will go better soon. Farmer Torfs has some good project to talk to you about. Do drink another cup of warm coffee; it will brighten you up and cheer you."

"The grovelling hypocrite, the sneaking rascal, who has his eye on my farm!" roared Jan Staers, in a voice choked by rage. "Let him come; I will very soon kick him out at the door!"

At these savage threats, Clara could no longer refrain herself; her cup of sorrow overflowed, and with a cry of anguish she sank down upon a chair, placed her hand before her eyes, and wept and sobbed aloud.

Her emotion pained her father deeply; he wrung his hands and ground his teeth in a paroxysm of impatience and rage, and at length said—

"I have a pain in my head, Clara, child; why will you worry me so with your whims and tricks? . . . . now, now, out with it, what do you want me to do?"

"Answer me, then!" he cried, angrily, after a brief pause.

"O father," said the poor weeping girl, beseechingly, "don't be churlish to Farmer Torfs. Listen to him with good nature; what he has to say to you will make you very glad."

"Have done, then, with your blubbering; I will listen to what he has to say, even if I burst with rage."

"No, no, father dear," sobbed Clara, "not so; you will listen to him with friendship and kindly feeling."

Jan Staers raised his head again, and remained a few moments without speaking. The thought was evidently very painful, and the struggle within, a violent one. At last he said suddenly and sharply—

"Let me alone; you will keep talking to me—it worries me, I tell you; your voice makes my head split: get along—be off from this; I will call you if I want you."

But when he saw that his words had made her tears flow afresh and more plentifully, he added, in a milder tone—

"Come, now, I will try my best to listen to the old hunks with patience."

The poor Clara raised her apron to her eyes, and slowly left the room. Jan Staers followed her with his eyes until she had quite disappeared. Then he rose up and made a few unsteady steps across the room; he then stood still, pressed his arms convulsively to his side, stamped with his foot, and seemed abandoned to utter despair.

Again he made a few steps, muttered some moody curses, and shook his head in deep thought, as though he were making a violent effort to recall some things which had escaped his memory. From time to time he shivered in every limb, and exclaimed, as if in pain or great uneasiness—

"Whew—how cold!—my brain is all on fire, and my body is quite frozen!"

All at once his eyes began to beam with a melancholy lustre, and an expression of deep suspense overspread his face; it was as if a sudden illumination had been cast on his mind. From his chest issued a hoarse rattling sound, and he struck himself passionately on the forehead with his clenched fist, as though he would have broken his skull.

Exhausted by this overtension of his powers, and subdued by pain, he staggered to the table, and let himself drop into his chair with a deep sigh. Then, with his bewildered gaze fixed on the floor, he exclaimed, in a forlorn, despairing tone—

"Damnable poison! curse of soul and body both! ah, he who invented you was a cruel enemy of his kind. Despicable drunkard that I am! what a wretched pass I have brought myself to! The blessed light torments me; my whole body is trembling; my very soul is dry and waste; I can neither walk nor stand, nor eat nor drink! In my head is a dark, hideous chaos of despair, of rage of guilt, of remorse, and of coward impotence and my child, my poor Clara! she is suffering she is pining uncomplainingly away; I requite her love with anger and surliness—I am her father, and I must be under constant obligation to her— and, oh cursed destiny! I am her murderer! in vile selfishness, I have blighted and wasted her young life! Were God to punish me—to kill me —it would be a blessing for her. How ghastly a thought that a father's death should be a blessing to his child!"

This last thought seemed to shock him terribly; he gnashed his teeth fiercely, and clutched the table so violently with his hands that it seemed to bend beneath the pressure of his fingers.

After this violent convulsive movement he remained a while quite still; and then his countenance began again to work with painful emotions. Holding his fingers pressed on his forehead, as though to coerce his refractory memory, his cheeks became all at once bloodless, under the impulse of a sudden alarm.

"Yesterday," he muttered, "yesterday I was to have gone to the town. Yes, I had some money —money to pay an instalment of my rent. But where did I go? what did I do with myself? how did I get here? let me see—can I have paid the rent?—ah! wretched man! I got drunk, I fell asleep—"

And with trembling haste he raised his blouse, and unclasped a leathern belt that was fastened around his waist. He shook a number of pieces of money out of the belt upon the table, his countenance the while bearing an expression of deepest anxiety. He seized several of the pieces, and tried to count them; and now his frame shook more violently still, and he felt as if each separate hair were standing erect on his head from sheer despair.

"Horror of horrors!" he exclaimed; "lost! stolen! I must count them over again; perhaps I have made a mistake."

He then tried hastily to arrange the pieces of gold in two rows; but his hand shook so tremulously, that it was with extreme difficulty that he at length succeeded, after a fashion; and many a bit-

ter word, many a deadly curse, rolled from his lips
during the operation.

His terror became greater still, and a cold perspiration broke out all over him; for he counted
and counted again, and still found himself a considerable sum short. And at length he was forced
to give up all hope that he was mistaken in his
reckoning. A violent tremor shook his whole
body; he tore his hair, and roared, in a tone of
despair—

"Fifty francs! fifty francs short! where can
they have gone? Ah, I had sold our last cow—
and the money was to have stopped the ejectment;
and now, now I shall be driven out of my farm,
and turned out into the street like a dog—and
then go and beg! I must be jeered—be despised
—be pointed at with the finger, as a contemptible
drunkard! And my poor Clara! what will become of her? perdition—may perdition seize
me!"

And he uttered a cry so shrill and so full of
distress, that it seemed as though his heart had
broken in twain within him

He then started up, strode furiously up and
down the room, struck his fists against the walls
until they bled, kicked the chairs in all directions,
and gave utterance to all kinds of cries of desperation and rage. Then, when he had exhausted
his passion, he stood suddenly still. An indescribable smile of joy and of derision lighted up
his features as he turned his glistening eyes toward

the door of his sleeping-apartment; and he exclaimed, as if beside himself—

"Ah, ah! light and clearness for the spirit, vigor
for the body, energy for the will,—there they are,
behind the door, in a flask! I have surrendered
my reason, my whole soul, to the demon of drink;
he alone can lend them back to me for a few moments. And I must, I must have them now.
Advise me, advise me—yes, for the last time, the
very last time; yet this once—only this once—"

And while finishing these words, he sprang
toward the door, and disappeared in the little
adjoining room. And now for some time there
was a silence as of death throughout the farm-
house; only, at intervals, a dull muffled sound, like
the gurgling of a liquid from the mouth of a flask
reached the large room.

When Jan Staers again made his appearance, he
was scarcely to be recognised for the same man.
His countenance was lighted up by a gentle smile,
his eyes were bright and wide open, his head stood
erect and firm on his shoulders; he no longer trembled and staggered, and his cheeks were suffused
with a warm and rich blood. His every gesture
betokened freedom, courage, and energy.

Approaching the table, he said, in a tone of
scornful merriment—

"So, so,—the miserly wretches,—they thought it
was all over with Jan Staers, did they? the stupid
blockheads! they clapped their hands when they
saw him turned out of the stone farm, did they!

Well, I am not quite done up yet. Ha! ha! 'it is poison,' whine the stupid scoundrels; exquisite poison, delicious poison, that courses through my veins like a living flame! Ha! ha! now I have sense enough; it is clear enough now here inside, in my head. But let us be quick. I have emptied the flask; it is too much, perhaps. Now let us make haste to count the money, and decide what is to be done to show that Jan Staers is not quite so easily to be thrown on his back."

Then he arranged the pieces of money, and counted them readily and accurately.

"Only forty francs short!" he exclaimed, joyously; "ten francs gained! but now, where can these twenty florins be gone? Ah, I know. Yesterday I didn't go to the town at all: I stopped short at the 'Golden Apple,' on the Crossway. It was a jolly company: I lent fifteen florins to Klaes Grills, the sand-digger. What ever makes me always play the rich man? Bah! it was only in jest; I shall get my money again. And the other five florins? Yes, I remember, they got them out of me: I paid all the reckoning. Well, come, come—there are no pots broken as yet. I will be off at once to the town, and carry this money to my covetous old landlord; I will go by the lower road, so as not to pass by any public-house. He will be glad enough when he sees his cash; else who will take off his hands this tumble-down house and these wretched barren fields?—who? Ah, yes, the old beetle, perhaps: the niggardly old

6

Torfs, who has been hankering after my farm this many a year, and splitting every farthing into four to manage it. But I'll let him see! To-morrow I'll begin to work, and I won't drink any more; no, on my life, not a drop more, till the brooks run gin. I will sell some of that useless rubbish there in the great glass wardrobe. My name is worth money still; I shall readily find a horse and a couple of cows somewhere on credit. And besides, I will drive such a trade in grain and in wood, and by care and intelligence I will so soon put every thing straight, that the envious fellows round me will burst with wonder and vexation. Ah, but who is that coming? The beetle, I declare, with his hypocritical face; oh that I could kick him out at the door!—but no, no, I promised Clara that I would receive him in a friendly way. Come then, I'm in a good temper now; I'll be a good boy, and hear out what the old rascal has to say. It will be uncommonly hard work, though."

With a smile of conscious pride, he looked at the old Torfs as he entered the room, and threw himself back in his chair, just as if he were some great lord who was receiving a beggar. A slight shade of vexation came over Farmer Torfs's countenance when his eye rested on Jan Staers, as he bade him good-day, for he saw how strange and fierce was the light of his eye, and how red his features were.

Going up to him with a friendly smile, he said—

"Farmer Staers, I am come here to ask something of you, and at the same time to make you
a weighty proposal. Are you prepared to listen
to me with calmness?"

"With calmness? what do you mean?" asked
Staers, contemptuously. "Do you think I have
lost my senses?"

The old man shook his head in displeasure, as
he continued—

"I should be sorry to say any thing to displease
you. The matter on which I am going to speak
to you is very serious; it demands on both sides
the greatest consideration. With your permission,
I will take a seat."

"What difference does it make to me whether
you sit or stand?" answered the other. "Only
make haste; for I must be off to the town in a
very short time. All these preambles and flourishes
make me impatient—the perspiration stands on my
forehead."

"There is no use in my remaining here," said
the old man, in a tone of vexation, and turning
toward the door, as if to leave the room. "I did
not come here either to jest or to be made a jest
of."

"Now, now, sit you down, neighbor," said
Jan Staers, with a friendly smile: "it is only my
way. Let us hear what you want."

"Will you listen to me a moment without
interrupting me? I like talking straight on,
you see, whenever I have any thing to say; but

in my turn I can hold my tongue and be a good listener."

"Say on, then ; and if I interrupt you, may—"

"There is no need of that!" interposed the old man, as with a gesture of his hand he kept back the oath that Staers was about to utter.

He then sat down on a chair, and said, with impressive calmness—

"Staers, you have a child, a daughter. It would be a pleasure to you to see her happy, would it not? You are a father. Always alone in this farmhouse, without company, wailing over bitter and painful things: you can conceive that her life must be rather weary and dull—now, don't be impatient; let me have my say out. Clara is a good lass, and deserves a better lot; and it would be indeed melancholy if she had to endure new sorrows; for an indelible disgrace would deprive her of the hope of a happy life—"

"What are you prating about all this time?" growled Staers, with kindling eyes. "Disgrace? what disgrace?"

"Only a few words more ; don't interrupt me," continued the old man, calmly. "You know my son Luke ; he is a fine lad, and works from morning to night."

"I can well believe that, for, if he didn't work, what on earth is he fit for else?"

"Well, now, neighbor, it seems that the young folks have had a liking for each other for a long time, and—"

"And, and?" said the other, scornfully.

"And I am come to ask the hand of Clara for Luke."

Jan Staers burst out into a long peal of laughter, which produced a very painful effect on the old man. It was evident that Torfs was deeply wounded; for he raised his eyes toward his neighbor with wonder and inquiry, and said, in a tone of irritation—

"I cannot see that there is any thing so very ludicrous in the proposal I have made."

"Nothing ludicrous?" shouted the other. "Ha! ha! the daughter of Farmer Staers is to marry the son of a cattle-drover! You stick your horns rather high, neighbor: God be praised, I am not come to that yet."

The aged Torfs was obliged to put forth all his strength to restrain his indignation at this contemptuous scoff. His lips were compressed with anger, and his hand trembled at his side. It was with a bitter calmness that he said—

"You were once a thriving farmer, and I was once a poor cattle-drover; but we are, neither of us, what we were."

"You will make me angry in a moment," said Jan Staers, still with a look of ineffable contempt and derision; "yet I don't want to heat my blood. So you think that I am fairly come to an end, do you? I'll let you see something yet you little dream of. He laughs best who laughs last!"

The old man had for some time noticed that

E   6*

the eyes of his neighbor glowed with a peculiar
fire; his smile, his gestures, were too remarkable to
allow him to doubt that Clara's father had already
drunk too much that morning.   And with this conviction, he made a movement toward the door;
but he thought of his son, on the impossibility of
putting off the matter, and he sat down again on
his chair, and said, firmly and decisively—

"You may interrupt me or not, as you please,
I will say out all I have to say to you.   In the
name of your child, I beseech you listen to me
with patience—"

"Now, now, go your own way; I am listening."

"Look you, neighbor," said the old man; "it
is useless to play with me, or have any disguise
with me; I know the state of your affairs too accurately for that.   I know, too, that to-morrow, if
not to-day, you will be ejected from your farm,
because you have not paid the arrears of your rent,
and the term of the writ is nearly run out.   I know,
too, that you have made away with your last cow,
but the money you got for it is not enough, and
consequently—"

Jan Staers struck his hand among the pieces of
money which were scattered about on the table,
and their pleasant chink echoed through the room.

"Money?" exclaimed he, with impetuosity.
"Money? there is money for you!"

"It is not the third part of what you must pay
if you would suspend the execution of the writ:—
if you will only be reasonable, I will advance you

at once what you want to make up your whole rent."

"You?" said Staers, with scornful incredulity. "How did you come by it?"

"Yes, I. And why not? Do you think that from twenty years of hard work and thrift there is not enough over, when one has had a good landlord?"

"Oh, yes, our landlord! he knows how to skin a man alive, the blood-sucker!"

"I will not hear that said!" indignantly exclaimed the old man. "He has never raised my rent over me, although I have very considerably increased the value of his land."

"Ah, you will lend me money!" repeated Jan Staers, in a softer tone. "Well, I should never have expected it from you. We shall become good friends, I see. How much will you lend me?"

"In case you will assent to the happiness of your daughter and my son, I will lend you enough to clear off your arrears with our landlord; and besides, I will help you to pay off all your debts by degrees."

"But, Father Torfs, you are only making an idle boast! you talk of money as if it grew on your back. Have you found a treasure,—or have you stolen one? It seems likely enough. Now don't be angry, neighbor; it is only my way of talking; I don't mean any harm. What were we saying? Oh, yes, you are to lend me money, plenty of money,—on condition that your son shall marry

Clara. Well, now, it is reasonable enough; there is my hand to it. It is a bargain. Luke can come and live with us, and work—there is land enough. Why do you draw your hand away? what more is wanting?"

The old man paused for a moment, and then continued:.

"It cannot be so, neighbor Jan. Let me once for all explain to you freely and fairly my whole intention. Without horses, without cows, this farm can never be cultivated properly. My son and you would work yourselves to death for nothing; you would not get half your rent off the land. Now this is my plan; I have some little money, and plenty of credit; I will take your land off your hands, and bring my horse and my four cows here with me. I will buy two horses besides, and gradually get as many cows as are necessary on such a farm as this. You shall live on with us in the stone farm-house. Luke and Clara will put up with my present little cottage, and I will take care they have enough to begin life in a quiet way. You will have no further cares upon your mind, and perhaps you would become fond of a dwelling in which my wife and I, through our example and our kindness, would try to make your life more pleasant and peaceful. And if you were once cured of the vice which is the cause of all your misery, then you would have good reason to bless God, neighbor Jan. Clara, who has nothing to look forward to but poverty and wretchedness, would find in my son Luke a virtuous husband, and live happily with him to the end of her days. Well, now, do you agree to my proposal? whole and entire, as I have laid it down?"

Jan Staers, whose head had already become confused with listening so long, had probably deceived himself as to the drift of the proposal; for he stood up with joy, and was throwing his arms around the neck of old Torfs; but the latter drew back in doubt and consternation, and declined the embrace of his neighbor. Nevertheless, Staers managed to raise both the old man's hands, and exclaimed: "Ah, you are a fine fellow, to help your neighbor so generously and nobly! It was time, indeed; for I could not see my way very far ahead—— well, yes, put up your horse and your cows in the stables here,—I give you free room; we will farm together and divide the profits. Each shall have half; that seems fair enough."

Shaking his head with vexation and compassion, the old Torfs observed, drily—

"You have not understood me: I am to be tenant here."

"What! what do you say?" roared Jan Staers, roused to a fury of passion. "You are to be tenant of the stone farm-house?—and what is to become of me?"

"You are to live with me. If you like to work, I will pay you for your work. If you prefer working for any one else, or would rather do nothing at all, I will give you free board, lodging, and clothing, until our children have to provide for us all, as the law directs."

Jan Staers seized in his rage the first object within his reach, and flung it with violence on the floor; the plate with butter lay in fragments at his feet. With a flood of curses, he shrieked out—

"What will come to me next? Ha, that is just the parable of our curé—the clay cot of the cattle-drover is to devour the stone farm-house of Jan Staers. You bite very close, you envious old hunks—but what hinders me from flattening your hypocritical old face against the wall? You are to be master, and I to be servant! To come here like a snake, wriggling, and curling, and crawling, to cheat me out of my daughter and my stone farm-house!"

"Cheat!" repeated the old man, with disdain. "These two years and more our landlord has wished to put me into your farm; I have refused, and have begged him to have patience with you, out of compassion for your hapless daughter—I see well what her end must be; but take good heed to my words, Jan Staers. I am willing now to consent to the marriage of my son, in case I can prevent the disgrace of your ejectment—but if that ejectment once took place, I should say, no, no; forever, no!"

"Be off, out of my sight, I tell you!" roared Staers. "You hideous old beetle, set your foot on my threshold again, if you dare!"

He raised his hand and made a gesture of

threatening toward the gray-headed old man, who was moving to the door. He was discomposed and ruffled, and wound the leather thong of his medlar stick around his wrist, and prepared to defend himself. When he saw that Jan Staers stood still, pouring out a whole volley of curses and revilings, he said, with indignant irritation—

"Ah, I have no fear of your threats; but you are in your own house, and I will not remain here against your will. I will say only a few words more to you; you may attend to them or not, as you like. Jan Staers, you are a heartless father; you have spent the inheritance of your daughter in vice and drunkenness; you are poor, the beggar's wallet awaits you. And the disgrace, the ruin, that you alone have deserved—you will force that upon your innocent child—to the very extreme of endurance—till drink has killed you—till misery has made her pine away. I came to rescue both you and her; I was ready to give twenty years of the sweat of my brow to make her happy. In your selfishness, in your pride, you have crushed her whole future—her whole life. Oh, remember that there is a God above us! He will punish you for your baseness; in the day of his terrible judgment he will ask you what you have done with your poor, hapless child!"

The firm and impressive tone of the old man— perhaps, too, the stout medlar stick—had at first struck and restrained Jan Staers. He listened with an air of disdain; but the concluding reproach stung him to the quick. A loud sound, like the roar of a lion, rolled from his throat, as he rushed with clenched fists at the old man. But before he could reach him, Farmer Torfs had stepped through the doorway, and found himself in the village street, along which some laborers were passing at the moment. Jan Staers hur'ed some parting execrations at the head of the old man, and then he flung his door to with such violence, that a large piece was broken off and fell upon the floor.

At a little distance stood Luke and Clara, anxiously watching. The sounds of strife had already filled them with anguish and terror; and when they saw the old man approach them, his face pale with suppressed passion, his eyes gleaming, and his fists clenched, they could scarcely summon up strength enough to ask him, amid their tears, how he had succeeded.

"Let me be quiet," murmured he; "I am chafed —I am trembling all over—my blood is boiling in my veins. I feel as if I should be ill: an apoplexy, perhaps! Alas! my dear children, no hope now for you: all is over—forever—forever."

Luke followed his father, moaning and tearing his hair; Clara walked beside them, with her face buried in her apron.

A few moments later, the door of the stone farmhouse was thrown open again, and Jan Staers issued from it. He ran, with hurried steps and unintelligible gestures, along the village street, and disappeared in the pine wood which lay along the road that was cut out of the hill-side. He was on his way to the town.

CHAPTER VI.

POOR Luke wandered back to the courtyard of his father's house. Now he stood still at the corner of the barn and looked out vacantly upon the meadow, toward the spot whence resounded the heavy blows of a hatchet; then he turned suddenly round and walked a few steps, then stood still again, crossed his arms, stamped on the ground with spite, and at length made toward the door of the stable mechanically, as if he were walking in his sleep. Here he moved slowly toward the cows, placed his hands on their necks in a kind of dreamy abstraction, and looked at them as if he would have told them all his piteous sorrow; then, still slowly and sadly, he shook some hay into the horse's rack, and finally stalked, in moody silence, into the cottage where his mother was busied in pouring water from a boiling kettle into the coffee-pot.

Luke let himself sink listlessly upon a wooden bench in the chimney-corner. He was quite crushed down with dejection; his limbs hung nerveless and loose about him, and his whole body seemed shrunk in and bent together. He kept

7

his eyes fixed on the smouldering fire in a mournful reverie.

Mother Beth was a little plump dame, with cheeks still blooming, and large, open blue eyes, the sweetness and animation of whose glance betokened the gentle goodness of her heart. Although she now and then shook her head in compassion whenever her eye fell on her disconsolate son, a gentle smile played on her lips, and it was remarkable that she did not seem to think the misery of Luke quite so extremely crushing as the young man's dejection would have led one to suppose it.

The coffee being made, she set the pot among the hot embers, drew forward her stool and her spinning-wheel, and soon the flax was running nimbly between her fingers. Then, with the hum of her wheel as an accompaniment and support, she began, in a soothing tone:

"Luke, lad, you sit there like a body who has done something very bad. Come, come, drive it all out of your head; it isn't as bad as you think."

"Not so bad?" sighed the young peasant, without moving a muscle. "Why then were we all so merry here yesterday? and why did you, mother, make me almost a fool with happiness by showing me all those beautiful things? Haven't you put back in the chest there all the things you meant to give Clara as a wedding-gift? Oh, mother, I was so happy—so happy——and I thought I could look so far on into my life, and all was so good, so bright, so heavenly beautiful—and you, mother, were you not obliged to wipe away the tears from your eyes, because we were all so beside ourselves with gladness?—There was father giving me advice, and making me wise— how I was to farm so as to get on. Oh, Clara, poor Clara! When I told her that you would be her dear mother, she fairly gave way; she burst into tears of joy, and was almost out of her senses with happiness. And now she is sitting there again alone within the silent walls of the stone farm-house, and is tearing her hair, perhaps, in utter hopelessness."

Some more painful emotion here smote his heart; he turned half round, and, wringing his hands in desperation, he sobbed out—

"And to dream about it a whole night long— not to be able to close one's eyes for joy—to jump up a hundred times and turn one's eyes to the win- dow to see if the sun of the long hoped-for day was not yet up—to feel one's heart flutter, to sing, to dance, to lose one's senses quite in an intoxication of joy and hope—and then, after all, to feel a cold knife run through one's heart, and to hear father say, 'No hope more! it is all over—all over for- ever!' Ah, look you, mother, you may believe it or not, but it is enough to kill one outright!"

"Luke, Luke, you are such a stiff-necked, obsti- nate lad!" said his mother, in a tone of vexation. "Why don't you hearken to what I say to you? Let father's anger cool down a bit; things will go

all right then. If you were in his place you would,
perhaps, be a great deal more angry than he is.
Only think—he goes to Jan Staers, to make him
an offer which was, perhaps, rather imprudent
and rash on our part. He offers to save him,
and to make Clara happy; and he gets for answer,
'grovelling old hunks, hideous old beetle!' he is
threatened to have his head beaten against the
wall, and to be kicked out of doors! Ah, Luke,
he is still your father, and you ought surely to feel
that he has good cause to be angry, yes, to be very
excessively angry!"

"Alas, dear mother, I know that well enough!"
exclaimed Luke, dejectedly; "but is it Clara's
fault that God has given her such a father?"

"Truly, child," sighed the old dame, "of a
surety, it is not her fault; but everybody must
bear his own cross. If I had been able to forecast
all this, you should never have made acquaintance
with Clara."

"Why, father says that Jan Staers has been
given to drink these twenty years; so you have
known it well enough all the time."

"I let myself be seduced, Luke—that is just the
word. I have always loved Clara, long before you
did, lad. It was always such a good lass from the
cradle—so pious, so industrious, and so unfortunate!—more by token she was so neat and
clean, and had such pretty black eyes. Look
you, Luke, that is the way with mothers: you
could scarcely both of you run alone, when I said

to myself in my heart, she wouldn't make such a bad wife for my Luke!"

Her voice had gradually become more soft and gentle; as she uttered the last words, the kind-hearted old dame put her finger to her eyes, and took away two blinding tears.

The youth sprang from his bench, seized her hand, and exclaimed—

"Oh, dear, kind mother, thank you, thank you! and you think so still, don't you?"

"That is to say, Luke, after a time, yes."

"What do you mean?—after a time?"

"Why, father is master; we must have no other thought than his. The thorn which has pierced him will not be very soon got out. We must wait, child."

Luke returned to his bench in great discontent, and muttered, in an irritated tone—

"Wait—wait! and in the mean time to know that she is unhappy, and has nothing in the wide world but terror and suffering! Wait—and fall sick, and die of vexation!"

"Look you, Luke, if you won't have patience, I can't help it. You must not put the cart before the horse, lad. There are a good many days in the year; and if it is bad weather one day, perhaps the sun will shine out the next."

"And father, who is so angry that I dare not look at him! I must not mention the subject. It is all over, all over forever, he says."

"Yes, yes, he may say all that just now, you

7*

see, just to give his anger a little vent; but I, who have dreamed for fifteen years long that Clara would be my daughter, I shall not let the notion drop quite so suddenly. We must give in a little bit at first, Luke; your father is master; we must not say a word against his will. You just let me alone: I will contrive to feel my way with a little hint, and bring the subject up again. Your father has a right good heart; his anger will lessen with time and patience."

Luke was just going to thank his mother for her tender consolation, but at that moment Father Torfs entered the house, and with one hand placed his hatchet carefully on the ground, while with the other he wiped the perspiration from his forehead. His countenance was severe, but calm; his greeting brief, but gracious withal.

He took his place at the table without saying another word. The good dame placed the coffee-pot and the bread on the table, and made Luke a sign that he should draw near and eat with them.

Father Torfs was evidently regarded with great respect and even awe by his household, for his appearance alone had effected an entire revolution in Luke's frame of mind. The lad seemed to conquer his sadness, and came to the table with his eyes cast down and an air of timidity; he sat down opposite his father, and, in spite of himself, it may be, ate and drank, that he might not vex him. An oppressive silence reigned in the little room, until the old man said, with a calm and measured voice—

"Luke, I told you not to work this morning, because I knew well enough that your head would not be fit for it, and I wanted to let your sorrow pass over a little. But now you must lend a hand to load the beech-wood on the cart. To-morrow you will drive over to the town, and deliver it at the house of our landlord."

"Very well, father; I will do all that you wish," answered the youth, submissively, but with a touch of sorrow in his voice.

His mother had risen up to reach something; she stood at the window a moment, looking up the village street. Her manner indicated curiosity and anxiety.

"Take courage, Luke," said his father; "it pains me much to be forced to see you suffer. I was once young myself, and I know that it is a bitter thing to be deceived in one's hopes; but I cannot help it. You must, by degrees, drive it out of your head—"

Suddenly they heard a noise as of confused voices, with loud and merry peals of laughter; it seemed to come from the street of the village.

"'Tis the laborers and lads of farmer Daelmans, who are coming from the field with the last cart-load of potatoes," observed the old man; "I saw them at a distance just now, hanging the cart with branches of green. This evening they keep

the feast of cakes. They are merry, sure enough,
Beth."

The good wife turned round. On her countenance one could read fear and deep sadness.

"I don't know," she replied; "there is a great
crowd at the door of Jan Staers, but I can't see
what is going on. The rural guard is there with
his sabre drawn!"

"Heavens!" shrieked Luke, springing up, "what
can it be? Clara, Clara!" He ran to the door,
and was about to leave the house; but his father
anticipated him, and said, with a gesture of command—

"You stay here, Luke: what happens there is
no concern of ours."

Rushing to the window, the poor lad pressed
his face against the glass, trying to make out
what was going on among the crowd of villagers
in front of the stone farm-house. The sight of
the drawn sabre of the rural guard, gleaming over
the heads of the lookers-on, made him tremble as
though he were quailing beneath some terrible
disaster.

"Good heavens! can Jan Staers have committed any crime?" cried he, in a tone of deepest
dejection. "Can they be fetching him to put him
in prison? Alas, alas! this is all that was wanting to complete my misery."

"Don't be afraid," said the father; "I think I
know what it is. The officers of justice are come
out of the town to seize his goods; the rural guard

is keeping the people away from the door. Look,
now he is driving the lads back, because they
were coming too near."

This movement allowed them to see within the
circle of villagers. All at once a shrill, piercing
cry of despair forced its way from Luke's deepest
heart.

"Oh!" cried he, "there is Clara sitting against
the wall, near the door, on a sack of straw; she is
holding her hands before her eyes; she is weeping; they have turned her out into the street.
Oh, misery of miseries! they are laughing all
around her; they are making a jest of her degradation—of her unhappiness! Father, father, let
me go; for God's sake, let me go!"

The old man bolted and locked the door, and
put the key into the pocket of his blouse.

"But, father," cried Luke, quite beside himself,
"how can you be so cruel and unfeeling? Clara,
—oh, the poor child!—she is sitting yonder in the
open air, without a shelter! she knows not where
to go. She is weeping bitter tears, I see them—
oh, and listen, they are laughing! She must—
tender, innocent lamb as she is—she must put up
with this disgrace, and remain sitting there, the
scoff and jest of the whole village! Have you
then lost all feeling, father?"

"It is very sad; but—"

"But, but, father," howled Luke, tearing his hair
violently, "you don't know what you are doing!
You are allowing your son's wife to be insulted!"

F

" Your wife ?"

" Yes, she shall be my wife, even if I die with vexation at causing you so much displeasure; she shall be my wife, I tell you that!"

And, terrified at his own boldness, he ran with streaming eyes to his father, raised his hand, and, laying his head on his bosom, said, with a beseeching, imploring voice—

" Oh, forgive me for daring to speak so; but, for all that, it is truth. She is suffering; she is unhappy. Oh, let me go, that I may rescue her from that terrible degradation."

" To fetch her, and bring her here?"

The old man shook his head, while he muttered, in perplexity and hesitation—

"And her father! her father?"

Dame Torfs had not yet had time to put in a word. Although the piteous lamentations of her son cut deep into her mother's heart, she had hitherto restrained her emotion, and listened in silence. But now she burst suddenly into tears, and said, with a deep groan—

" Look you, Torfs, you are really too cruel; you cannot stand out any longer. You can't drive our Luke quite into his grave; and this luckless lamb,—oh, the poor dear!—sitting there before everybody, under the blue heaven, and weeping! Can you look on in cold blood and see her there—like a stone without a soul or a heart? Yes, you have more sense than we have; I know that; but, after all, perhaps it is better to be some-

what more merciful, come of it what will. We
are, after all, Christian folk, Torfs; don't you
know that?"

"Oh, father, do listen to mother; let me fetch
Clara?"

The old man seemed quite overcome by the
rebuke of his good wife.

"One moment," muttered he, with his finger on
his forehead, and his eyes fixed on the ground,
"one moment; let me think—"

He hastily took the key from his pocket, and
opened the door.

"You are making me commit a great folly,"
said he; "but, in the name of God, then, go and
bring Clara here."

Luke and his mother rushed out at the door,
and ran in haste toward the throng of idle gos-
sips who were gathered around the door of Jan
Staers's dwelling. The young man made his way
by main force through the crowd, thrust back
some laughers with angry impetuosity, seized the
hand of the maiden, made her stand up, and said
to her—

"Come, come, my mother is here; she is come
to fetch you; you must not stay here. I will
take care that your clothes are brought to you.
Cheer up, Clara dear; Luke will never forsake
you."

Mother Torfs had already grasped the other
hand of the weeping damsel, and was now leading her along the village street toward her cot-

tage, saying all manner of soothing, comforting
words by the way. Luke remained at the stone
farm-house, and made there a terrible commotion
among those on whose face he had surprised a
smile of derision.

"What!" shouted he; "are you wicked enough
to take pleasure in another man's affliction? You
see the poor Clara — goodness, loveliness, kindness itself—pining in tears, and you stand by and
laugh! Fie on you! I am ashamed that you are
men."

"Now come, Luke, don't you get up any bad
blood, lad," said a burly peasant. "We are not
laughing at Clara's misfortune; far from that;
but surely you would not have us make a long
face because the proud, drunken scoundrel, her
father, has got his deserts, would you? Jan Staers
has planted his nose well in the mud now. It
serves him right; he has long deserved it. And
now the village will be clear of the filthy beast."

"It is wonderful," remarked another villager;
"I met him this morning there away in the dell;
he had a whole sackful of five-franc pieces with
him, and said that he was going off to pay his
rent."

"Pay his rent!" said a third, with a laugh; "as
if there were not too many public-houses on the
road for that! I'll bet any thing he is sitting now
in the 'Spotted Cow,' so fuddled and blinded by
drink, that he remembers nothing of God or his
commandments."

"Silence, friends, silence!" said Luke, with angry impatience; "who among you will lend me a hand? I should like to stow away the bedding and the wearing apparel in our barn."

Three or four young lads sprang forward, and expressed their readiness to help him in any way.

When Mother Beth reached her house, leading Clara by the hand, her husband was no longer to be seen; she thought that he was gone out into the back court, and paid little attention to his absence. So, leading the weeping girl to the bench by the hearth, she made her sit down, and said—

"Clara, child, it is a sad job; but you must not despair. We shall be able to help you a little bit."

"Alas! for me it is no matter," said the girl, with a voice interrupted by sobs; "I can work, and can easily earn enough to get a bit of bread; but father, oh, poor father, what will become of him? Where will he sleep? No dwelling more —to be turned out in the street like a beggar! Oh! Mother Beth, it would be a good thing for us, perhaps, if we both had died a good Christian death!"

"Child, child, you must not wish any thing of that kind," remonstrated the good dame, in a tone of rebuke and sorrow.

"And only yesterday so full of joy!" sobbed Clara, lost in her own thoughts; "to fall, as it

were, out of heaven, and tumble down into hell
—into disgrace, into poverty, into hopelessness!
Oh! oh! And my father, my poor father, what
will he do now?"

"Yes, truly, Clara," answered Mother Torfs,
shaking her head slowly; "that is indeed the
worst of all. We would gladly take care of you,
and put you up a little bed in the attic until something else turned up; but your father—you see,
child, that is quite another thing. I won't have
him in my house; and Torfs would rather
leave the house, and be off, than — how shall I
say it? — than sleep under the same roof with
such a savage. You must consider, Clara, that,
when your father is drunk, he is a very awkward
man to deal with. He would turn the house upside down in the middle of the night, and rave
and swear, and perhaps call my good man ugly
names again. Torfs, too, is rather short and
quick in his way; he would not put up with it
long; and—who knows? — they might do each
other a harm in their passion. No, no; Jan
Staers must never set foot over this threshold; it
cannot be."

"O Lord, help me! I know that well, Mother
Beth," pleaded the poor girl; "but, for God's
sake, don't say it. It cuts me to the heart. To
know that my poor father is everybody's scoff; to
hear him jeered for his misfortune; to see people
clap their hands for joy because we are turned out
of our house — and no means, no hope, of bet-

tering our lot!—it must go on and on so, until, perhaps, it ends with something awful. Oh, Mother Torfs, say now yourself, would it not be better that God should take us both out of the world?"

"Drunkenness is indeed a fearful evil," muttered the old dame, pensively. "And certain it is, that the vile habit of gin-drinking is gaining ground in our villages like a contagious sickness. In our neighborhood it is not so very bad yet; but there, away in that direction, toward Kempen —there the men run in crowds to make their wives and children miserable, and to hang the beggar's wallet round their necks in the end—"

She was interrupted in her discourse by the entrance of Luke, who went up straight to the weeping girl, took her hand, and said to her, with an accent of consolation—

"Oh, Clara dear, don't cry any more; things will turn out much better than we think. I have put the chest and the clothes in the barn, and spread out the beds in a corner on some straw. Your father will be able to sleep there till tomorrow morning; and then mother will put in a good word with father to help you out of your difficulties. And after all, you see, it will be all the same, whatever turns up. I shall, in any case, be glad to see you stay here."

"So! what are you talking about there, Luke?" interposed his mother, in a tone of rebuke. "Jan Staers to sleep in our barn? On my word, I think you have lost your senses. Suppose the whim takes him to smoke a pipe? And then that infernal invention of phosphorus matches—in the straw! We should have house, and barn, and all burnt to ashes. Don't speak of it, for God's sake, before your father."

"But where is father?" asked the lad, looking round in all directions.

"Indeed I don't know. When I came back with Clara he was gone, and I have not seen him since."

"Good heavens! he is vexed, perhaps."

"Possible enough, my boy; you have said many things too, look you, which were rather strong. And you know of old, your father will be treated with due respect."

"But, mother," said Luke, with a mournful voice, "I do honor father all I can; I love him and look up to him for his goodness and his wisdom; but how can I help it, if my heart will run away with me in my vexation—"

He ceased suddenly, for at this moment his father entered the house. The young man went up to him, and said, in a supplicating tone—

"Oh, father, you are not vexed with me? You must bear with me a little, and forgive me; I didn't well know what I was saying."

"Sit you down!" said old Torfs, with an im· perative voice and gesture, "and listen all of you with attention; I don't like to be interrupted. '

Luke and his mother obeyed in silence; and as

if they guessed, from the old man's tone of voice, that he was going to say something very important, they fastened their eyes on him with intense curiosity and anxiety.

"You think that I am vexed with you, Luke?" said his father. "You are wrong. I feel too much pity for your trouble, and my one wish is to see you happy. While you and your mother were gone to fetch Clara, I thought over the course we must take. Look here what I said to myself:— We all love Clara, and it grieves us much that she must suffer—the innocent child! If she were alone, the thing would be soon done; she should never shed another tear about it, for I would not allow it. But we have no right to separate father and daughter; where she is, there he must be too. Jan Staers shall not set foot in my house! I have hit upon another plan; and though it may cost me some money, I have not grudged it, in the hope that the God who is above us will reward me. There behind, near the brook, is a little laborer's cottage, belonging to our bailiff Putkop. I have hired it for three months; you must move the bedding and things there; Clara can live there with her father—"

Luke made a movement as if he was going to speak; Clara extended her hands in grateful acknowledgment; but a sign from the old man drove the words back into their mouths.

"I will make one last effort," he continued. "It may be that Jan Staers's misfortune will bring

8*

him to a better mind. Clara, you will tell him that I mean to come to have a talk with him to-morrow forenoon; try and persuade him to lay aside his pride, and to look at things as they really are. If he will accept my proposals, and fulfil the conditions I mean to make, then, my children, nothing is lost yet, and all that we were dreaming about yesterday may still become reality. I have a kind of hope that all will go right. This is all I had to say."

Luke and Clara sprang up at the same moment, and seized, with tears in their eyes, the hands of the old man. The maiden murmured some unintelligible words of thankfulness.

"Oh, father," exclaimed Luke; "an angel cannot be better or kinder than you are. Thank you, thank you! How can I repay you?"

"Continue to be virtuous, Luke," answered the old man, with deep emotion; "and when I am old and worn out, then remember how I have loved you, and what I have done to prove my love. And you, Clara, if God is so good to us as to give you to us as our daughter, love your new mother, and tend her with care to the end of her days."

The girl threw her arms round Mother Beth's neck with a cry of joy, and exclaimed—

"Oh, if I am doomed never to see you again after to-day, I shall never forget all your goodness. I shall remember you in my prayers, that God may bless you, and grant you a long, long life!"

Rousing himself from the effects of his emotion, the old Torfs then said—

"Come, don't let us lose any time. Beth, bring with you all that is necessary for a good cleaning out: a bucket, a broom, and all the rest. Go with Clara, and touch up the cottage a bit, that it may look a little tidy. Carry over what is wanted for housekeeping. The rural guard will stay close to the stone farm-house, to show Jan Staers his new abode. Go you, Luke, take the wheelbarrow and carry off the bedding. There is the key. I must go again to say a word to the bailiff Putkop. Anyhow, be sharp; for evening will draw in very soon."

When he saw that each was in movement to carry out his injunctions, the old man stepped out at the door.

CHAPTER VII.

It was about ten o'clock in the morning, when Farmer Torfs closed the back door of his cottage behind him, and went along the field toward the new dwelling of Jan Staers. He had scarcely gone a good bow-shot, when he saw Clara in the distance, coming toward him. The girl seemed to him quite sprightly and full of energy, for she held her head upright, and walked on with a light, firm step.

This sight gladdened the old man, because it encouraged him to hope for a favorable result from his efforts; and so it was with a smile on his lips that he saw the maiden come up to him.

"Well now, Clara, has your father borne his misfortune patiently?" he asked. "Is he become more reasonable?"

"It is quite wonderful," answered the girl. "A great change has come over father. It was not late last evening when he came back from the town; and he could not have drunk any thing, for he allowed himself to be led by the rural guard to our new house without a word of opposition. He spoke to me a few calm and affectionate words, advising me to go to rest. Little did I sleep, however, for I heard that my father was awake, and was pacing up and down his room. When I rose and came down-stairs, I found him sitting in a corner, with his arms folded on his breast, and looking sadly down on the ground. I became pale, and uttered a slight groan as I took him by the hand; but he consoled me with great tenderness, and asked my forgiveness for all the wrongs he said he had done me."

"It is indeed wonderful. At this rate he will mend."

"He declared, again and again, that he would never more enter a public-house, never taste another drop of strong drink — not a single drop more! He takes his lot very submissively, and

says that he will go out to work as a day-laborer
to earn us a living."

"And do you think that he really and truly
means it?"

"Certainly: there is no reason to doubt it. He
has borrowed a spade from the shoemaker; and,
since an early hour this morning, he has been busy
digging the little bit of ground behind our cottage.
Ah, Father Torfs, I ought to lament over our misfortune and ruin, ought I not? But I cannot,
you see I am so gay, so happy, that I could jump
into the air for joy. Now my father will drink no
more! If we were as poor and bare as the stones,
that would still be a great happiness to me. And
if we both go out to work, we may, perhaps, manage
to earn enough to pay the rent of our cottage and
get on in a small way. I feel so much energy—I
can't tell you how much. If I did not fear it was
wrong, I should thank God with all my heart for
having cast us into such a deep of misfortune!"

The old man shook his head thoughtfully, and
muttered to himself—

"Hum, hum! it is rather sudden!"

Then, turning to Clara, he said—

"So, then, he has said that he does not mean to
drink any more? That he means to go out as a
day-laborer? It is a very good resolve, and it is
just the thing I want to talk over with him."

The girl pointed forward with her finger.

"Look, there behind the hedge is father, busy
digging," said she.

"Have you let him know I am coming?"

"Yes; he will listen to you with respect; he has promised me."

"Now, then, Clara, you go along home to our mother, and wait there till I come to you; I must be quite alone with your father. Courage, lassie! if what you say is true, we will all go to church together to thank God for his mercy."

The maiden turned back along the field-path with slow steps, while Father Torfs entered the court-yard of the little cottage.

When Jan Staers saw his old neighbor coming, his face burned with a fiery crimson, and his lips moved with a peculiar expression. Was it only shame on account of his wretched condition, or was it also a bitter vexation of soul? This conjecture did not escape the old man; but it made no very unfavorable impression on him, for he could well understand that this meeting must be humiliating to Clara's father—quite enough so to occasion him a little temporary discomposure.

Jan Staers had stuck his spade in the ground and left off his digging. While muttering a sad and somewhat cold greeting, he walked with Farmer Torfs into the cottage. Placing a chair for the old man, he said, with an emphatic and constrained voice—

"Farmer Torfs, you have had the kindness to provide me a home; I thank you on behalf of my daughter."

"On behalf of your daughter!" repeated the
old man.

"Yes; for certainly you would not have done
it for me."

"Look you, neighbor, you must not look at it
quite in that light," remarked the other, with a
firm and assured voice. "I admit that I was for
some time very angry with you; for, certainly, it
was not likely I could look on in cold blood, and
see you thoughtlessly wasting your inheritance
and rendering your daughter wretched; but, believe me, if you will only get the better of your
unhappy vice, and say farewell forever to strong
drink, then will I show you that you cannot have
a better friend on earth than me."

"It is very possible; but I will take good care
that I will not eat my bread out of any man's
hand," said Jan Staers, with a sullen, secret emotion of repressed anger and jealousy. "I mean to
pay the rent of this cottage; and so you shall not
have to bestow an alms on Jan Staers."

He laid a marked and peevish stress on the
word *you*, as if to show that no assistance he might
receive from any other person would humiliate
him so deeply as the idea of being beholden to
Farmer Torfs. There was an unfriendly and
quarrelsome expression in the tone of his voice,
in the very sound of the words.

"Neighbor, neighbor," said the old man, shaking his head, "pride is an evil counsellor. I had
intended making you again a proposal which has

no other end in view than the happiness of your daughter and your own welfare; but I see clearly that your affliction even has not changed you. It is a great grief to me; but, after all, I cannot do what is impossible. In the name of God, then—."

He stood up as if about to take his departure, and sighed profoundly.

"Poor Clara!" he exclaimed.

Jan Staers now placed his hands before his eyes and began to weep bitterly, as though the bending and crushing of his pride had affected his whole frame; his limbs moved convulsively, and a mournful cry issued from his oppressed bosom.

Father Torfs looked at him for some time without speaking. His countenance bore an expression of deep sympathy and compassion; he hastened to lay his hand on his neighbor's shoulder, and said, in a tone of consolation—

"Now, Jan Staers, moderate your grief; hear me out; I will tell you what I wanted to propose to you."

"Alas! I am a contemptible rascal, a venomous reptile, a reprobate abandoned of God!" exclaimed Jan Staers, in wild despair. "I am doomed to perish. I shall sink down into hell, and burn there forever and ever, like a wretched fiend that I am! All this night I have not been able to sleep; for, for the first time these many years, I had drunk nothing, not a single drop. My father, my mother, my wife, all rose out of their graves and stood before my eyes; they reproached me with my disgraceful conduct, and accused me of having embittered their lives—of being the cause of their premature death—"

"You are wandering in your mind. Don't make yourself out more guilty than you really are," murmured the old Torfs, gently.

"*I* wander in my mind!" repeated Jan Staers, with a bitter scoff. "Fifteen long years I have been the scandal and disgrace of the whole village, and have lived like a beast. I have wasted the sweat of my father's brow, and the inheritance of my child, in vile debauchery. I have cursed, and sworn, and blasphemed, as though I would rise up against God himself out of the deep mire of my drunkenness. Alas! I have received the care, the love, the mournful solicitude of Clara with utter unfeelingness. I have crushed her young life under heavy shame; and, as her sole recompense, I have cast her down upon the straw of poverty, into an abyss of frightful degradation. Damnation! my soul is lost—there is nothing within me but a loathsome mass of brute instincts, of selfishness, of base cowardice, and of pride. You come to offer me help—you wish to make my Clara happy, to raise her in tenderest affection out of her poverty and humiliation — and I, abominable monster that I am, I am not able to command myself so far as to feel grateful to you. Far from that; my abject soul spurns the benefit you would confer, and chafes that your kindness degrades it. Wretch that I am! leave me; I am not deserving

G   9

of your goodness. God has laid his curse upon me!"

The old Torfs was so deeply affected by the despairing confession of Jan Staers, that his eyes were filled with tears of compassion. He remained silent for a short time, then sat down again on his chair, took the hand of his neighbor sympathizingly, and said to him, with a kind and soothing voice—

"Jan, there is no guilt so great but that it may be done away by true repentance. Although I quite enter into your distress of mind, I am filled with extraordinary pleasure that your eyes are at last opened to your past sinful conduct. It is a great gain. Let me now ask you a few questions: we shall perhaps soon get at some happy conclusion of all your trouble. Tell me, how much money have you left from the price of your cow?"

"Nothing," answered Staers; "I gave it all yesterday into the hands of our landlord's steward, and no sooner had he put it away in his money-box than he told me that the writ of ejectment had been already issued."

"That is no great matter; your debts are so much the less. Clara has been telling me that you have resolved never to drink again. Is this really your irrevocable determination?"

"If I ever drink again—one single drop—" exclaimed Jan Staers, clenching his fists, "may God—"

"No, no, don't swear about it!" interposed the old man; "your word is quite sufficient for the moment."

"Drink!" exclaimed the other again. "So firmly have I resolved that I will never again set foot inside a public-house, that I would not do it to gain any sum of money—never—never!"

"Come, that is good; and you have made up your mind to work like a right-minded, independent man?"

"Ah, neighbor Torfs, I don't know whether I ought to say so to you, but I am longing to die; for my death will make my child happy. And since that is the only good I can do her, I shall try to put an end to my wretched life—"

"What, what! put an end to your own life!" exclaimed the old man, with horror. "Surely you have lost your senses! Don't you believe, then, that you have a soul, and that there is a God in heaven? Wretched man! your words make me shudder."

"You deceive yourself," remarked Jan Staers; "I don't mean that. I have resolved to work, to slave, so hard and so continuously, that I shall sink under it—that my body will waste and give way—"

"Oh, come, is that all you mean?" said old Torfs, with a sigh of relief and of joy. "You may make yourself quite easy about that; the work men do with a hearty good-will never yet killed anybody; on the contrary, it makes them strong and healthy. But, neighbor Jan, you are not wise to be so impetuous. Even in good things cool counsel is best, and the golden mean is the best way to reach the goal. Are you really resolved to sacrifice your miserable liking for drink to the happiness of your daughter? Begin, then, by taking your affliction patiently, and look your humiliation courageously in the face. Break down your pride; it is that which makes you speak so harshly and rise up in rebellion against your inevitable lot. Listen to me now, calmly; I shall make you see that you have no reason to abandon yourself to despair. Yesterday you did not behave quite well to me, and I had firmly resolved never to speak a word more to you. But the sorrow, the disgrace, of Clara, who sat weeping at the door of your house, have overcome me. All is forgiven and forgotten. I have been pondering it all the night, and now I have hit on a plan to be of use to you and to your daughter. The first condition I make is, that you shall leave off drink—because, if I knew that you ever once—only once—tasted gin again, I should certainly leave you to your fate, and never trouble myself with you any more than if I had never known you."

An expression of rising vexation passed over Jan Staers's face; he made an evident effort to control himself and get the better of this feeling. It was nevertheless observable in his words, for he said—

"You wish to raise Clara out of her poverty? Well, now, take her into your house, or provide for her in some other way. I will leave the village, and seek my bread of bitterness somewhere else, until I need it no longer."

"Always proud!" growled the old man. "No, no, that won't do. In case you ever get drunk again, you would be coming back and giving me trouble that I would not—and could not—put up with."

"But I tell you that I mean never to drink any more—never!"

"That is just what we must first of all see— you as well as I. Listen attentively, and don't interrupt me. You have nothing at all left; and if you don't wish to beg you must work—work as a day-laborer. Well, now, look you here what I propose to you. You shall work for me; I will give you the very highest wages, and I shall not mind if you take a holiday now and then."

"Work for *you? your* day-laborer, *your* servant?" muttered Jan Staers, with fierce desperation.

"Is it not all one whom you work for?"

"No, it is not all one to me," was the answer. "I cannot help it; the thought of it kills me with shame."

"I understand; you have always had a grudge against me. But was it my fault? Have I ever done you any harm?"

"No," exclaimed Jan Staers; "it is envy that

was consuming me. Your success was the ever-lasting rebuke of my indolence — I could not digest it—nor now either. I would rather work for anybody else."

"It cannot be, neighbor; for your own welfare it is necessary that I should help you in the effort to overcome your unhappy vice. Don't be too proud; it is not enough just to say, 'I won't drink any more,' to cure oneself of so terrible a failing. So, if you work for me, I ask this pledge for the space of three months. It is not that I want to be your master; on the contrary, it is on my part an effort to enable myself to become your true friend. So it is seriously agreed between us, is it not, that for that time you will not taste gin, not one single drop? For, you see, however firm your resolve may be now, once put your lips to the glass—and the devil has you safe enough again in his clutches! Well now, will you accept the test?"

A scornful smile played on the lips of Jan Staers.

"It is of no use," replied he; "you may be sure I shall never drink again."

"But do you submit to the test with good-will and in all kindliness?"

"Yes, since you wish it."

"Now I will say something more. If you keep your word, and avoid all drink for three months, then you will have gained mastery enough over yourself to do your duty henceforward as an honor-able man and as a father. We will then begin to talk about our children, and consider whether it is

not advisable to let them marry after Easter. You
should never remain a day-laborer then, Jan Staers.
My son would have to call you father, and you can
fancy that we should not let you remain in a degrading position. My first project—the one you so
scornfully rejected—will come forward again to be
talked over. We will put our children into a little
cottage, and you should then come and live with
us, not as a laborer or as a servant, but as our relation, as a member of our family."

While the old man was speaking, Jan Staers
looked at him with an unwonted expression; his
features seem transfigured and brightened by a
gentle emotion, and his eyes glistened, as though
the words of his neighbor were pouring a healing
and comforting balm into his soul. The old Torfs
remarked this favorable change in his state of
mind, and it was with a more tender accent, and
a sympathetic deepening of emotion, that he thus
continued:

"Jan, hitherto every one in our village had
laughed at you and despised you; you have behaved very shockingly, and have given yourself
up blindfold to drink, in order to drown the reproaches of your conscience there within you; is
it not so? Ah, well, now only carry out your
good resolution, and you will see how happy your
life will be from this time. All the lads will be
edified by your amendment: people will esteem
you for your wise resolve. Meanwhile all the
past will sink and be forgotten; and, in the feel-

ing that you are doing your duty toward God and toward man as you ought, you will find strength and courage; you will be able to carry your head up again, and look everybody honestly in the face. We shall be good friends; we will work together for our children, for they will inherit all we have, won't they? We will make ourselves glad in their love, in their happiness; and when the Lord of heaven shall at length call us to his throne of judgment, we shall appear there with an assured confidence in his mercy and compassion!"

Jan Staers was profoundly moved by the pathetic tone of the old man, and great tears trickled fast over his cheeks.

"You are too good," said he; "I don't deserve it."

And raising his hand, he exclaimed—

"Ah, I shall now be able to rise out of my shame and degradation! It is not too late to expiate my past guilt; I shall have around me a family that loves me; I shall work for my Clara, make myself worthy of her love, see her happy! Ah, Torfs, noble, generous man, you give me my life back again, you restore peace to my soul, and trust in God's goodness! Thanks, thanks!"

"Give me your hand on it," said the old man; "the hand of kindness and firm resolution."

The pressure of Jan Staers s hand was most violent; and, as if he could not be temperate in any thing, he now overwhelmed his neighbor with all kinds of fervent expressions of thanks to such an

extent, at length, that old Torfs, wishing to put
an end to these demonstrations of gratitude, interrupted him, by saying, with calm earnestness—
"Jan, I have confidence in the sincerity and
firmness of your resolve; but you must allow me
to speak for a moment, as if it were just possible
that you should again yield to temptation. What
I ask of you is the price of your daughter's whole
future and happiness. If you ever once let yourself be overcome with drink I shall, without mercy,
break off every engagement between us, and forbid
my son ever to see Clara again, even though I have
to use all my power and authority as a father to
compel him. I am not wanting in strength of will;
what I have once decided after mature thought is
infallibly done. But I feel assured that you will
never be so inhuman a father as to crush the life
of your daughter for the sake of a miserable vice.
You must remember that there yawns before you
an infinite abyss of shame, of poverty, and of male-
diction; you will never leap into it and drag your
child after you, now that deliverance and happiness
smile upon you?"

"No, no, you need not fear," said Jan Staers,
beseechingly; "I will follow your advice; I will
let you lead me like a child; I will submit myself
to your will, and serve you with gratitude, and
with respect and veneration. More than this I
cannot say: words fail me to express, as I wish,
the feeling of gratitude that fills me and unnerves
me. But be very sure, for all that, I will never

drink again, never any thing stronger than water."

"And coffee and small beer, which you will have with us. You must not run on too fast with your resolves, neighbor; it is dangerous. He whose arrow flies over the target misses his mark quite as much as he who falls short."

The old man rose from his chair, and, pressing once more Jan Staers's hand, he said—

"I am very much pleased; a joyful hope fills my heart. Take courage, neighbor; we shall get on. We shall live many happy days together in the world yet. When will you come to my house and set to work?"

"To-morrow, if you like."

"To-morrow! I would much rather you should come to-day, after dinner; for you see, Jan Staers, hard work is the most mighty weapon against all kinds of vice, and it is not good for a man to be left too long alone with his own thoughts. When a man is idle, good and bad thoughts run alike through his head."

"Well, then, this afternoon; I will do any thing you like."

"We will thresh some new corn together, and you will feel how hard work clears the head and cheers the heart! Till the afternoon, then."

Farmer Torfs left the cottage in a very happy frame of mind. Though he could not help being a little anxious about his efforts and their possible consequences, yet he inwardly rejoiced that he had

resolved to make them. The thought that he was
going to confer a very great benefit on a fellow-
man filled him with a sort of joyous pride. And
with this there mingled a sweet and delightful
satisfaction that he was thus securing his son's
happiness, and sparing him much sorrow and
bitter pain. So he stepped out through the fields
with unusual vigor and speed, and soon reached
his little cottage. There he found his wife and
Clara at the door, looking anxiously and inquir-
ingly at him as he drew near, and taking comfort
from the smile on his face. Both came a few steps
toward him, and asked him eagerly how he had
fared in his visit to the cottage.

"It is all right; I am very much pleased;" said
the old man. "After all, there is good feeling,
even virtue itself, in Jan Staers. I have a good hope
that every thing will turn out just as we wish."

"And has he agreed to all you have proposed
to him?" inquired Mother Torfs.

"Yes, he has. It cost him a little effort at first,
though; but after all, you see, Beth, we must not
ask too much of a man who is in trouble. Cologne
and Aix-la-Chapelle were not built in a day. We
shall do now; we shall do, I see. I am very glad
that God put the notion into my head; I am sure
it will turn out well." He took the hand of the
poor girl, who stood by, devouring his words with
tremulous eagerness. "And you, Clara," said he,
with considerable delicacy and affection in his
voice, "you too will help us a little, and strengthen

your father in his good resolve by your love and care. Ha! look up, and be a little more lively; the gay dreams of yesterday will come true after all. You will be to us a very dear child; we will all live together in affection and in unmingled joy and happiness."

The maiden was so deeply moved that she turned away her head to hide her tears. Sud-denly a distant sound seemed to have caught her ear, for she raised her head and looked away over the fields in the direction from which came the sharp crack of a well-known whip. With a cry of joy she raised her hands above her head, and waved them in the air like the sails of a windmill.

"What are you about, Clara?" asked Mother Beth, in amazement.

"Look, look," said the maiden, "yonder in the lower road Luke is coming with his cart! oh, how glad he will be!"

She continued all the while making signs to Luke.

"Ha, ha, he sees it! he sees it!" she exclaimed, "Listen, how merrily he is cracking his whip! here he comes! here he comes!"

And in sooth Luke was cracking his whip so vigorously in the distance that the sound came on the breeze like the modulations of a lively song.

"Oh, the vagabond!" roared Father Torfs, stamping his foot with anger; "the hair-brained vagabond, he is making the horse go at full gallop! He will break his neck or his limbs in another minute. Just look how the cart is thumping and jolting along the road! he'll break it all to bits! sure enough, he'll never reach home with a sound skin. The stupid blockhead! I'll pay him out for this. Oh, these young folk—these young folk —there is no holding them in! Just look—look!"

"No, no, don't be vexed, Father Torfs," said Clara, coaxingly; "it is all joy—all for gladness. I'll run on and tell him to drive a little more gently."

"Now, look there; only listen how my poor old cart is creaking and rattling along!" growled the old man. "The blacksmith will get a good job out of that, I see. Yes—there's so much gone of my precious money. There now, there, the horse is off full gallop again!"

But Clara had ceased to hear the wail of his lamentation; with the speed of an arrow just free from the bow, she was off over the fields, running at full speed, shouting and waving both arms, to meet the reckless stripling.

CHAPTER VIII.

AFTER dinner Jan Staers presented himself in the cottage of his old neighbor, to begin his career as day-laborer. Farmer Torfs placed a flail in his hand, and led him to the barn, where

10

they and another hired laborer were to thresh the new corn.

When Jan Staers entered the barn, a thrill of painful surprise ran through him; his lips were compressed together with vexation, and his fore-head glowed with the scarlet of shame. He had recognised in the laborer one of his own servants in times gone by, whom he had discharged in a fit of drunkenness and with very harsh and brutal treatment. And now this poor day-laborer greeted him with a familiar smile, and in that smile was a slight touch of revengeful derision; so at least thought Jan Staers, whose heart was suddenly charged with bitterness at this unexpected appa-rition and at his haunting suspicion.

Matters became still worse when Jan, either through distraction or because he was not accus-tomed to work, did not wield his flail scientifically enough, and so struck out of his turn. Then the laborer would utter some little joke, and make merry over the unskilfulness of his former master. Poor Jan made very great efforts to restrain his anger; he kept his eyes fixed in a wide stare on the straw which covered the barn-floor, and did not look at his fellow-laborer again.

The old Torfs thought nothing of the perti-nacious silence of Jan Staers, or rather he thought it a natural consequence of his sadness and of the trouble he was in. During the whole afternoon he used every possible effort to raise the spirits of his companion; and whenever a new sheaf was laid on the floor, the good old man took the opportunity to say a few merry words to him, and thus, if possible, entice a smile to play on the lips of his gloomy neighbor.

But all was in vain. Jan Staers worked until the perspiration streamed from his forehead, and soon he turned out his work in a much better style ; but he answered the old man's demonstrations of friendship only by brief, abrupt monosyllables, and never spoke a word unless when it was absolutely necessary in order not to seem rude or stupid.

And so things went on until evening closed in. Then Jan Staers took leave of his neighbor with a cold greeting, and he took himself to his own little cottage. When the poor day-laborer had wished him good-evening in a friendly, cheerful tone, Jan had turned his head sulkily away, and returned him no answer.

The second day, and the following days, matters did not at all mend. On the contrary, now that Jan Staers had to work in the open fields, and sometimes to drive through the village in the cart of his new master, his lofty pride was ever receiving fresh and deeper wounds. The peasants who met him looked at him with a sort of curious wonder, which tortured him and made him wild with shame, as though he regarded every look and every word of his fellow-villagers as a scornful jest on him.

He was yet more annoyed and irritated when,

as sometimes happened, he observed that the
farmers would come running out of their barns and
stables to look at him as he drove by, and seemed
to whisper and smile to one another about his degradation and humiliation. His heart really bled
within him; he was consumed by a secret vexation, which rose at times to a desperate but sullen
rage. Seeing no means of relieving these bitter
torments of soul by words or deeds, he gradually sank deeper and deeper into a moody silence.
At all hazards he resolved to abide the test—to
keep his word;—the happiness of his daughter!
this was its price. He made every effort, therefore, that his indomitable pride permitted, to
please Farmer Torfs, and with most painful
submission carried out accurately all his com-
mands.

The deathlike silence of her father grieved
poor Clara excessively. She spared no exertion to
infuse courage and hope into his breast. Whenever he came home for his dinner at mid-day, or
returned in the evening with wearied limbs, she
surrounded him with every invention of affectionate care, spoke to him the tenderest words to
comfort him, and in cheerful accents set before
him the joys of a brighter future.

He answered her affectionately, and appeared to
be grateful for her tender affection: then he usually
broke off the conversation abruptly, and drove the
poor girl to silence by his impenetrable coldness.
Then he would go into a corner, and sit with his

head buried in his hands, and remain lost in gloomy musings, until, after a brief good-night, he went up-stairs into the attic in which his bed stood, and bolted his door behind him.

This singular behavior began to fill Clara and Luke with uneasiness. Their blissful dream began to enfold itself with clouds as they gazed on it; and, although they knew not what they had to fear, their hearts would often beat with intense anxiety about the future.

Quite different were the feelings of old Torfs. It was true, indeed, that the melancholy abstraction of Staers did not please him very much; yet it was enough for him that he kept himself from drink, and did his work regularly and well. He thought they could not expect more of him at first, and it would pass away by degrees as he got used to his new position. Besides, if he stood the test well, and really remained victorious over his fatal propensity to drink for three months, then he would not be compelled any longer to work as a day-laborer; on the contrary, he would be the relation, the inmate, and the equal, of Torfs himself. This improvement in his condition, the affectionate friendship of his new family circle, the happiness of his child,—all this, he said, would raise Staers out of the dejection which kept him so low.

So the old man used to say to his son and to Clara: he tried to make them see that every thing was going on very well—could not go on better—

H   10*

and, in order to dissipate their gloomy forebodings, he would at times laugh and jest with them on their causeless fears and fancies.

What inspired him with this comforting hope was the evident submission of Jan Staers to his slightest command, and the painful timidity and gentleness of his voice whenever he said any thing to him or asked any question of him.

Could the old man have seen how Clara's father whenever he was alone, would gnash his teeth by fits and starts, and stamp with his foot, and mutter bitter words between his teeth, then perhaps he would not have deemed the fears of his children quite groundless. But in his presence Jan Staers repressed every rising feeling of impatience or of vexation, and assumed a sad but calm and cool exterior.

Ten days had thus gone by, and Jan Staers had manifested no tendency toward strong drink; and it was commonly thought in the village that he had really overcome, by an unwonted energy and persistence of will, a vice which is generally most difficult of cure, if not entirely hopeless. But, at the end of that time, there appeared some indications which began to disquiet the old Torfs, and to excite in him suspicions and doubts whether Clara's father had accepted the test with good will and free concurrence. Whenever he went to see him in the fields, he was pained and surprised to find him standing with his arms crossed; and, at the end of the day, the very small amount of work done showed that he must have passed many hours in idleness.

The two vices which old Torfs hated the most were idleness and drunkenness. It grieved him to see that Staers, while he seemed to get the better of his drunkenness, remained still the slave of indolence. Nevertheless, the old man made as many excuses for him as he could; he thought he had noticed that Clara's father had been paler than usual the last few days, and that his cheeks had become visibly thinner.

Torfs had spoken to him about it, and told him that if he did not feel quite well he should not hesitate to say so, and then he might stay a few days at home to rest himself thoroughly; but Jan Staers had made reply that he was quite well, and felt himself strong enough to do any work that farm-laborers usually did.

The twelfth day—the morrow was a great holiday—Father Torfs was returning from the town, to which he had been summoned by his landlord. At the end of the lower road he did not follow the pine avenue, but took a footpath which would lead him along a field where he knew that Jan Staers was employed in spreading a great heap of manure. When he had reached the field, and come to Clara's father, he took him by the hand, and said, in a light and joyous tone of voice—

"Don't be cast down, friend Jan; take courage, man; things will all come right. Shall I tell you something that will give you great pleasure?"

He then gave him a slap on the shoulder, and said—

"What would you think, eh? if I were to tell you that you would sleep again—much sooner than you think for—in the stone farm-house yonder?"

"*I* sleep there? is the new tenant in want of a servant, then?" muttered Staers, with a forced effort at a jest.

"You don't catch my meaning; I mean that you will live again in the stone house, as you used to do formerly."

"But the new tenant is Franz Vleugels, from the forest farm."

"He has, indeed, offered a good deal for it; but the man—do you see, Staers?"

And the old man raised his hand to his lips, and made a movement with it to imitate a man drinking.

"So you see, neighbor Jan, the landlord won't hear of him. He would rather let the farm at a much lower rent, if he can only be sure that it will be regularly paid, and that his impoverished fields will be improved and well farmed. Guess, now, who the new tenant is?"

"What business is it of mine?" growled Jan Staers. "I should like never to hear the stone farm mentioned again—the wretched hole where I was slowly ruined!"

"Now, now, be a little more calm, neighbo. Jan; *I* am the new tenant."

"I knew well it would end so!" exclaimed Jan Staers, with a forced laugh, which was meant to simulate joy, and expressed envious derision.

"And I have got it at a very reasonable rent," continued the old man. "I give very little more for it than you did. It is a mine of gold, my friend. The landlord, who has a liking for me, because he has known me these twenty years as an honorable man, and is sure that I shall improve his property, opened his money-box, and said I might take what I wanted. I am to buy cows and horses, and hire laborers as many as I like. Yes, we shall do, now; we shall have to tuck up our sleeves, now! Eh, neighbor, our children will have room enough in the world, now; for if we don't get money *now*, people may well say, ' They were too stupid or too idle to become rich.'"

During this glowing exposition of the old man's projects, Jan Staers kept his eyes fixed on the ground, and his arms seemed to tremble by his side.

"Well, now, what do you say of this news?" asked Torfs, astonished at his silence.

"Good! it is very good! I wish you good luck!" muttered Jan Staers.

"You must have a better heart," said the old man, with increasing joy; "the appointed time will soon run out; then you shall leave your cottage, and come to live with us in the stone farmhouse. We must not put off the marriage of our young folk much longer, or the little farm-house will have to stand empty. It is a good thing that winter is coming on, and that there is a good deal of plastering and patching up to be done in the stone house; for the landlord wishes to hand it over to me sound and in good repair. Monday we will go together there, and have a look over it, and see what we can do to prepare the fields to yield a good harvest next year. The land has had a good fallow, friend Jan; it will work well, depend on it! Come back to the house in something less than an hour; we will have a cup of coffee, and bespeak one of mother's best rye-rakes. Good-by; within an hour!"

Jan Staers leaned on his pitchfork, and with a fixed and gloomy look followed the old man with his eyes until he had disappeared in the distance. He remained in this attitude as though stunned, sunk in the depth of despair, and with a bitter sneer on his countenance, until he heard over the fields the echo of gladsome voices in the house of old Torfs: they were welcoming the glad tidings.

All his muscles quivered with a sudden convulsion. With an unintelligible growl, he threw the pitchfork angrily away from him. He stamped his feet and clenched his fists; the sounds which escaped his lips were formless, but they sounded like fierce and terrible execrations.

He remained a short time overmastered by this transport of rage. But soon he relapsed into his former immobility, and, as though his reason gra·

dually gained an insight into his true situation, his limbs became again relaxed, and he said to himself, in a dejected tone—

"Wretch that I am! He brings me happiness for my child—and I am bursting with envy! abject coward! I am lying prostrate in the pit of misery I have dug for myself, and I hold him for my enemy who reaches out a brother's hand to raise me from my degradation. Oh, that drink, that drink! It numbs the heart—it slays the soul. But I will overcome it; I will strangle this demon of pride which possesses my heart. Come on, Farmer Staers, you contemptible drunkard, you are to be a servant in your father's stone farmhouse! You must be obedient, and toil and wear yourself out for others, in the very house where you used to command as master. The men will laugh at your humiliation; they will make a mock of you; they will rejoice, in their envious gibes, over your misfortunes; but you must stoop and crouch, and digest your misery as best you can, and drink the poison draught of shame—drink it in full draughts—until you burst!"

He went a few steps, took up his fork from the ground, and began to work again; but there was something so wild and feverish in his way of working, that one would have said he was cooling his rage upon the heap of manure. He stuck his pitchfork into it with furious violence, threw it hither and thither without order or moderation, and behaved himself like one out of his senses.

After about a quarter of an hour, the perspiration was pouring from his brow, and his breath
was short and thick with extreme weariness.
But still he continued, and at intervals a gloomy
sound issued from his mouth, as though he were
goading himself on to persevere in this desperate
conflict with himself, until he sank exhausted and
powerless.

Then all at once he heard the voice of Farmer
Torfs, who was calling to him from a great distance to leave his work and come to drink the
promised coffee.

"Perdition!" growled Jan Staers. "Go—and
sit down at the table—look on—and see how glad
they all are—how they clap their hands for joy!
See how your own child exults in your disgrace!—
and chatter, and laugh and be merry; or else you
will be driven away like a servant, who is not
servile enough in his master's eyes! Come, come,
—crawl along—reptile that you are!"

And with slow steps he went, and murmured as
he went, toward the abode of Farmer Torfs.

CHAPTER IX.

IT was the day after this scene, and about two
o'clock in the afternoon. Clara stood ready, with
her prayer-book in her hand, to go to church. She
spoke to her father, and said, with her sweet voice—

"Now, you will go out, won't you? and walk a bit in the fields to freshen you up? The sun is shining so clear; it is so beautiful and so fresh out of doors. Here you sit all day long, moping; it is not right, father. You will make yourself ill. Farmer Torfs said, too, that you ought to get a little fresh air. Ah, if you won't do it for your own sake, do it for mine. It is not so very great a kindness, and you don't know how glad it will make me. To think you are sitting there on that chair all day long, with your head in your hands, dreaming away—do you think that that is no grief to me?"

"To run right into men's faces, and have to answer all sorts of jeering questions!" muttered Staers.

"But, father," observed the girl, "it is a festival; almost all the men will be in church; you won't meet anybody. Besides, if you don't wish to see anybody, go away toward the forest; you may be sure of being alone there. But the clock is striking; I must make haste."

She pressed his hand, and, looking coaxingly and imploringly into his eyes, she asked—

"Father dear, won't you now? won't you take a little walk?"

"Well, yes. What difference is it to me? It is all one to me—every thing is," answered Jan Staers, impatiently.

"And if you are not at home when I come back from church, I shall go to Mother Beth's; she has

11

begged me to come. You will come on too, won't
you, father? You know that we are all to have
a game of cards quietly in the early evening;
Farmer Torfs said so."

"Very well," growled Staers. "Take care you
don't be late for the service: people will think you
are lazy and idle."

Repeating hastily her greeting, the girl ran out
at the door.

Jan Staers remained a little while longer, sitting
without moving a limb. A grim, sour smile was
on his lips; and he was gazing wrathfully into
vacancy, as though a disquieting spirit stood before
his mind's eye.

"Play a game at cards!" he muttered. "Yes
—play with the cards—and gnaw your own heart
the while others are merry and glad. Go out to
walk; yes, show yourself out of doors: Jem Pas-
mans will ask you, as he did you yesterday, how
much you get a day with the old beetle. The
broom-maker—a mere begger—he will pity you,
and tell you it is a miserable and humiliating
thing to go and work as a servant in your father's
farmyard; and the drunken blacksmith will put
his hand to his mouth, and laugh and shout to
you from a distance—'Jan, Jan, my lad—this
comes of—the glass!' All the children will be at
your heels as if you were a strange sort of animal,
and they will whisper scornfully to one another
about Farmer Staers, the great fool, who was rich,
and drank himself poor."

Now he held his peace a while, and his morbid fancy charged these irritating thoughts with yet more vivid and maddening colors. Then an expression of deepening despair succeeded to one of envious hatred on his countenance, and, with a laugh of fierce and bitter derision, he continued—

"And to-morrow I am to go and work in the stone farm-house—help the masons to put new tiles on the roof. I shall have to stand up aloft, on a ladder, right out in the street. The whole village will see me; fathers will point me out to their children as an example that they must lay up in their terrified hearts. My story will be told again and again a hundred times; and I, the while, dying of shame and spite, shall have to sit up there on the roof like a martyr on the rack; and down below in the street they will be laughing, jesting, scoffing, and calling out aloud that I have deserved it. Oh, half of one month is gone; and I feel myself quite conquered already—ten weeks more! ten ages of horrible suffering, of infernal despair!"

All his limbs were convulsed and shaken in a paroxysm of passion. He rose with a groan, and strode up and down his little room like a madman, shouting aloud—

"No, no! it cannot last. I must put an end to it. Clara!—but if I were dead she would be happy. Nothing could hinder her marriage. My body would be scarcely cold before the Torfses would begin to talk of the wedding. Ah, I should be

set free from all my shame; I should have no more
feeling than a stone; no more conscience to gnaw
me; no more heart to feel."

He sprang forward, put his hand on the bolt of
the cupboard, and opened the door of it with violence. Something like the glimmering of bright
steel struck his eye. He stood a moment looking
at it with a shudder; it seemed to kill him with
terror and fear; for he closed the door with a jerk,
and sprang backward with a dull, sad cry.

Then, as though he would escape from some
perilous thought, he began again to run rather than
walk up and down the room, and roared all kinds
of disjointed words without form or sense.

Suddenly he stood still before the window and
looked out. A smile of peculiar joy illumined his
face, and he sighed with longing for something the
sight of which seemed to cause him indescribable
pleasure.

About a bow-shot off, on the farther side of the
brook, was a public-house, above the door of which
hung a sign. A swan was painted on it, and beneath the swan a pint full of brown beer, and a
green flask surrounded with little glasses. And
on this flask Jan Staers kept his eager eye fixed;
he stood with open mouth and panting breast, and
then he said, with a shudder—

"Gin!—Ah, to be dead—no more consciousness
—no more pain; to drink, drink, drink, and then
fall down without reason, without soul! to feel
the flame rush through one's veins! to be rich,

happy, valiant, and strong! to forget every thing
—all—every thing—come, come!"

He felt his pockets and fumbled about them with
feverish eagerness.

"Money!" murmured he; "I have no money.
The old beetle won't pay me till to-morrow. He
distrusts me; I might go and drink with it to-day.
Ah, I saw some money yesterday!—it must be
there still. There, in Clara's box!"

He stooped toward the box while saying these
words, and took out a little casket, the contents of
which he shook out into the palm of his hand.

"Silver!" said he, with glee. "Silver! one,
two, three francs, and a half; enough, enough to
live, to die—"

But, as if the pieces of money had uttered an
appealing, expostulating voice, he put them back
into the little box hastily and in terror, and began
suddenly to shiver and to totter on his legs, so
that he sank into a chair to prevent himself from
falling.

With his bewildered eye still fixed upon the
money, he said, gloomily—

"Vile Judas! go—sell the soul of your child!
Wretch that I am, what am I going to do? Poor
Clara, she has worked so many nights in secret for
this. The brewer's wife gave her some shirts to
make; she has hoarded the wages of her toil,
penny by penny, all in secret; I was not to know
it. But Luke has betrayed her. She is going to
buy me a fine Sunday neckerchief; she wants to

surprise and gladden me with this grand present! —and this money, this money of love and affection,—it will serve for—oh no, no! never! never!"

Springing up hastily, he replaced the pieces of money in Clara's box. While he was stooping to do this, a strange sound smote suddenly on his ear. It was a distant noise, as of some one who was coming along, singing as he walked. Jan Staers stood upright in the room, and listened with marvellous astonishment to the song, which seemed to him more and more distinct, although the false notes, and the confused and stammering words, must have been uttered rather by an idiot than by a reasonable man.

"The sand-digger!" muttered Jan Staers, with a bitter expression of envy on his countenance. "How jolly *he* is now! He has had his drink; he sings, he runs, he has plenty of courage, he knows nothing of humiliation or of shame! He has no daughter; *he* can drink—drink as much as he likes."

The song came nearer and nearer; the door of Jan Staers's cottage was opened, and his old boon-companion stood before him.

Klaes Grils, the sand-digger, seemed uncommonly merry, and in good spirits; his eyes rolled wildly in his head; his cheeks and his nose glowed with a fiery red; he felt with his hands in the air, and at last he said, with a loud peal of laughter—

"There he is! Good God, he is alive still! Jan Staers, lad, I thought you were gone to live in a mole-track. These ten days we have had such a drinking-bout! it is so good just now, the gin at the White Calf. I wanted to lead the wheelwright's son home, but he would lie down in the middle of the road, and I can't make him get up. So every one to his taste, say I."

Jan Staers stared at his old companion with a peculiarly steady and fixed look; there he stood, tottering and reeling about, and making all kinds of strange grimaces.

"But, bless me, friend Jan," continued he, "you are making a face as if you wanted to eat me up! What are you up to now? Where do you go for a drink? or do you manage matters like great folks, and mix your glass at home to your liking? I'm going to try that to-day; I have a little green flask; when it is full it holds over a pint."

He put his hand in the pocket of his blouse and drew out a flask. Reaching it out to Jan Staers, he stammered—

"There, that comes out of the White Calf. Just taste it. Only a drop; don't be greedy; for that's something to make a dead man jump up out of his coffin."

He kept his hand stretched out toward Jan Staers, who stood trembling with inexpressible anguish, and following every movement of the flask in the sand-digger's unsteady hand.

"Is your throat bunged up?" said the latter, jeeringly. "Or do you think it is some of that wretched stuff from the Blue Dog?"

"Go away, go away! take the flask out of my sight!" roared Jan Staers, although he involun tarily put out his hand as if to seize it. And in truth a fearful conflict was raging within him. The memory of the simple but deep affection of his daughter stayed him a while on the brink of the awful precipice; but the fatal flask shone be witchingly before his eyes. It smiled on him; it seemed to him surrounded with all kinds of en- chanting images of happiness; it drew him on and on with irresistible force, as the magnet draws the needle.

However, the brutal and repulsive face of the sand-digger, which grinned behind the flask, would probably have given him strength to gain the vic- tory over his passion, had not his companion at that moment withdrawn the flask, saying, with a scornful laugh—

"Ah, ah, I know how it is; they were talking of it at the White Calf. You would catch it well, wouldn't you? The old beetle would send you about your business, if you drank only one single drop."

"Here, here!" howled Jan Staers, suddenly springing forward, and grasping the flask with his hand, as a wild beast clutches his prey.

"Stop there! halloa!" cried the other, running after him round the room; "only one drop; I know you of old; you have no bottom to your mouth. Give me back the flask! give it me!"

Jan Staers put the flask to his mouth, and

pushed the sand-digger violently from him. For a moment there was a kind of scuffle, until at length Jan Staers, drawing a deep breath, gave back the flask and sank down on his chair exhausted.

The sand-digger looked alternately at the empty flask and at his panting comrade, in mute wonder.

"Oh, be off with you, begone! Fiend that you are, you have stolen my soul, you have murdered my daughter," moaned Jan Staers, as if beside himself, and shuddering in his chair.

"Well, that is good!" grumbled the sand-digger. "What rubbish are you saying now? You shall see whether I won't make you pay for your drink. Here I am assaulted and robbed in broad daylight, as if I were in a wilderness. Ah, you don't like it; you are afraid it will burn your lips! I shall go up yonder, up the hill, to the Spotted Cow, and drink a pint of the best, and put it to your account. If you won't pay it I will bring you up before the magistrate, as sure as my name is Klaes Grils. Stealing is stealing; they locked up Frank, the dung-carter, for six months for finding a loaf worth twopence on the baker's counter."

The sand-digger took two steps toward the door, as though to leave the cottage; then he turned, and asked again—

"You will pay it, won't you? Then we shall still be good friends, anyhow. Jan Staers, lad, how ugly you look with your great, glassy, staring eyes! If I didn't know what it is owing to, I

I

should run away from you as from a mad dog.
The devil, who is up in the church in the picture
of the Last Judgment, and you—why you are as
like one another as two drops of gin—no, I mean
two drops of water. But Jan, I forgot to ask you:
is it true what they were talking about in the
White Calf, that the old bcetle has taken the stone
farm, and that you are going to work with him as
his servant? on your own property—that is, what
was your own property? I wish that word 'was'
didn't come in, don't you, Jan? What a number
of beautiful franc-pieces we should have, which
are gone now! So, so—the curé's parable, which
used to make you rave so, when you were half-seas
over—the parable is come true! The clay cottage
has, after all, eaten up the stone farm-house! IIa!
ha! the curé, lad, is a clever man, to tell true
fifteen years beforehand! So, you are to be
servant to the old hair-splitter! I'm sorry for
you; you'll have to work like a slave—and gin?
yes, indeed, you will draw your gin out of the
well with a bucket!"

During this jeering address, Jan Staers had remained sitting in his chair, with his unmeaning
gaze bent on vacancy. Not a limb, not a muscle
of his body moved; but his features worked with
impetuous emotions, and at each wound which
the sand-digger's gibes inflicted on his pride, he
clenched his teeth more rigidly together, and his
eyes sparkled and glowed with an ever intenser
flame of anger. It was also observable that the

drink had begun to fire his brain, for his accus-
tomed paleness was now replaced, even on his
forehead, with a warmer tint.

"Farewell!" grumbled the sand-digger, turning
again toward the door. "Tell your master—the
old beetle—that I laugh at him and despise him,
for all his being tenant of the stone farm-house."

Jan Staers sprang up, and, running after the
sand-digger, pulled him back into the room.

"Wait, wait a moment!" he exclaimed, with
warmth, as he bent over the box; "I will go with
you; I will pay you for the flask—up yonder in
the Spotted Cow."

"Come, now, that's something like! ah, you
nave some money in a box? While you are about
it, bring a little more. Let me see—silver!"

"Come along!" exclaimed Jan Staers, dragging
the sand-digger toward the door.

But when he set his foot over the threshold, it
seemed as if a restraining thought occurred to
him; perhaps there stood before his disquieted
spirit the image of his daughter, standing with
uplifted hands, imploring him to have pity on
himself and on her. He leaned against the door-
post, and stood for a moment trembling; but the
sand-digger pushed him out into the street, and
followed him, carefully closing the door behind
him. Jan Staers walked on with uneasy and painful rapidity, and made for an oak coppice, as
though he were afraid of being seen by any one.
When they reached the open field, all was still and

solitary; so far as the eye could reach, there was
no living being in sight.   The sand-digger reeled
and staggered after him, and muttered, quite out
of breath, "Eh, Jan, are you on fire anywhere
that you run so fast? but I'll beat you yet; my
legs are good yet.   Oh, there I go, down in the
mud!   They call this keeping the roads in order—
an honest man can't go up to the Spotted Cow
without breaking his neck!   Here I am, in for it.
Jan, Jan, wait a bit; we must rest a little there
at the corner of the wood, at Jem Snoeks's."

Running on thus, and stammering as he went,
the two boon-companions disappeared rapidly behind the angle of the pine grove.

A quarter of an hour later, large numbers of
men were seen leaving the village, and returning
homeward through the roads and lanes and over
the fields.   The service was over.

When Clara entered the cottage, a joyous smile
played on her lips.

"Ah, father is gone out to walk," she said, gayly.
"This is the first time.   Now things will go better.
He will come round by degrees, and the bitter
vexation that gnaws him will vanish gradually.
The brewer's wife has given me some more work.
What a beautiful neckerchief that was in the sa
cristan's window! it was so gay, it quite dazzled
my eyes.   I shall manage it famously; and father
shan't know a moment's peace until he puts it on
and goes with me to church; as for the worn-out

rag he has on his neck now, it is quite a disgrace
to be seen in it. And he knows nothing about it.
I work while he is in bed. Come, I will run off
to Mother Beth's and tell her the good news—and
this evening we will have such a nice game at
cards — and the loser is to have a cleft stick fitted
on his nose. Oh, how merry we shall be! how
we shall all laugh!"

Swiftly as a bird she ran out at the door, and
disappeared behind the wall of the cottage.

CHAPTER X.

"Good-day, Mother Torfs; what fine weather,
isn't it?"

"Because you look at it with such merry eyes,
Clara."

"Yes, yes, I am very well, too."

"Sit down by the fire, then; we'll have a little
chat. Does all go well yonder?"

"Mother Torfs, my father is gone out to walk.
This is a sign that he begins to get used to his
position, and that he is shaking off his gloom."

"Gone out to walk? Clara, child, it is a holiday; all the public-houses are wide open."

"No no, Mother Beth; he is only gone for a
stroll in the fields to get a mouthful of fresh air.
The public-houses? don't be alarmed about them

12

If my father had wished to drink, he might have
done so any day; but, be sure, he stands firm in
his good resolution; and if he becomes a little
more cheerful in mind, I don't despair but that he
will quite get over his bad habit."

"It is my notion, too, Clara, that things will go
on well. Perhaps something *may* turn up wrong,
but anyhow Luke shall not be prevented from—
from enabling me to call you my daughter. Look
you well, you wouldn't say that Luke is much
like his father outwardly; but inside, they are
as like as two pins. Luke seems patient, and
gentle, and easy to manage as a child, doesn't he?
Well, for all that, Luke has a hard head on his
shoulders, Clara; and, like his father, whenever he
takes any thing into that head of his, you will
never make him give it up. Say what you like,
and try all you can, both of them always come
back to the point they started from. They are
a little bit obstinate, sure enough: it runs in the
blood of the Torfses—they always were very hard
to manage."

"But, Mother Torfs, I thought Luke was to be
here after the service?"

"He is gone with his father to the St. George's
Guild. They meet to-day. I dare say it will be
an hour before they come back."

"I have heard say that they are going to choose
Father Torfs as Dean of the St. George's Guild; is
it true?"

"It seems so; but Torfs hesitates. He does

not like to have his head troubled with cares. You see the Guild is not on a very good footing, and if Torfs became dean he would want to set it all right: for he would rather not touch a thing than leave it half done."

"But it would be such a nice thing for Farmer Torfs to be dean. Only think, Mother Beth, what an honor for the family!"

"Ha! ha! Clara dear, you make me laugh. You good-for-nothing girl, you are always caring for the honor of the family! You seem to think it is Palm Sunday, and that Easter is at the door! —But, laughing aside, I was saying just now that the Torfses are made of very stubborn stuff. If you were to say that obstinacy was wrong, you would have them both down upon you. You must know, then, that they never decide on any thing without keeping it at least four-and-twenty hours working in their heads; sometimes they will run about with a thought in their brains for months and years before they say it must be done. And if you find fault with them,—oh, it is *manly*, and they can't see any harm in it. But, after all, the Torfses are capital workers, and they do their duties carefully and accurately both toward God and toward man. Yes, often so good and so strict, that you may happen to get a good scolding if you hint they are wrong in any thing they do."

"I've got something in my head, Mother Beth. Couldn't they make Luke dean of the St. George's Guild?"

"Oh, you little goose, he is much too young. I don't know what you sit there dreaming about. Clara, Clara, you mustn't be so proud. Honor and renown, look you, all that is but wind. Just blow on your hand; you will feel something, and think it is something real, and it is nothing after all. I was saying the Torfses had a will of their own. You must know how to manage them when they take a whim in their heads. Look: if things should ever go so far as that you should sit here by the fire, and be called Dame Torfs—you laugh, eh?—then you must take good care to notice what Luke has in his head; and if you think that he is going to do or undertake any thing that is hazardous, then begin betimes your observations on it, and never give over;—you may have to talk a long time, but never give over, till he has given up his project. If you can't get the better of his whim, and if he has once made a resolution, don't bother him any more. You'll never move the Torfses."

"Oh, mother, where people love one another, every thing goes smoothly."

"No, no, child, nothing in the world goes smoothly. What you must take care of especially is, that you never—never, do you hear?—allow him to remain a quarter of an hour in a public-house from the time of your marriage. As soon as you notice any thing of that kind, then begin to be vexed, and peevish, and look sour, and scold, and so on, without ceasing. Men can't stand out

against that, and they will do any thing we like to
be quit of our everlasting seesawing on one thing,
as they call it.   Of that curse of our villages, of
gin, I shall not say much to you ; you have had a
melancholy example of its consequences before your
eyes all your life long, and so has Luke ; but who
knows ? some bad luck, or some trouble ; they take
a drop to drown their vexation, they say, and then
it is all over with them.   Just look, in the village
over yonder, on the Lysterberg, the weaver Tist
Mees ; he was for forty years an honest man, who
earned his bread honorably.   He had five children,
and one of them was killed by a kick from one of
the brewer's horses.   Tist Mees was almost beside
himself with grief; by the advice of some bad
friends he tasted gin for the first time, just to cheer
himself up, as they said.   It was all over with him :
the poor weaver became a drunkard, and went fast
to ruin.   To console himself for the loss of one
child, he has brought the four others to beggary,
and made them miserable.   Clara, child, if things
don't mend in our villages with this wretched gin-
drinking, depend on it we shall hear of some sad
doings.   If it were only the drunkards themselves
who suffered, we might say that it served them
right—they reaped as they sowed ; but that wife
and children, sometimes even father and mother,
should have to suffer hunger, and shed tears of
grief and shame—that is not as it should be ; and
I say that drunkards can have no hearts in their
bodies, to forget their poor lambs in such an inhu-

12*

man way, and knowingly and willingly make them suffer so much. You are sitting so still, Clara; I dare say you have not been listening all the time, and are thinking of something else."

"I am sad, Mother Beth: your words make me afraid. You talk as if Luke could ever get a liking for gin. There's no reason in that, now. Oh, God! is the world then so far gone that we cannot be sure of those we love from one day to another?"

"You must not be vexed about it, Clara; but for all that, look you, you must always keep your eyes wide open. One thing more you ought to know well. The wife seems to be the slave in a family, and always to be obedient; but it is only in appearance, child. Of a hundred households, ninety are just what the wife has made them, or allowed them to become. So you must always be up very early, earlier than the servants, and take care that everybody goes to his work in good time. Never let them stay up longer than necessary at night; it only wastes oil, and makes them lazy at their work. You must give a good example to everybody; for where the farmer's wife likes sitting about, or crossing her arms, there the cart runs out of its proper track, and the horse remains in the stable uselessly nibbling his hay. You must be neat and clean in every thing, Clara; cleanliness in a household cheers the heart and gladdens the soul. And economy, Clara, economy is the first duty of a wife. Men, you see, are not

strict enough about it; but they are always glad,
after all, to see a little heap of money in a corner
of the chest, though they never ask how it has
been gathered, by care and economy. Let nothing
be lost; every thing has its value. In the town
there is a man who became rich only by collecting
old iron and worn-out clothes. A plate that has
lost a piece may still last some time; and when
it breaks in pieces at last, you see, it breaks instead of the new one that you might have bought.
Anyhow, it is a plate gained; and so it is with
every thing. When Luke wants to throw away
his waistcoat or his blouse because they are worn
out, just put a patch here and there, and they will
last six months longer. And then you must be
careful not to spend a penny at the milliner's.
Out of an old pair of father's trousers, mother can
easily make a new waistcoat for her eldest boy;
and when the eldest is grown out of it, just pass
it on to the next, and so on, till you can do
nothing more with it but cut out a good pair of
socks for father. But you see, Clara, there is one
thing you must not be too saving in, and that is
eating. I don't mean that you should have dain-
ties on the table; no, but there should always be
enough. It is a mistake to try to save out of the
mouths of your servants; it never answers in the
long run. He who works hard must eat well, or
he will never hold out. What you lose in victuals
you gain twice over in work. And the same with
cattle Look you, when we bought our horse, it

was lean and out of condition, and scarcely fit for work; and though we got him cheap, we thought we had made a very bad bargain. But we treated the poor beast well, and he got round, and became very strong again. You may go all round the neighborhood, and you won't find a horse that will do so much work, and with so much spirit. But the cows, Clara, the cows, if you don't care for them and look after them as if they were your own children, you will never get on in farming. Cows, do you see, are the main thing in farming; and it takes a good deal of skill to get out of them all that is in them, and improve their condition all the time. I'll tell you how to manage it. I once heard the curé preach—I don't remember now what it was about—but he was telling us about the false gods of some of the folk that lived a long time ago. Some went and bowed down to the sun or to the moon, some to an elephant, some to a bird, or any thing else; but there was one country where they had a notion that cows and oxen were gods, and so out of reverence they would not kill them nor eat them. Thinks I to myself, these people, poor creatures, they don't know any better, but they weren't so far wrong after all; for you see, Clara, the cow is the queen of all cattle, and the greatest benefactor to men. Without the cow, man would never be able to work the land; and like too many, even now-a-days, they would eat one another up for hunger, if God hadn't created the cow. Clara, child, what ails you now? You look as if you had a tear in your eye."

"Oh, it is nothing," stammered the girl; "I was thinking of my poor white mammy, who supported us so long, and then was killed at last before her time. All you say is very true, Mother Beth."

"Yes, if you have been listening to all I have been saying. I fancied your wits were wool-gathering a little bit; Luke was skipping about in your head, wasn't he, now? Well, well, it is natural enough."

"No, Dame Torfs, you are mistaken; I have been listening, listening very attentively, and I thank you a thousand times for your good advice. Your words made me feel a little sad; I did not know that it was so serious a matter to be mistress of a house, but now I begin to have a little notion of it."

"Yes, yes; this book isn't so easily read through. Only wait a bit till we come to the chapter on children. We had three, but my little Mieken and Pietje went to heaven when they were about seven years old. It is too early yet to talk about them; you will find it all out soon enough. I was going to tell you something about the stable and the sheep, but I fancy I hear Torfs's footstep. Come, we will get out the cards."

CHAPTER XI.

OLD TORFS and his son entered the house at that moment. Luke went straight toward Clara, who had risen as they came in, and talked quietly with her. The sweet smile which lighted up both their faces, and the joyous gestures of Clara, showed that the maiden was busy in telling her lover how her father had gone out to walk in the fields to refresh himself a little.

"Well, now," exclaimed Mother Beth to her husband, "how have things gone up yonder? you are surely not dean?"

"No, no," said the old man with a laugh, "they spared no pains indeed, but—"

"Yes, yes, father; but tell it right out," said Luke, interrupting him. "Ay, indeed! only fancy, mother, they had elected father, and there he sat pondering and weighing, like he does when he is in doubt about any thing. I saw by the shaking of his head that he was going to accept it, but I stepped gently on his toe, and then he said: 'I thank you for the honor you have done me, but my last word is—no!' Everybody knows father; so there was nothing more to be said but, "Tis a great pity!' and so they all said."

"Well, come, come, Torfs! said Mother Beth, jestingly, "your mouth watered after all to be dean, did it?"

"There *is* something in it," answered the old man. "When you sit down among all your old friends, who beg you and coax you, and mean to give you a token of their respect and affection! I was affected by it a great deal, and it gave me great pain when I found my refusal vexed them. But don't let us talk any more about it; let us rather have our game—that will put the matter out of my head. Where is Jan Staers? I asked him to come at half-past three, and now 'tis four o'clock."

"Father is gone out to walk in the fields," said Clara. "He wanted to get a mouthful of air to freshen him up. I told him, Farmer Torfs, that you wished him to go out to walk, and then he did it with pleasure. He will come in a moment; perhaps he hasn't heard the clock strike."

"So! he is gone out? that's all right. But we will begin while we are waiting for him. Sit down at the table—no, no, Luke mustn't sit by Clara; they help one another; we must play fair."

They arranged themselves around the little table, and old Torfs took the pack of cards and began to deal.

"Three of trumps!" exclaimed Clara; "twenty. Knave and queen, sixty! I shall win. I knew you would lose, Luke. I'll fit you, this time, a saddle on your nose, which shan't be made of straw, I assure you. You had better look sharp, lad, I've got it all ready."

She held up a thick piece of wood with a cleft in it, and said, with a loud laugh, "Look, there is a saddle for you! this will pinch your nose so that you will cut twenty different faces in a minute!"

"Bless me! is it possible?" said Mother Beth, laughing: "you have got the thickest stick from the bakehouse. Suppose I lose?"

"Oh yes, then we will make the cleft a little deeper and easier for you. This is only for Luke. This will teach him how to tease me again, as he did the other day."

"Come, come, do you call this playing at cards?" drily remarked old Torfs.

"My nose is beginning to be sore already," muttered Luke. "I believe you have sorted the cards on purpose for me. Eights and nines, and not a single trump!"

"Ten of spades!" exclaimed the old man, throwing the card on the table with an air, after the peasant fashion, much like a sledge-hammer.

"Ace of spades, and—the trick is mine!" said Mother Beth, exultingly.

"Queen of hearts," she continued.

"I won't take it," said Clara; "Father Torfs shall get one trick. There, nine of diamonds!— and now my turn. Knave, nine, ace of trumps— one, two, three,—all mine. Luke hasn't got one single trick. Here, my lad, hold up your nose."

Luke was obliged to sit with the cleft stick on his nose, without touching it with his hand, until the second game was played out.

The piece of wood which Clara fixed on his nose must have pinched him well; but, though the tears almost came into his eyes, he made such odd faces —probably to amuse the others—that they all burst out into a peal of laughter. Clara especially clapped her hands, and filled the room with her merry voice.

All was suddenly quiet, and Luke, as if ashamed, took the "saddle" from his nose and threw it under the table. The others stood up, for the door was opened, and Master Knops, a farmer of the village, entered the room.

"Ah, you are playing?" said he. "I am vexed to have to spoil your merriment; but I come to tell you something you ought to know. I must tell you; you would rather know it than not."

All looked at him with cool curiosity.

"You see," he continued, "I went up to the Spotted Cow to look after our Thomas, for they are always trying to lead our young folk astray. Eighteen years old, and he is already a slave to gin! 'Tis enough to turn all my hair gray! I didn't find Thomas there; but as I came back I went over the hill and through the pine grove to look for Thomas at Jem Snoeks's. I heard a noise behind the stone cross, and whom should I find lying there, so far gone that he couldn't stand on his legs—"

All his hearers turned deadly pale. Clara rested her trembling hand on the back of a chair.

"Who? why, the sand-digger," continued Master Knops.

"Ah, thank God!" shouted Clara, with her arms uplifted toward heaven.

"Thank God!" repeated Knops. "Yes; but I hadn't gone five steps before I found another lying there. I took him by the hand, and shook him violently to rouse him. Well, it was no use; there he lay like a stone; he had scarcely a breath left in him. You may guess, perhaps, who it was? It was Jan Staers."

Clara fell into the chair with a piercing shriek, and covered her face with her hands. Luke and his mother stood pale and motionless, as if stunned, in the middle of the chamber. The countenance of Farmer Torfs had meanwhile become crimson, his lips were compressed with an expression of contempt and indignation, and he stamped his foot heavily on the floor.

"I have only to say further," remarked Master Knops, moving toward the door, "that you would do well to take a wheelbarrow to fetch the drunkard home to his house: else he will lie there all night. As for leading him home, you need not think of that: he has no feeling nor motion left. Good-day, all of you."

Clara sprang up, and, stretching her hands imploringly to Luke and to the old man, she exclaimed, amid a flood of tears—

"Oh, Master Torfs, oh, Luke, come—help me—
go with me! Anyhow, my poor father can't be
left lying there!"

"*I?*" shouted the old man, furiously. "*I* go, in
the face of everybody, and drag this ungrateful
drunkard along the road? I would rather—I know
nothing of him any more; I have never known
him. All is broken off between us. And you,
Clara,—it grieves me much; but, whatever grief it
occasions me, I know no more of you, either, my
poor child."

Luke stood with his eyes bent on the ground,
transfixed by this unexpected blow, and trembling
violently.

"But," continued Clara, anew, "I cannot carry
my father by myself. Let all be broken off between
us: perhaps I may afterward die of it—but now—
now—you are Christian men, are you not? Do
one last act of Christian charity and pity for me!
I assure you, Father Torfs, never again will I set
foot over your threshold; I understand well enough
that all is lost—lost—and I have too much regard
for Luke ever to—O Lord! O my God!—I implore you, go with me. Bring my father to his
house—and then abandon us to our bitter fate!"

Luke had at the same time clasped his hands,
and seemed to be imploring his father's permission
to follow Clara. Mother Beth looked at her husband with a sad and inquiring expression, but she
dared not speak.

The maiden fancied that she saw old Torfs waver

in his decision; she fell before him on her knees,
and exclaimed—

"Oh, I shall go and live with my father in another village—far from here: you will never see
us again!"

The old man raised the girl from the ground, and
said, with his head erect and fixed—

"Well, then, out of love to you: but it is the
last time. Come, Luke, we will go and see. But
that I should ever dream of such a thing! Let me
never hear of him again—of him or of any thing
that belongs to him—whether here or at a distance
—else I will make you know, Luke, that I am
master!"

Mother Beth, overcome by her emotion, sat down
on a chair and began to weep, as she saw her husband and her son go out at the door with Clara.

The shortest way to reach the hill where Jan
Staers was lying, according to Master Knops's state-
ment, was through the village street, and Clara, in
her affectionate impatience, tried to lead old Torfs
in that direction; but he took the way through the
fields, without paying any attention to her, and
thus soon reached the pine grove. Here he slackened his speed, and resumed his ordinary pace, and
broke the silence by saying, in a tone of deepest
dejection—

"It is such a pity, too! All was so nicely
arranged! I had planned every thing beforehand
in my head: how I should behave to make him
feel that I was indeed as a brother to him, and

convince him that he should be quite on an equality with me. You would have been married before Easter, children; you would have lived on this little farm; and Jan Staers was to have lived with me in the stone house, and we should have worked together to leave you a fair inheritance! Ah! it was a paradise of delights to us all; and the reckless, the dastardly drunkard—he has bartered the happiness of his child for a drop of gin! You weep, Clara! my dear child, you may well weep; you are indeed in a miserable plight. God will recompense you there on high for all your sorrow and trouble in this world."

Neither Luke nor Clara uttered a word. The poor girl sowed the dreary path with bitter tears; the lad, lost in utter despair, strode along by his father's side without consciousness of feeling; only at intervals a deep sigh relieved his laboring breast.

The old man continued, in a melancholy tone of voice—

"You see, children, you must be reasonable. You know I have done all that was possible to see you happy; but if you don't put every thought of the past out of your heads now, do you know what the consequences will be? You will then darken and embitter the life of the poor worn-out old Torfs and of Mother Beth; and their last days will be days of shame, and vexation, and sorrow."

"Oh, don't imagine it!" exclaimed Clara, with a voice almost smothered with tears and sobs. "I know well what will become of me; my little

13*

corner in the churchyard is marked out already. But it is all the same; I will never make you unhappy,—you, my dear benefactor; I shall forget Luke—forget him and never think of him any more—except only to pray God on my knees to grant him a long and happy life."

A suppressed groan broke from the breast of the young man.

"And you, Luke," sobbed the poor girl, "forget me too; it must be so. And if you will show me a kindness when you shall see me no more, ah, think of my poor father in your prayers, that God may at least have mercy on his unhappy soul before he dies!"

"Clara, dear child, you talk like a reasonable girl," said the old man, deeply affected. "I feel it much; I love you so well that I would give half my property to deliver you from your miserable condition; but God has decreed otherwise. Luke, my dear boy, be you too of good courage; accept your lot with patience; assure your old father that you too will lay aside a vain hope."

The youth stood still in the road, his every limb convulsed with emotion, and, turning toward his father, he said, with a firm voice and resolved countenance—

'Lay it aside? forget her? no, never! Clara is deceiving you; she tells a lie. Forget me? she can't do it! I lay my life on it, let her try as much as she likes, she can't do it! Ah, do you think, father, that 'tis enough to say, 'I will never think of her again'? The faithless thing, she may forget me, if she can;—Luke, mind you, is no weather-cock, to turn whichever way the wind blows. It has grown right into my heart, and it cannot be rooted out, as long as I live!"

"Luke, Luke," murmured the old man, re-proachfully, "you will then make your old father and mother wretched?"

"No, no!" exclaimed the youth, with fiery im-petuosity. "I will never again speak of Clara, never see her again, avoid her—out of love to you, father; but never, never shall I love another. I will wait, wait long years; even if my hair grows gray in waiting. Clara shall be one day my wife—unless death shall remove one or both of us from the earth."

The maiden had listened to these words of despair with a shudder. Unable to restrain her emotion any longer, she sprang to Father Torfs and threw her arms around his neck, and let her head fall on his bosom, and then, as though she would deprecate the wrath of the old man, she said, in a beseeching tone—

"Oh, Torfs, forgiveness!—forgive him!"

The expression of the old man changed suddenly; he put the girl aside with gentle force, and said—

"Silence! people are coming yonder. Come, let us make haste."

And all stepped out along the road with quick-ened pace. They cast down their eyes, and did not look about them, hoping that the peasants who

were coming toward them would pass by without
interrupting them or remarking their emotion; but
already one of the villagers began to shout from
a distance—

"Ha, you are looking after Jan Staers, I suppose? He has sat it out well this time! But you
won't find him in the Spotted Cow; he is gone off
with the sand-digger—if you can call it going, for
they were tumbling about like blind people, feeling
with their hands from tree to tree."

"Look you, now," said a second, with a sneer;
"didn't I tell you, Farmer Torfs, that you could
never wash a blackamoor white?"

The old man passed them quickly, without returning any answer, and at length reached the foot
of the hill, on the top of which stood the cross
which preserved the memory of the wretched
Durinkx. Having reached this eminence in the
pine wood, they looked a while among the trees,
and very soon found Jan Staers, lying stretched
out at full length on the ground.

Clara's father must have moved about in some
violent way. Perhaps he had been seized with
cramp, or with strong convulsions; for, as he lay
there on his back, the ground at his feet was quite
ploughed up with the stamping of his heels, and
each of his clenched hands was full of grass and
fir-cones which he had seized in clutching at the
ground and had crushed between his fingers. His
eyes were open and glassy, his lips blue.

Clara uttered a mournful cry, and, falling on her

knees, she took her father's hand and bathed it
with tears. The old man and his son knelt also
by the side of Jan Staers, called him by his name,
shook his head and his limbs, but could not succeed in eliciting the least sign of feeling or life.
With tears on his countenance, old Torfs shook his
head in deep thought. He made a sign to his son
to keep quiet, and then stooped his head over the
breast of Jan Staers, as though to listen whether
he still breathed.

"Loosen his neckerchief," said he to his son;
"it will relieve him."

"Eh! what are you at there?" stammered a
voice from between the trees. "Go your own
ways, and let people sleep quietly."

"It is the sand-digger," muttered Luke, angrily.
"The despicable scoundrel is the cause of all this
misfortune!"

The sand-digger had meanwhile raised himself
on his elbow, and gazed with wonder and derision
on what was taking place beside him.

"Yes," he hiccuped anew; "call him again!
you won't get him home till morning. He wanted
to drink gin against me! I'll soon lay him on his
back. Don't you see that, old beetle? holloa!—
Farmer Torfs, I mean. You cunning old fox, you
would pay him to-morrow, would you? that the
bird mightn't take wing to-day. Ah, well, but he
had a little box in his chest—"

A shrill cry broke from the hearts of Clara and
of Luke at the same moment.

"What is the matter?" asked the father, in amazement.

"Oh! it is—it is horrible!" shrieked the youth. "Clara's money! the pence her love had saved—for which she had worked all night long. Oh, if he were not Clara's father, I would run away from him. God has cursed him!"

The poor girl, sobbing and wellnigh fainting, laid her hand on the young man's mouth.

"Come, come," said the father, tormented by an indescribable anxiety, "let us go away from this. We will try to drag him down the hill. There below, at Master Vlym's, we can get a wheelbarrow."

The old man took the insensible body in his arms, Luke held his legs, and so they dragged him along slowly and with difficulty over the uneven ground, and down the hill. Clara followed in silence; her tears flowed in streams over her cheeks, and when she heaved a sigh it sounded like a wail of utter despair.

At the foot of the hill Jan Staers suddenly drew up all his limbs together, and a hoarse rattle was heard in his throat. The two who were carrying him uttered a cry of joyful surprise; they laid him down on the ground, and, together with Clara, stooped over him to trace on his countenance the signs of returning life. But the hope was vain; not the slightest movement could be detected in his now extended body.

Farmer Torfs grew pale. A melancholy conviction took possession of him; he concluded that this last sign of life in Jan Staers was really the convulsive shudder of death.

"Run, run, Luke! fetch the wheelbarrow!" he exclaimed; "quick—make haste!" He laid his hand on Clara's head, and said, with a sigh of profound commiseration, "Poor Clara, hapless child, God be gracious to thee!"

The sorrowful girl knelt again by her father without reply, and held his ice-cold hand pressed to her lips, calling, amid her sobs, "Father, father!"

Luke soon came running with the wheelbarrow; he helped his father to place the nerveless, relaxed body upon it, and set forward without delay along the field path that led toward the cottage of Jan Staers.

The old man had taken Clara's hand, and was trying to alleviate her distress by words of consolation. He concealed from the poor girl his own apprehensions, and tried to persuade her that her father would be all right again after a long night's rest. Moved by pity, he assured her that he would help her in secret, and never forsake her in her hour of need, so long as he could assist her without involving his whole family in misery and in shame.

The maiden murmured some few signs of quiet gratitude, but had not strength to express her feelings in connected words. She kept her eyes on the pallid face of her father, in deep suspense, and was frequently so agitated by fear and alarm that her hand trembled and shook in that of the old man.

They were fortunate enough to arrive at Jan Staers's door without meeting any one. They lifted the body from the wheelbarrow and laid it on a bed. The girl drew a chair forward, sat down, and with a bitter groan let her head fall on the breast of her father. But the old man took her by the arm and forced her to rise, saying—

"Clara, quick, run for the doctor; tell him I will pay him double if he will come at once, without a moment's delay."

The maiden looked at him bewildered, as if she did not understand him; then at length her consciousness seemed to return, and she said, running to the door—

"Ah, thank you! yes—the doctor!"

Farmer Torfs looked after her sadly; then, turning to his son, he said, with a solemn voice—

"Luke, it may be we are standing beside a corpse! quick, make haste and call the curé. If life remains in him he may yet have time to make his peace with God. Who knows, on the brink of the grave—"

But the youth had not waited for the close of his father's sentence, and was already far on his way.

Then the old man turned toward the bed, crossed his arms on his breast, and remained thus, with his eyes fixed on the face of Jan Staers; and from time to time he shook his head and murmured to himself—

"There are so many who begin with a little drop, and anticipate no misery, no punishment; but who of them can say, 'My call shall not be like this'? Poor soul! perhaps thou standest already shuddering before the judgment-throne of God!"

CHAPTER XII.

It was in the year 1851, in the first week of October. Enticed by the bright autumn days, I had ridden into Kempen, intending to amuse myself by rambling a while in Hageland. There, in a village amid the ironstone mountains, dwelt one of my old friends, who was the vicar of the parish.

He had taken a favorable opportunity to give me in a letter such a poetical description of the beauty and healthiness of his village, that I had felt ever since a strong desire to accept his pressing invitation and pay him a visit.

And there I was, in this lovely country, where the ground is so varied with hill and valley that it seemed as if the waves of a raging sea had been suddenly arrested and petrified during a tempest.

I had been taking a walk with my good friend the vicar round the neighborhood, and we sat down at the foot of the stone cross on the hill to rest ourselves for a few minutes.

We talked over our youthful days. He told me
14

of his studies in the seminary, and of the inner conflict between the world and God, and of his trying to choose some other course of life, of his final victory, of the tranquillity of his mind, of the calm happiness he now enjoyed.

I told him all about my soldier life, the melancholy death of some of our old friends, who were killed by my side at Louvain by a cannon ball, the ups and downs of literary life, the hot contentions of political parties, the resuscitation of Flanders, our too long degraded fatherland.

And thus gossiping of poetry and of poets, of the beauties of nature and reminiscences of our earlier life, we saw the mist of evening rise slowly at the foot of the little wood, and creep higher and higher, and spread itself out over the meadows, until the sun had sunk far below the western horizon. The rising moon was glowing like an enormous ball of fire over the tops of the dusky pines.

We betook ourselves leisurely to the presbytery, where I was to enjoy a night's hospitality. After supper we remained a long time listening with great interest to the stories which the octogenarian curé told us about the "Besloten Tyd,"* or time of concealment, and about the "Peasant War."

---

* The "Besloten Tyd" is that time in our history when the French republic had closed the churches, because the clergy refused to take the oaths required of them. They said mass and preached, during this time, in cellars or in stables, in woods or other concealed places.

Persecuted and hunted down by the ferocious sansculottes, he had sought refuge among his armed countrymen, and remained among these so-called "brigands," up to the time of their destruction. By a chance which seemed almost miraculous, he contrived to escape when the bodies of his companions lay around Hasselt, pierced with sabres and weltering in their blood.

This was all very interesting to me, as I was then occupied in collecting materials for writing a tale founded on this last and famous effort of Belgian freedom against a foreign tyranny.*

It might be about eight o'clock when the good curé finished his narrative. We sat talking a little while about one thing and another, until the curé looked at his timepiece, and said to his vicar—

"Don't forget your promise to Farmer Torfs."

The vicar rose up and put on his hat, and, taking a book from the table, he said to me, "Friend Conscience, I must go in haste to a cottage a little way off. It is there behind the brook, a few minutes from this. I shall be with you again in half an hour. In the mean time you can chat with Mynheer the Curé."

But I had been for some time looking with longing eyes at the upper panes of the window,

---

* The tale here referred to is "The War of the Peasants: a Historical Sketch from the Eighteenth Century." It will shortly appear in this series.

through which the pale moonlight streamed in so enticingly, and so I rose from my chair, and said—

"How lovely it must be out of doors now! Let me go with you; I will wait for you in the road, and store up within me the impressions of this beautiful country in a still moonlight night. Mynheer the Curé, I am sure, will not take it amiss."

"Oh, by no means," said the aged priest: "my hour has struck; I am off to bed."

Scarcely had the vicar led me a gunshot through the field path, when he pointed out to me a little cottage, which stood alone on the margin of the brook, surrounded by trees.

I could not help admiring the humble cottage which rose so solitary and forlorn out of the level meadow into the calm night, and glittered and sparkled like a diamond beneath the moonbeams. It was as though the torch of night had concentrated all its keenest lustre upon it; its little . windows were touched up with many-tinted light; the vineyard behind the gable shook its tendrils gently on the sighing breeze, and the tops of the trees waved like masses of molten silver over the roof.

"How beautiful!" I exclaimed. "It stands there like a work of enchantment."

"I will tell you presently, as we walk back to the presbytery, the history of that little cottage," said my friend, in a tone of sadness; "it will furnish you with matter for a touching story, if

you will only change the names of persons and
places so that no one may recognise them. This
cottage, you see, friend Hendrick—three days ago
there was in this cottage a young girl who dreamed
of happiness; who looked out into the future, and
saw every thing radiant with the glad light of her
hope. She loved; she was to have been united
to the beloved of her heart after Easter. In her
simplicity she could not keep in the happiness that
awaited her, after a whole life of suffering and of
shame. When she met our old curé she told him
all that was in her pure and innocent heart, and
how she could not sleep for joy. She was to be
rich, to be a mother, to thank God, to make all
about her happy, and to scatter around her the
treasures of her loving soul like an aureole of
quiet gladness and energy—and now!"—

My friend was silent. I listened for more, for
the tone of his voice indicated something very
serious and thrilling.

"And now?" I repeated, with curiosity.

We were close to the cottage; a few steps, and
we should reach the threshold.

"And now!" continued the vicar, leading me
toward a side-window. "Keep still. Look; thus
is it now!"

I looked through a pane of the window. A shuddering came over me, and I could scarcely restrain
the cry of anguish which forced itself from me like
a stifled groan.

The moon filled the room with a bluish light,

L   14*

and gave to it a dismal, ghostly appearance. On a table stood a crucifix, between two tapers of yellow wax, whose tiny flames flickered like two corpse-lights. Three or four persons—an elderly dame, an old man, and a youth—were kneeling on the floor. I was alarmed at their silence and their immobility. They were like stone statues, without life.

In the middle of the room, on two chairs, lay a long wooden chest—a coffin—and at its head a young maiden, whose dishevelled hair fell down in waves upon the coffin, and from whose cheeks a flood of bitter tears streamed on the fatal wood.

The vicar took my hand, and said, as he led me from the window, "Go off to a little distance; walk up and down there in the path. Within a quarter of an hour I will rejoin you. I have to say some prayers here. Preserve the impression of what you have seen; I have a melancholy story to tell you." He had his hand already on the latch of the door.

"Who—who lies there?—in the coffin?" I asked, quite unnerved.

"A drunkard!" said he, as he entered the cottage.

When my friend left the lowly cottage, he found me standing a few steps from the door, with my arms crossed on my breast and my eyes fixed on the ground. He then began to tell me about Jan Staers and Farmer Torfs, about Mother Beth, and Clara and Luke. The history was tolerably long, for we were already sitting in the large room of the presbytery before I knew who the personages were that I had seen gathered around the coffin.

My friend advised me to write a story of these incidents. The materials seemed touching enough, but my heart revolted against the notion of bringing before my readers a picture which could excite no emotion but disgust.

The vicar made many attempts to get me to understand that one might describe vices in all their mournful hideousness, if only true feeling and delicacy guided the pen, and if one's aim were simply to inspire a horror of vice and a love of virtue; that, besides, my tale would be useful to villagers, and that, if only one single man were rescued from destruction, it would be a sufficient recompense to me.

I observed to him that my style of writing led me to aim at vivid and striking pictures, and I could not make up my mind to use the colors of my palette in sketching from nature so degrading a vice as drunkenness; that I could not help finishing my pictures, and should run a risk of presenting scenes which would brand me as a man of degraded fancy.

He then adduced the instance of the ancient Greeks, who, on certain days of the year, made their slaves drink to excess, and exhibited them to their children in that state, to root in their tender minds a disgust of this contemptible vice.

The matter remained that evening undecided.

When I was leaving the presbytery the next
morning, my friend renewed his efforts. Although the night had somewhat changed my
views, I did not venture to make him a decided
promise, but, after a hearty farewell, I left him
with these words: "I will think it over; perhaps
you are right."

————

THREE years have gone by since the event just
related. The coffin and the weeping maiden have
often crossed my fancy, but I never ventured to
attempt compliance with my friend's wish. But
now I had finished my larger work, " Clovis and
Clotilda," about two months since, and I was looking out for something fresh ; it was to be a story of
village life, a tendril the more to entwine into the
wreath of hedge-flowers that I had promised to
weave for my friends.

While I was sitting musing, with my head on
my hand, the postman brought me a letter. It is
from my friend the vicar. What can he have
to tell me? Since my visit to his lovely village I
have not heard of him. The letter made inquiries
touching my health ; then went on to speak with
wonder and animation of " The Dream of Youth,"
of Flanders' glorious poet, Van Beers, and at last
concluded thus :—

" —This is not, however, the true motive of my

etter. Can you guess why I write? Perhaps you
may yet remember the coffin, and the story I told
you in connection with it. I have waited with
some impatience, but waited all in vain, for the
tale you were to write about it. I had almost forgotten it at last; but yesterday it all came back
again fresh as ever, and I have been turning it
over in my mind all the day. I baptized a child
yesterday, a plump and lively youngster. Guess
now, if you can, who are the father and mother.
Luke, the young man, who was kneeling in the
room of the little cottage, and Clara, the girl with
the flowing hair, who lay bending over the coffin.
They were married about a year ago, and they
live in the stone farm-house with Farmer Torfs
and Mother Beth. They are happy, and are doing very well. There is some talk about making
old Torfs burgomaster of our village at the coming
election. Do come and see me once more; I will
take you into the stone house, and we will drink
some coffee there. Well, now, there's a conclusion for your tale. Won't you write it, after all?"

The next day I despatched a letter to Hageland.
The first lines were: "I am coming; I shall be
with you the day after to-morrow, and shall be
overjoyed to shake hands with Father Torfs and
Mother Beth, and Luke and Clara. I will begin
at once to write the tale. May it be a lesson and
an example to some poor villager; I ask nothing
more."